LOST BOY

HANNAH GRAY

Copyright © 2023 by Hannah Gray
All rights reserved.

Visit my website at www.authorhannahgray.com
Cover Designer: Amy Queau, Q Design
Photographer: Renie Saliba
Alternative Cover Designer: Sarah Grim Sentz,
Enchanting Romance Designs
Editor and Interior Designer: Jovana Shirley, Unforeseen Editing,
www.unforeseenediting.com

No part of this book may be reproduced or transmitted in any form or by any means, electronic or mechanical, including photocopying, recording, or by any information storage and retrieval system without the written permission of the author, except for the use of brief quotations in a book review.

This book is a work of fiction. Names, characters, places, and incidents either are products of the author's imagination or are used fictitiously. Any resemblance to actual persons, living or dead, events, or locales is entirely coincidental.

playlist

Listen to the music that inspired *Lost Boy* on Spotify.

"Cover Me Up" by Morgan Wallen

"Sober" by Bad Wolves

"Don't Think Jesus" by Morgan Wallen

"Wild Horse" by Warren Zeiders

"Pain Killer" by Warren Zeiders

"I Remember Everything" by Zach Bryan, featuring Kacey Musgraves

"Weeping Willow" by Warren Zeiders

"Chasing Cars" by Nate Smith

"Broken" by Lifehouse

"your place" by Ashley Cooke

"Tourniquet" by Zach Bryan

"Me + All Your Reasons" by Morgan Wallen

"Enough Is Enough" by Post Malone

"Mourning" by Post Malone

"Chain Smokin' " by Morgan Wallen

prologue

CADE

I lie on my side, staring out the window, wishing like hell I could get out of here but knowing deep down that I'm exactly where I need to be. *At fucking rehab.*

The image of my mother's face flashes in my mind as I think back to when she and my father dropped me off here last week. She was crying. She felt terrible for lying to me and bringing me here. But instead of easing her mind, I was a dick. Because in that moment, I wasn't concerned with her feelings. I just knew I didn't want to be here. I didn't want to go through withdrawal or be stuck in a rehab facility for weeks upon weeks.

The moment I'd figured out where they were bringing me, I was so desperate to change their minds. I knew there was no getting through to my dad, so I preyed on my mother instead. I needed to go back to my house. I'd get clean. I would. But first, I needed to snort something just one last time. I cried, yelled, and begged. Nothing had worked. I guess, eventually, I realized my ass really wasn't going home with them. It was stay here and get clean, or take off and be off the team ... forever.

On the plus side, I'm now on the other end of withdrawal. I no longer feel like I'm going to die, which is nice. Puking, shitting, sweating, and the worst body aches you could ever imagine while you deprive your body and mind of the one thing it is convinced it needs? *That* will make you almost wish you were dead. Every time I go through the withdrawal process, I tell myself the same thing. *Never again will I touch another drug.* Yet here I lie, wishing I could have something to take the edge off while my nerves are going crazy.

Before my parents came and got me at Brooks, Haley tried to talk to me. I knew she had told Hunter that she was worried and that I was doing drugs. It had to have been her—she was the one who had fucking walked in on me when I was about to snort a line in the bathroom. But the day I left, I was still fucking mad at her. After all, it was her fault that my parents were crying. So, when she came to me that morning, begging for me to talk to her, I ignored her. She tried to grab me, but I pulled away.

I left her crying, and I didn't care. Not because she'd ended my run with drugs. But because she'd turned my life upside down. My teammates would never look at me the same. My parents would be back to not trusting me. And not to mention, my body would fucking hate me over the next few days, if not weeks. It was her fault that I was starting to feel like absolute shit. It was her fault that I was letting my team down by going to rehab instead of being on the ice with them. Everything was her fucking fault in that moment. And because of that, I couldn't look at her. Even if she was an angel sent from heaven just to save my ass.

But even though I felt like I hated her, I knew I loved her too. I guess I had loved her since the night she had found me having a breakdown in my bedroom less than a week ago. Maybe even before. She could have walked— no, run—out of the room and away from me. Instead, she told me she loved me. I didn't say it, but I knew I loved her right back.

But I don't love her enough. I don't know if I ever could. Because my brain was wired to be a selfish man. And I've always put what I needed before caring about anyone else.

Even her.

And do people ever really change? I fucking doubt it.

HALEY
FOUR MONTHS EARLIER

I look around my dorm room, silently stewing while grinding my back teeth together, staring at the damage from when the bottom floor of this building flooded, thanks to the worst rain and windstorm I have ever seen.

I stuff some things into my bags, knowing that I won't be able to stay here for a while. I like it here. I adore rooming with my best friend, and I love that this building is centrally located to most of my classes.

Remi walks into our room, pacing around nervously, dragging her hands through her hair. "What the hell are we supposed to do? Classes started weeks ago. There are no available dorms left. Oh, and on top of it, I got an email, saying it could be months before this is cleaned up."

Remi and I have been best friends since we were kids. So, I'm well aware that she is someone who gets worked up easily. She likes things to be perfect, and when they aren't, she sort of—okay, she really freaks out.

Her phone rings, and she quickly answers, sounding frantic, of course. "Hello?"

I can't hear who is on the other end, but when I see her bobbing her head up and down, eyes wide, I know it's likely something to do with our future living arrangements. She chats for a few minutes before ending the call.

"They have space for one of us in the east dorms." She swallows. "You take it. My parents are only an hour and a half from here. I'll commute."

"What? No. Absolutely not." I shake my head. "My brother has an open room. I'll just crash there until they repair this place." Looking around, I cringe. "Which might be a while."

"Are you sure?" She comes closer, putting her hands on my shoulders. "I mean, Hales, he lives with another hockey player. Won't that be totally awkward for you?"

"*Two* others actually." I laugh, holding up two fingers. "And, no, it will be fine. I highly doubt any of them are home much anyway." I give her a weak smile, dropping my hand down. "It will be all right. And you and I, we'll still meet up and hang out, right?"

"Duh!" She nods. "All the damn time."

"Good." I smile, taking my phone out. "Time for me to break the news to Hunter that his baby sister is crashing his house!"

"Are you sure about this?" She sighs, looking nervous.

"No, but it'll be fine." I nod. "Heck, maybe even fun. Who knows?"

I inhale slowly. Because I'm not nervous about living with hockey players. I'm just scared of looking like a total idiot in front of Cade Huff because his very presence turns me into a twelve-year-old girl.

A babbling, fidgeting, blushing twelve-year-old girl.

Because, yeah, he's *that* hot.

CADE

After feeding the monster inside my brain, I drag the back of my hand across my nose and collapse onto my bed. It's gotten bad. My relationship with drugs. Part of me knows that I'm getting out of control, but then the less … intelligent, more stubborn side wants to keep telling myself it's all fine. And that this is only temporary.

I want to believe I still have control of the situation—the situation being drugs and me. But the truth is, I think I might be worse off than I was when my parents sent me to rehab the last time.

I'm spending more money. And faster too. The money I had saved from working at my dad's garage this summer is dwindling fast. And I know it's only a matter of time before I start using the debit card my parents gave me for emergencies. That's their fault though. Why would they give a recovering addict a debit card? *Because I promised them I was fine—that's why.* And, goddamn, I'm good at convincing people of that.

I roll onto my side, staring out the window at the rain pelting against the glass. It's been raining off and on for days now, bringing me back to when I was a kid. The summer before fifth grade, it rained every single day. Right up until the last three days before school started back up. And then we were forced to cram months of fun into a few measly days. Which, obviously, was impossible.

I remember my mother looking out the window of what had to have been the third week of waking up to rain. She sighed and said that it was like it was Groundhog Day. At the time, I didn't get it. I wasn't sure what she even meant. Now, I do. Because these days, it's Groundhog Day every fucking day of my life.

I guess when something bad happens that forever changes you, life has a way of putting this bubble around you, keeping you inside of it. You can only fit a little bit of happiness into the bubble, and if you have any more than that, you'll be consumed with guilt. Because why should you be happy? You don't deserve it.

On the outside, I look like a normal college kid, living his best life. I'm a Wolf, playing for one of the best college hockey programs in the country. I have the best of friends and the most badass teammates, and on top of it, I'm surrounded by the prettiest women, who are more than eager to climb in my bed and show me a good time.

It sounds perfect, right? Wouldn't you trade your left nut to be me?

Yeah, I guess I wouldn't blame you either. But the truth is, sometimes, I'd trade *everything* to be anyone else.

I'm not naive enough to think I have the worst life of any motherfucker around. I know there's a lot sadder shit out there than mine. And maybe it makes me a weak person because I'm stuck in the past, blaming all my bad choices on one night. Maybe I'd still be putting shit up my nose even if my best friend hadn't died in my arms. Who knows?

One thing is clear. That little voice of reason, telling most people when something is a bad idea and to pass on it … yeah, I don't have that. If I want to get fucked up, I'll get fucked up.

Slowly climbing out of bed, I pull a pair of sweatpants on and head downstairs. And I'm thankful there's no practice until this afternoon. Morning practices aren't my friend.

"Are you just waking up, man?" Watson scowls from the couch. "Aren't you supposed to be in class?"

"Wasn't feeling it." I shrug. "Hey, can you haul your titty out and let me have a sucky-suck?"

"What?" He scowls. "What the fuck are you talking about?"

"Well, if you are going to act like my mother, you might as well pump out the titty milk." I shrug, yawning. "I like mine warmed up too." I pat my stomach. "Better on my tum-tum. Oh, and I'll take some cookies with it too. Nothing like milk and cookies."

"Fuck off. You're so stupid." He groans. "Just be careful, missing class, Huff. You know how Coach feels about that shit."

Pretending to be sucking a titty, I eventually stop and shake my head. "Yes, Mommy," I mutter, grabbing a bottle of water just as Hunter strolls into the kitchen.

"Yo." I nod. "What's crackin', Thompson? You lifting more lately or what?" I wink. "You're looking extra bulky, my man. I'm diggin' it. So ... muscular and manly."

Hunter glances from Watson to me. "Look, guys, my sister's dorm flooded. She needs a place to stay, and I told her she could crash here until they get it fixed." He looks nervous as he completely ignores my sweet-ass compliment. "Is that cool with y'all? I guess I should have asked first."

"Hell yes," Watson says, nodding. "You know I don't care."

"Watson, maybe you'll be able to show your candle collection to Haley. Chicks love candles." I point to him.

"You love my mama's candles too, Huff." He raises his eyebrows at me. "Don't even lie."

"Fucking right I do, big boy. But that damn apple pie one makes me want to go to my grandmother's every time we light that shit up. And that's a problem because she lives too damn far away."

"From the looks of you lately, I should light it more often." Watson narrows his eyes. "You look like you've lost some weight. Everything all right?"

My shoulders instantly tense. But before I can say anything, Hunter intervenes because if there's anything he hates, it's when his friends and teammates don't get along. Hunter is one of those guys who can't stand for anyone around him to feel uncomfortable.

"Hales loves candles," Hunter says. "So, you're in luck, Gentry."

"Who would look at Watson Gentry, our six-foot-two goalie for the Wolves, and think, *That guy right there is heading home to light some fucking smelly candles?*" I say, shaking my head and grinning. "You're a real gem, Gentry. Martha Stewart would be proud."

"Hey, I'm confident in my manhood. I ain't afraid to enjoy some smelly soaps and candles." He shrugs. "And you guys secretly love the candles and the hand soaps my mom gives us too."

"It's no secret, my man. I'll love your candles loud and proud." I nod. "I'd have sex with the vanilla cupcake one if I could find a way to stick my dick in it. But that's probably illegal or some shit. And that'd be one really embarrassing charge."

"Jesus Christ," Hunter mutters, rolling his eyes. "One thing we're going to do is establish some ground rules. First, don't hit on my sister. Second, don't try to bone my sister—"

I raise my hand before he can finish, and annoyed, he waves toward me. "What, Cade?"

"Wouldn't rules number one and two technically collide into the same rule?" I wink, glancing at Watson and rubbing my palms together. "Wondering how many rules I'm fixin' to break."

Holding his middle finger up, he narrows his eyes. "Shut up. Don't even think about it. Rule number three is, be fucking respectful. She's a good girl. She's been through a lot the past few years, and she doesn't need living here to be another thing she has to recover from. So, please, for the love of all things … try to act civilized and not like complete cavemen. And keep your dick in your pants."

"Well, I have to take it out sometimes, or it would never get oxygen. And if it didn't get oxygen, it'd probably fall off. And how awful would that be, not just for me, but for the entire female population?" I sigh. "Not to mention, you'd lose me as a player because I'd have to go join the women's hockey team." My face lights up. "Buuut … I could get access to the locker room. I could look around and not even have to worry about popping a chub."

Hunter gives me a murderous glare, his jaw tightening, and I shrug.

"All right, all right. Aye, aye, Captain." I grin, saluting him. "I will … under no circumstances … *not* bone your sister."

"Huff," he growls. "Cut the shit."

"Okay, I will not bone your sister, dammit! Now, make Watson swear it too. I feel singled out. You're discriminating against me and not the candle lover."

Turning toward Watson, he doesn't even get a word out before Gentry is shaking his head, frowning.

"I won't fuck your sister, man. Don't worry. Besides, I've got my sights set on someone else."

"Ahhh … big daddy has a lady!" I clap, dancing around like a moron before slapping his shoulder. "Who is the mystery lady, Gentry?"

"It's no one," he grumbles, rolling his eyes. "She basically hates me anyway."

"The ones that pretend to hate you will ride your dick the hardest," I say with a cocky grin. "It's called hate fucking, and it's the bomb. So, consider yourself blessed, my friend."

Times like these with my friends, joking around and giving each other a hard time … I almost forget. For a moment, that hunger to get high leaves my brain, and I forget that my life is pretty well fucked right now. But then, when I stop laughing and the room's quiet again, I remember that without a little pill every so often, I'll be puking my guts out. And not only that, but I also won't even feel normal. I would know—I've tried to stop numerous times over the past few months.

I'm not even in the driver's seat of my own life right now. I'm just a passenger, stuck between jumping out and hanging on just to keep myself from having withdrawal.

I snap back to reality when Hunter makes us promise to be polite to his sister just before he heads out the door. We both agree. And I can't speak for Watson, but I plan to do what I promised.

I just like teasing Hunter when it comes to his sister. I mean, shit, I haven't seen Haley Thompson in well over a year—when she was still in high school. She was sweet—and far too innocent for me. And the last time I saw her, she still had a baby face. So, unless she's grown up overnight, I think Hunter is safe.

I mean, how much could she have changed in a year?

Haley

I glance around my new bedroom. My eyes land on the queen-size mattress, and I can't help but wonder how many girls have been boned in the bed. After all, this was some other hockey player's bedroom, who graduated last year, and it's a known fact that hockey players tend to sleep around.

I moved in yesterday, but I just finally finished putting everything away this morning. Watson was here when I arrived, but I have no idea where Cade has been because I haven't seen him yet. And with that boy, it's hard to tell since I know he's a bit of a ladies' man and, from what I've been told, a party animal. Not running into him too much is for the best; I'd likely just embarrass myself because he makes me so incredibly nervous with his panty-melting grin and his confident swagger.

Ever since my brother was a freshman here at Brooks, I've been completely enthralled by Cade. His energy is always off the charts, and his smile lights up any room he walks into. He is so shiny and happy and has this magical ability to get the attention of everyone. And I … I'm just not like that.

My whole life, I've felt like I'm not where I'm supposed to be. Like I'm running toward something—to wherever I belong. I've always longed to just finally feel at home. But I haven't found it. I'm not sure I ever will either.

Seeing someone like him, a person who seems so sure of himself, it's as charming as it is infuriating. But when you're as pretty as him, who *wouldn't* want to look and smile at you? With his stupidly chiseled body, ocean-blue eyes, sharp jawline, and short brown hair, he looks like he walked out of a magazine. I have been around athletes my entire life because Hunter's life revolves around hockey. But Cade … he is different from everyone else. He's captivating while being his true self.

I glance in the mirror. My dirty-blonde hair hangs down past my shoulders in thick, sun-kissed waves. As much as I like to straighten it to make it smoother, it takes too long because I have too much damn hair. My green eyes have always seemed a smidgen too big for my face, and the light-colored freckles splattered across my cheeks and nose are just annoying. I am pretty, but not breathtaking. Not like the girls who usually surround Cade.

My stomach growls, telling me it's time for some lunch. I grabbed a few groceries last night, but I'll surely need to go to a store again soon. Especially living here with three dudes. If they are anything like Hunter, they can eat like bears.

Heading downstairs, I open the refrigerator and take out everything I need to make a BLT—minus the T because tomatoes are gross. Rifling through the cupboards, I finally find a frying pan and start cooking the bacon.

"Don't burn my house down, please," Hunter says from the living room before sitting down on the couch.

"Oh, shut up. You know that was one time when I was thirteen, and I've never set anything on fire again."

"You grabbed your toast from the toaster oven with a paper towel …" He widens his eyes. "Paper. Hot oven."

"Yes, and you've never let me live it down." I groan. I have grown to love both cooking and baking. And I am certainly capable of cooking bacon for a damn sandwich. I point my spatula at him. "If I'm such a terrible cook, I guess you won't need any of this bacon for your own sandwich, will you?"

Before he can answer, a shirtless Cade strolls downstairs, walking into the kitchen.

"Is that bacon I smell?" He inhales before his eyes find mine, and he unapologetically looks me over. "Well, shit, Haley baby. You done went and grew up."

"Huff," Hunter growls. "Remember our little chat?"

"Yeah, but that was before I saw that she wasn't a little kid anymore, but a *woman*." He winks at me. "Lookin' good, Haley baby. Lookin' real good."

My cheeks burn, but I don't know if it's from the nickname Haley baby or if it's because he said I looked *real* good. I feel my body prickle with nerves just because he's paying me any attention. "Uh ... thanks." I swallow before remembering the bacon, taking a few now-crispy pieces from the frying pan and setting them on a paper towel.

I glance nervously at him as he reaches into the fridge and pulls out a water bottle, and I watch him chug it, his neck moving as the liquid slides down his throat. His hair looks like he just rolled out of bed. His gray sweatpants hang dangerously low on his hips. I can't help but ogle the insanely prominent V on full display, and a stupid image pops into my mind of me running my tongue along it.

Forcing my mind to get out of the gutter, I finish the bacon and glance at Hunter and then Cade. "Help yourselves. I cooked two packages." I look around. "Where's Watson?"

"Right here," he calls, walking around the corner and patting his stomach. "I smelled bacon. And when I smell bacon, I show up."

"Hey, where's the tomato though?" Cade looks confused as he grabs a plate and begins building his sandwich. "Can't have a BLT without the T. That just wouldn't make sense."

"Haley doesn't like tomatoes." Hunter laughs. "So, when she goes to restaurants, she orders a BLT without the tomato. Oh, and extra bacon."

"I like bacon. Bacon is good." I shrug before pointing to the refrigerator. "There's a tomato in the crisper. I just didn't take it out because, well, I'm not going to eat it."

"Sweet!" Cade pulls it open and takes the nasty red vegetable out. After slicing it up and adding it to his concoction, he takes a huge bite and moans. "Damn, that's good bacon. Crispy. Thick. Warm." He bobs his head up and down, moving side to side as he eats, standing up. "*Haley baby, you're the one. You make lunchtime so much fun.*" He sings the words loudly, grinning my way.

"Damn right you do." Watson nods in agreement. "The only sandwiches we get around here are peanut butter and fluff."

"Watch it, asshole. I've made you a shit ton of grilled cheeses," Cade tosses back with a scowl. "Don't act like you didn't enjoy them. Buttery goodness and all."

"And I love your grilled cheeses. But bacon just makes it next level. Add bacon to your grilled cheeses, Cade, and I'll never mention this BLT again," Watson says with a shrug.

Ignoring them, I nod toward the burning candle. "Oh, and I have to say, I love the selection of candles in the cabinet. I went with lemon pound cake." I giggle. "But now, I need to know, who has a girlfriend? And I know it's not my brother. No offense, Hunt."

"None taken," he says, engrossed in his lunch.

Watson looks slightly embarrassed but quickly grins. "It's my mom. She always had our house smelling either like a season, a holiday, or a baked good when I was growing up. So, when I moved in here, she bought me, like, fifteen candles." He rolls his eyes, but I can tell he loves his mother. "And now, when she visits, she brings at least four with her each time."

Sweet lemon and other fruit scents have always been my favorite. I have never been one to enjoy the smell of strong perfumes. But a sugary fruit scent? That I will inhale all day long. And lucky for me, it seems like Watson's mom feels the same way, judging by the endless candles.

"Well, tell your mom I approve. I was basically huffing candles for half an hour before making lunch." I laugh, taking a bite of my sandwich. "It's like I'm a kid in Bath & Body Works again."

"Yankee Candle is her favorite place." He takes a sip from his water. "She spends an hour there, easy, every time."

As the boys finish their meal, Cade rinses his plate before sliding it into the dishwasher. Walking toward me, he rests his hand on the small of my back and leans forward to look at me. "Thanks, Haley baby. That was damn good. Guess I'll let you stay after all," he teases before giving me a lazy wink and strutting out of the kitchen.

Watching his back muscles glisten in the sun, I have to remind myself not to drool. Or ogle him.

"Cade, you riding with us to practice tonight?" Watson calls behind him. "Yesterday, we gave up waiting for you and left. You were almost late, man."

He glances back, his eyes flashing with something I can't place, and he shrugs. "Uh, yeah. Sure, I'll be ready."

He looks at me once more before heading up the stairs. And dammit if my heart isn't still thundering in my ears as my mind flashes back to him touching my back and that damn wink.

It's fine that I'm checking out my brother's best friend. I mean, who *wouldn't* have a crush on Cade freaking Huff?

CADE

I walk into my room and close the door behind me.

Christ almighty, Haley Thompson went and grew the hell up. Like ... really grew up.

The way her tits were straining against that T-shirt she was wearing or how her shorts hugged her ass like they had been made just for those scrumptious, round cheeks ... I couldn't help but look at her even though I felt like a pervert for it. I mean, hell, she's my best friend's little sister. Which practically makes her my sister. Only ... technically, if I wanted to, I could bone her without it being called incest.

Of fucking course I want to.

But I can't.

Hunter would literally kill me if I thought with my dick on this one. And my dick thinks she's fucking smokin' hot, and she has some pouty, plump lips that would feel awesome, wrapped around my cock. And, hell, she'd look great on her knees. I feel myself harden a tad, just thinking about it.

But Hunter is protective of his sister. And while I'm sure he'd secretly be okay with Watson going after her, I know I'm not the dude he's going to give his blessing to so I can hook up with his baby sister. He knows me. He knows I'm a fucking mess.

A while back, Hunter told me and Watson that Haley had a stalker or some shit last year. And it ended up with her being kidnapped and assaulted. Luckily, she made it out of there safely, but, holy shit, that had to leave a scar.

She's gorgeous, no doubt. But she's been through enough without me thinking with the wrong head and making her living situation awkward. I mean, it wouldn't be awkward for me because sex is sex. A time to blow off steam. *And my load.* I'm friendly with a lot of chicks I've fucked.

But she's a good girl. And sex with a good girl is fucking complicated. They expect things. They hope for things. Things I don't do. Besides, she's like sunshine. And I'd darken her light. She doesn't need me lurking around, ruining her. I'll stay clear; I'll just look from afar.

My phone rings, and I don't have to look to know it's my mother. She's called eight times in the past twenty-four hours, and I've ignored all of them.

Feeling guilty, I slide my thumb across the screen. "Hey, Ma."

"Cade! There you are!" She sounds more worried than pissed. "Why haven't you answered your damn phone? I've called so many times." She stops. "Where were you last night?"

"I passed out early," I lie. "Practice was a rough one. LaConte's trying to kill us, I swear."

There's a short pause.

"Cade, if something is going on, if you're struggling ... you need to tell me. Or your dad. Just don't keep it in or hide things from us."

"Relax," I say quickly, trying to keep my voice soft, though that's a struggle. "I'm good, I swear. You think I'd do anything to fuck up my spot here?"

"Language," she groans before her voice breaks. "I feel like I'm losing you again. Your calls are few and far between. You hardly message me back. Maybe I'm being crazy. I know it's not fair, me not trusting you." She sniffles. "I'm just so scared."

"Mom, I'm good." I feel a pang in my chest. "I promise."

She sighs into the phone. "All right. I love you, but please, just pick up your phone before I drive to Brooks."

"Yes, ma'am," I say quickly. "I gotta run. Tell Dad I said hi, and y'all don't miss me too much. Love ya."

"Love you more." She sighs. "Talk with you later."

"Bye, Mama," I drawl and end the call.

Dragging my hand down my face, I collapse on my bed. Because if there's one thing I hate doing ... it's lying to that woman.

Yet there I went. Doing it like it was my fucking job.

The truth is, my senior year in high school, I made some pretty bad choices. One was thinking that I could self-medicate the guilt and sorrow I was feeling out of my body. Months later, I found myself in rehab—against my will. But it's no secret that hockey is hard on the body. And when I fucked my knee up from overtraining this past summer, I needed something, anything, to train through the pain. I knew better because I had only been clean from pills for a year. And aside from a few beers here and there, I hadn't touched any drugs. But I didn't want to let the guys down by playing like shit if my skills got rusty from resting.

A few OxyContin later, I might have temporarily numbed the pain in my knee, but I knew I had fucked up my sobriety, moving forward. Because a few turned to weeks of daily use, which turned into months. And before I knew it, it was hockey season. And how the hell was I supposed to go through withdrawal when my team needed me?

Exactly. I couldn't.

I will get clean someday soon. But right now can't be that time. Even if I know that playing college hockey and snorting pills don't mix well.

But still ... here I am, continuing to do it.

So, I don't blame Hunter for not wanting me to get too close to his angel sister. I'm a bad guy. And bad guys should stay away from good girls.

3

Cade

Opening game is something the entire team waits for. It's like getting ready for a hunt, and we're anxious to take down our prey. The locker room is filled with equal parts excitement and nervousness. It's different this season though, and I think we all feel it.

We don't have Cam Hardy or the crazy motherfucker Brody O'Brien sharing the ice with us. And that sucks because Hardy was an incredible center and a true captain. And O'Brien? Well, he was slightly insane when he stepped onto the ice. He'd take out anything that got in his way of winning. Like me, he was a defenseman. And I think the entire team felt safer with the two of us on the ice together. Because if you fucked with any of our boys, we'd make sure you felt the wrath of it.

From what I've observed since being a part of the hockey world, some of the best defensemen have a few screws—or ten—loose. That's a trait he and I share. Aggression is our outlet. A way to blow off steam without getting in *too* much trouble.

I think I always felt closer to him than some of the other guys on the team because I knew he'd been through some shit in life. Probably not the best thing to connect on, but, hey, darkness usually finds darkness. If it surrounded itself with light all the time, it would just be swallowed up and forgotten.

Link Sterns, our new team captain, is a senior. He was offered a spot in the NHL last year. But his girlfriend, Tate, still had a year of schooling left here at Brooks. So, lucky for us, he put off going into the pros for another year to wait for her. That's a good fucking man. He's got more consideration in his left nut than I do in my entire fucking body. The only decent thing I might do for a chick is to make her come twice instead of just once. And even that usually isn't out of the kindness of my heart. It just *happens*.

There are enough drugs in my system to keep the pain in my knee at bay. But not so much that I'll be useless for the game. It's a balancing act. One that, if I'm being honest, is fucking exhausting. Yet here I am, already worrying that I'll need more in the middle of the game.

Thank God for intermission.

I haven't really thought about what I'll do if I get chosen for a drug test. It could happen at any given time. Last season, it did, and thank fuck I was behaving myself when it happened. It will happen at some point this season—that's obvious. But I guess I'll cross that bridge when I get to it.

"All right, all right," Coach LaConte says, strutting into the locker room. "I'm seeing a lot of fucking off in here. So, that'd better mean you all are ready for this opening game."

"Yes, sir," everyone calls out, nodding.

"I hope so. We know how important game one is. I don't need to tell you that this sets the tone for tomorrow night's game against this team. Hell, sort of sets it for the entire season, to be honest. If we come out swinging tonight and bring home the win, the others will know we aren't a team to take lightly. If we are sloppy and they see our weaknesses, they'll use that to their advantage. Not just tonight, but tomorrow night too." His eyes sweep the room, his lips in a firm line. "In practice this week, you guys looked good. Not great. But good. We have a long way to go, but I think tonight, this win, well, it'd be a fine place to start."

LaConte always reminds me of the coach from this show my mother used to watch when I was younger. It was called *Friday Night Lights* or some shit. I'd pretend like it was awful, but the second I sat down when it was on, I'd find my dumbass getting pulled into the drama of it. I'd never admit that to her though. Christ, she'd force me to rewatch the entire series with her. And I'd do it because I'm her only child. And because she's always been too damn good to me.

LaConte jerks his chin toward Link, who's leaning his back against a locker. "Take it away, Sterns."

Standing up straighter, he takes a breath. "Y'all already heard my spiel the other day at practice. We know this feels different without Hardy and O'Brien. And that's okay because it is different. Look around the room. This is your team. *Our* team. So, let's go out there and show them this *team* isn't one to be fucked with. What do you say?" Holding his hand out, he gives us a slight smirk. "On three."

As we all move in a circle, putting our hands over his, we look around. "*One, two, three … Wolves!*"

"Let's fucking go!" Link yells before heading out the door, the team following behind him.

When I get closer to the arena, I hear "Kream" by Iggy Azalea and Tyga blaring, and my heart rate picks up.

As we follow Link onto the ice, the sounds of music and people screaming for us fill the air. It's in moments like this that I think of Eli.

He would have fucking loved this.

He should be here instead of me.

HALEY

My brother played so well tonight, and as I watch him and his teammates all hugging, acting like animals, grinning like fools, my heart squeezes for him. He's really found his place. And that place is on the ice.

My parents have always pushed for both of us to become doctors. For our oldest brother, Holden, who passed away from cancer years ago, it wasn't a question of if, but when. He was going to be everything my mom and dad wanted him to be. He had the brains. The drive. And was basically a mini version of my father. For Hunter, all he's ever wanted to do is play hockey. Despite the pressure from my parents to become a doctor, it's clear that isn't the career he wants.

Me? I'm at Brooks with the intent of going to med school. But to be honest, that's not really what I want to do either. But the problem is, I don't have a clue what I actually want to do with my future. And until I do, I figure I should probably go with the flow. And the flow is pretending I really do want to be a doctor to appease my parents.

I watch Hunter blow a kiss to Sutton, knowing damn well it's all for show because they came up with the *super-intelligent* idea to fake date each other. Who even does that? Well, besides in romance books that I read, that is.

My brother—that's who.

I will say, the books with that trope in them are some of my favorites. And I suppose they usually do end with a happily ever after. But Sutton and Hunter aren't a damn novel. And I don't want to see my brother get hurt.

I move my gaze to Cade Huff. His smile is so bright as he throws his arm around my brother's neck, dragging him closer. He's truly a ray of sunshine. Someone I find so intriguing because of the way he seamlessly floats through life, brightening everyone's day.

"You're really ogling that number four with the name Huff on his back," Remi says, nudging me. "As in … *Cade* freaking Huff. As in … your new roommate. As in … Hunter's best freaking friend!"

I elbow her, looking around to make sure no one heard her. "Remi! Shut up!" I hiss. "I was not!"

"Oh, you were." She tucks a strand of brown hair behind her ear. "I don't blame you; I'd probably be looking too. Okay, I'll admit, I was looking." She pouts. "I'm a horny bitch who can't help but sit here and salivate over the man meat."

"Except you have a boyfriend, you little whore!" I tease her, poking my finger into her arm. "One all the way in California."

"Please, we all know my boyfriend is checking out the bitches of SoCal." She squints her eyes and scrunches her nose up, making one of her many animated expressions. "Probably in their crop tops and booty shorts with their big hair and pouty, over-glossed lips. So, yeah, I can take a little look-see too, right?"

Deacon and Remi have been dating since our sophomore year in high school. He plays baseball and was devastated that she wouldn't come to college with him in Cali. But Brooks has an incredible swimming program, and I'm pretty sure that girl is part mermaid.

"If you say so." I roll my eyes, letting them drift back to Cade.

As the huddle breaks apart and he's left alone, I watch as his smile fades. What replaces it is something I actually recognize.

Emptiness.

His body language changes, and his shoulders slump. Gone is the picture I painted in my head of this sunshine boy who was full of nothing but goofiness. And what's left is someone who appears lost and, honestly, kind of broken.

I can't help but wonder … *Why haven't I noticed that look on him before?*

With my fake ID, I order a drink. Since it's fall, Club 83 has some caramel apple martini goodness, and I'm pumped. Taking a sip, I nod at Remi as she downs most of her White Claw.

"Dang, that's good." I inhale, setting it down on the bar just as the waitress puts our cheese curds and fried pickles in front of us. "Not as good as *that* is going to be."

"You're going to burn your mouth, Hales. Would you just let them cool off?" Remi scolds me like I'm five years old as I reach for a piping hot curd, damn near burning the fingerprints off my digits.

Dunking it in ranch to cool it off, I blow a few times before popping it in my mouth. "Dear Lord, I love these things," I utter, trying to chew through the pain of the burn. "Hot."

"No shit they're hot," she deadpans before grabbing a pickle and waving it around so that it actually cools.

Remi's household eats only the healthiest of foods, and she always says I corrupted her with my love for junk food. She's not wrong, I guess.

My parents always tried to keep everything in our household extremely healthy. But our nanny wasn't nearly as much of a stickler. And when I asked for something, she'd usually deliver. Not to mention, when I got my license and had the ability to drive to any fast-food joint, that was exactly what I did. Far too often too.

Grabbing another curd, I pop it between my lips and start chewing when someone leans over me, snatching a fried pickle and dunking it in the ranch dressing. Looking up, I see Cade grinning at me.

"Sharing is caring, Haley baby." He nods, narrowing his eyes in an almost-seductive way. "Your bacon is still better. I'd eat the shit out of that all day, every day." He winks before taking another. "But ... not bad."

"Cade," I say, smiling a cheesy, embarrassing smile that literally hurts my cheeks. "Good game."

"Thanks. I saw you there, snacking on some Sour Patch Kids with your big ol' soda." His grin grows. "Next time, you probably should wear my jersey when you come watch me play."

"Oh, yeah? And why would I do that?" I raise a brow at him.

"To let everyone in the arena know who you're there watching. Duh." His eyes shimmer with amusement, laced with flirtation. "Plus, you know, angel, you'd look damn good in my number."

My neck continues to crane so I can look up at him. His smirk reaches right up to his eyes, matching that same charismatic energy I knew was in there despite his look of sadness earlier. He's confusing as hell. But with him this close, I can't even try to pull away. That is, until my brother shows up.

"She came to watch her brother, you dumbass," Hunter chimes in, taking the seat next to Remi and helping himself to our food. "Oh, cheese curds, fucking right."

"Keep telling yourself that, Thompson." Cade shrugs. "Whatever helps you sleep tonight."

"Y'all had better order more food for us if you're gonna eat all of ours," I warn them both. "I'm serious. I waited the whole damn game."

"I saw you, babe. It looked like you'd found something to hold you over," Cade jokes. "Sour Patch Kids. And I think I even saw popcorn." He widens his eyes at Hunter. "Wasn't a small one either."

I try not to let myself get caught up in the fact that he looked up at me enough to know what I was eating. But then I also want to crawl under my chair because he was watching me while I stuffed my face. *Literally the entire game.* Not to mention that I'm messy as hell when I eat. Or do anything in general.

"Haley girl don't play when it comes to her cheese curds," Remi teases me. "Or any food for that matter."

"Yeah, I know. She cried once because I'd eaten her shitty caramel apple she had gotten at the fair." Hunter shakes his head. "It wasn't even that good."

"Then, why did you eat it?!" I all but screech, smacking my palm on the counter. "I'm still mad about that, by the way. Mom and Dad had finally let us attend a fair, and you went and ruined it by eating the apple I'd snuck home!"

"Dude, it was, like … ten years ago. Time to let it go," my brother groans. "I'll buy you a new one."

"You're the one who brought it up, dickwad," I mutter, rolling my eyes. "And, yeah, you should buy me a new one."

Out of the corner of my eye, I see a female approaching us. When she reaches Cade, he steps back from me, and I hear a flirty, husky voice talking to him. Slowly, he walks away from our group and follows her. I bite the inside of my cheek to stop myself from sulking, which clearly doesn't work because when I look at Remi, she gives me a knowing look.

The night went from fun to shitty in about thirty seconds flat. All because a guy who I have no ties with walked off with another woman. It makes no sense and perfect sense, all at the same time.

Because for some reason, I really, *really* hate the thought of him hanging out with other girls.

CADE

The sexy chick and I take a few shots together before I let her lead me out onto the dance floor. I'm drunk. And high. And not in my right fucking mind at all. But we won our game, and my teammates are happy. So, right now, I feel like I'm on top of the world.

Hunter abruptly left a few minutes ago. But before he did, he made me and Gentry both promise we'd watch his sister and make sure she got home safely. I know he worries about her. And I guess her coming out and dancing isn't something she's done since she was kidnapped. But she seems to be having fun. And judging by the pink in her cheeks, she's feeling a little buzzed too.

Gripping her hips, I pull the chick I'm dancing with closer against me. Thankful as hell when her ass grinds against my cock, letting me know she's game for whatever the hell I want to do. Her hair is jet-black, and her skin is tan and silky smooth. She smells like tequila and too much perfume, and my head whirls as she cranes her neck to lick my neck. Dragging her tongue against my flesh, she stops on my jawline and gazes up at me with *fuck me* eyes.

"That's not all I'm hoping to lick tonight, babe," she says in a sultry tone. "And this drink isn't all I'm going to swallow either."

Fuck. Me. That's hot. When they offer to swallow from the get-go? That's a done fucking deal. Not every chick can handle it, and I don't really blame them. Not sure how I'd feel about a mouthful of cum either.

I open my mouth to speak, but my attention stays on the angel across from me as she dances with another dude. Just before I can answer the swallower herself, Haley catches me watching her. She quickly looks away, continuing to move her perfect body against her dance partner, who I'd love to punch in the face for no reason other than he's dancing with her.

My eyes stay on her. Just as they have for God knows how long since she's been dancing with that fucking football player. Her cutoff jeans are too damn short, and his hands are too fucking low on her hips. She spins around to face him, and I watch her rest her arms on his shoulders as they grind on each other in an eye-assaulting way.

Haley fucking Thompson … when did you become such a bad girl?

The girl I remember was sweet, innocent, and mousy. The woman I'm watching now is a fucking dirty girl, disguised as an angel. And, fuck, I'd love to take her into the restroom right now and dirty up her knees and fuck that halo right off of her head.

When the song is almost at the end, I release the beautiful girl in my arms and give her a wink. "Thanks for the dance, gorgeous. I'll catch up with you later." *Probably not.*

"I'm holding you to it!" She pouts. "Don't forget what I said," she says before dragging her tongue around her lips.

I give her a grin. I have no doubt that she can suck dick with the best of them. I mean, her lips are like a damn inner tube, and I'd love to feel them wrapped around me as I fucked her face. But right now, I've got other shit to worry about. Other shit like Haley Thompson dancing far too seductively with a dude who isn't me.

I head toward Haley, stopping in front of her just as the music switches to a slower song. "Can I cut in?" I ask, never sparing the sorry motherfucker a second glance.

Her eyes widen, and she swallows before looking nervously at the dude. "Uh … do you mind?"

"Nope," he growls, glaring at me before stalking off.

"Ooh, someone is salty," I tease. "Sorry, you looked bored. Figured I'd save ya."

She gives me a look, telling me I'm full of shit. "Mmhmm. Sure I did."

Slowly, I pull her against me, feeling her hesitate to put her arms around my neck. But eventually, she does, resting her head on my chest.

Unlike the chick I was just dancing with, Haley smells like lemon bread or some shit. I breathe her sweetness in, feeling like I'm at a damn bakery. In some way, I feel this need to protect her, like she's my little sister. Or maybe that's what I'm telling myself. Because let's face it—I'm not looking at her like a sister right now.

"Did I interrupt anything?" I say like I'm oblivious. "Was he getting ready to tell you about how many balls he's held in his soft man hands?"

"Shut up." She rolls her eyes but giggles against me. "And how do you know his hands were soft?"

"Strikes me as a dude who has lotion next to his bed." Dipping my head down, I wiggle my eyebrows. "I mean, not *that* type of lotion. Everyone needs a little rub and tug sometimes. I'm talking hand lotion. So, tell me, were his hands soft?"

She bursts out laughing. "Fine. Yes, they were pretty soft."

"Ha! Knew it!" I cheer. "You need a real man's hands on your body, sweet thing."

She's innocent. I'm not. I should stay as far away from her as I can. And maybe I'll start. *Tomorrow.*

"Hunter's going to be mad if he sees you dancing with me," she says. "Consider yourself warned."

"He already left." I shrug. "Besides, you should know I've never been one to read warning signs."

"Wait, he left?" she says, surprised.

"Don't worry; he told me and Watson both that we aren't allowed to take our eyes off of you until you're home safe." I shake my head. "Basically threatened to chop our nuts off if we didn't agree."

"Sounds about right," she huffs. "How are you getting home?" Her eyes narrow. "Were you planning on driving, Cade? You seem drunk."

"I ain't that drunk," I say. "And, no, I wasn't planning on driving." I shake my head. As much of a dumb fuck as I am, that is one thing I don't do. Drink and drive. I'll either walk or get an Uber when I'm fucked up. "Watson's not drinking. He's DD tonight."

She feels so good in my arms, and I'm enjoying this dance far too much.

For so much of my life, I've had a thing for mischief. I've always liked the feeling of knowing I was doing something bad and dangerous. But she's the furthest thing from any of those things. She's a damn angel. However, her brother finding out that I'm almost grazing her ass with my fingertips? Now, that's bad. And dangerous.

But that's not what stops me from gliding my hands further down her back to her ass. Or cupping her cheek with my hand and kissing her plump pink lips. What stops me from doing either of those things is the fact that I'm a fucking loser. Scum. A lowlife. And Haley? Well, she's perfect. Too perfect for me to be dancing with.

The song ends just in time, and I step back, dragging my hand down the back of my head awkwardly. "Thanks for the dance. I, uh … am going to go find Watson if you're about ready to head out."

First, she looks stunned. And then hurt. Nodding slowly, she averts her eyes. "Uh … yeah. I just need to go find Remi."

I've never been one to make good decisions. But even I know that looking at Haley Thompson the way I have tonight is a very bad idea. And I'm not going to do it again.

Maybe I'm turning over a new leaf. Because, for once, I'm not giving in to something I want.

4

Haley

So far, freshman year at Brooks is the complete opposite of what I thought it would be. First off, I'm not rooming with my best friend. Second, I'm living with my *brother* and his friends. Which is so not something I foresaw happening. Ever. And third, I have a crush. Like ... a fifth-grade, *doodle on your journal, butterflies in your stomach, stare too long, try to run into them in a hallway,* and *smiling like something is wrong with you when they look your way* kind of crush. I've always thought Cade was hot, but ever since we danced a few weeks ago, my weirdness has gone to a whole other level.

It doesn't help that for some fundraiser thing, the hockey players have apparently teamed up with some ballerinas to perform a dance. Cade's original partner, Lindsey, from what I hear, is in a committed relationship. Which would have been a relief, except she got injured. So, now, Cade is paired with the very beautiful and very single Poppy Huxton. She's known to be kind of bitchy. And of course, I stalked her on Instagram, and sadly—for me—she's *really* pretty. She must be at least five foot nine. Her legs are long and toned. At five foot two ... I have legs that are anything but lengthy. And when I move, I certainly don't look nearly as graceful as she does. In fact, I'm that girl who trips over her own two feet. Usually at the *worst* time.

Like my high school graduation. Now, that was really fun.

So, even though I have no right to be jealous when it comes to what Cade does and who he does it with, I can't help myself when it comes to him and his dance partner. After all, Cade Huff could charm the skin off a snake. I have no doubt that, soon, they will be, if they aren't already, hooking up.

I haven't seen him bring anyone home since I've been living here. Then again, it would be hard to know for sure because he's sort of like a rare unicorn. You never know when you'll see him. When you do, it's exciting, but it doesn't last long before he's gone again. You sort of wish you had taken a picture to make the moment last longer, but that would be considered odd. So, instead, you take mental photographs of him when he's shirtless ... which makes you an even bigger creeper.

Either way, I have no idea where he goes when he leaves, but he isn't at the house nearly as often as my brother and Watson are.

As I finish my homework, propped at the bar area in the kitchen, I realize it's about to be one of those rare days because I see his truck pull into the driveway and I watch him walk toward the front door.

Pushing the door open, he doesn't greet me with his usual grin. Instead, it's almost like I'm not even here.

"Hi," I say, making sure he sees me. Which, let's face it ... he has to.

"Hey," he answers quickly, not sparing me a glance before he heads toward the stairs.

I hear him trudge up the stairs before his door shuts.

"Well, okay then," I mutter, closing my laptop and stacking my things into a neat pile. "Nice to see you too, grump ass."

Cade

The water in my shower is so hot that I feel like it might melt my skin off. It burns my body as it pelts my flesh, but I stand here, not wanting it any other temperature.

I raced home after the team workout today. A lot of the other guys, Hunter and Watson included, were going to get a bite to eat. I was growing more agitated by the second, and I needed a little something at home to get me through my knee screaming at me for overdoing it.

I feel bad that I was kind of a dick to Haley when I first got home. She was just the only thing standing between me feeling like shit and me feeling a tiny bit better. I didn't have time to chat with her. I needed to get upstairs.

Now that I can actually concentrate, I feel like a douchebag. I mean, shit, I didn't even look her way. I'm going to make it up to her though. I might not be able to look at her the way I did the night we danced together, but I can still be her friend.

Shutting the shower off, I grab a towel and dry off before wrapping it around my waist. I walk into the hallway just as she comes up the stairs to head to her room. When her gaze lands on my bare abdomen, her cheeks pinken, and her eyes widen a fraction. Catching herself staring, she quickly puts her head down and heads toward her door.

"Haley baby," I say sluggishly. "I need to run to the grocery store for some shit. Ride with me?"

I don't acknowledge that I was a jerk to her when I got home. Because honestly, it doesn't matter all that much. I don't owe her anything. At least, that's what I keep telling myself. Besides, she probably didn't even care or notice.

Slowly, she glances at me. Keeping her eyes solely on my face. "Why?" her sweet voice squeaks.

"Because I want to hang out with you, duh." I wink. "But if you're too cool for me, I understand." I wave toward my upper body. "Just so you know, if you decide to go with me, the store has a *no shirt, no service* policy. So, go on and get your ogling out now, babe."

"I wasn't *ogling* you," she says, narrowing her eyes. "You're being cocky. And annoying. Just so you know."

"You were. But it's cool. I'd check me out too. Also, if you walked out of the bathroom without a shirt on … I'd ogle the fuck out of you as well." I smirk. "So, what do you say? You going or not?"

Watching me for a moment, she eventually nods. "All right, I'll go. I guess."

"Good. Meet you downstairs in five." I point to my stomach again. "Last chance before the shirt goes on."

"You're such an arrogant asshole!" She scoffs, shaking her head. "For the final time, I wasn't looking at your stupid six-pack!"

Her hair is doing that thing it does when it's humid out. It frizzes, and I notice that she always tries to pat it down. I like it when it's this way. She's got all of these things that she probably considers imperfections, but they make her damn near irresistible to me. She's kind of messy. She's short. She's got thick thighs. Wavy, untamable hair. And those handful of freckles sprinkled across her face. She's the furthest thing from textbook. And I love that.

"Whoa, whoa, whoa." I raise an eyebrow, running my fingers against my chin. "So, now, you're saying I've got a six-pack. You must have been really lookin', huh, Haley baby?"

"Don't make me change my mind, Huff!" she growls before heading into her room and closing—no, forcing—the door shut.

When we pull into the parking lot at the grocery store, she giggles when I park really far away from the building.

"You're just like my brother. Scared to death someone will ding your door if you park too close."

Grabbing my hat from the dashboard, I pull it onto my head. "Hell yes, I am. Half these motherfuckers here don't give a fuck about other people's shit. They'll ram a cart against a car and be like, *Whoopsies! Tee-hee-hee!*" I scoff. "Yeah, no. I'm not taking any chances."

Pushing our doors open, we head toward the building.

"So, you'll just walk, like, half a mile instead?" She laughs.

"Fucking right I will." I nod. "What, are you one of those people who parks right up front?" I raise my eyebrows at her. "Bet you have dings and paint missing too."

"Cade, I'll park *next* to a cart return. I don't care." She shrugs.

I stop, my mouth hanging open. "The fucking cart return? Really? That's like asking to have your shit run into." I shake my head. "I was disturbed that your brother said you wear socks while you sleep. But this? This shit is worse."

"My feet get cold," she says, laughing. "Why do people get so weirded out about socks at bedtime?! I don't get it."

"I was with a chick once, and she had wool fucking socks on, and I didn't realize it until we were ... you know." I stop, clearing my throat. "Do you know how quickly it can soften a chub to feel a fucking nanny-knitted sock run up your leg?" I grimace. "I went from steel to cooked spaghetti in seconds."

"Eww!" She swats me. "You're so gross. And, FYI, it's not like I bring a dude to bed and leave my big, fluffy socks on while we get it on!" She shakes her head. "Geesh."

Something about what she said throws me off. I don't want to hear about her talking about fucking another man. I know I was telling her my story about the *wool socks* chick, but I can't even remember what that girl looked like. Just that her socks were fucking gross. But Haley's words make me realize she can sleep with whoever she wants. I don't like that. Not one bit.

Just because I can't be with her doesn't mean I want anyone else to either. Because I sure as hell don't.

As we make our way to the motion-detecting doors, a big-ass dude exits through the entrance, smashing his ginormous, Sasquatch-sized shoulder right into Haley's tiny one. She almost falls over, but I quickly catch her before she does.

"Watch it," I growl at him, standing her up straight. He continues walking, not giving a fuck that he just took a chick out who is only a fraction of his size. "You all right?" I ask, cupping my hand over her shoulder. "Fucking dick ran right into you."

"I'm good. Really. It looked worse than it was," she says with a smile, but when I touch her shoulder, she tries to hide a grimace.

I drop my hand from her shoulder and start walking behind the dude, but she grabs my hand, stopping me.

"Cade, it's fine," she whispers, her eyes begging me to let it go. "It isn't a big deal. Please, let's just go."

I watch as he gets into his car—a piece of shit parked up front in a handicap spot even though he doesn't have handicap plates or a sign hanging from his rearview mirror. I know she's right. Not walking away from a similar situation is what got my best friend killed. I can't risk something like that happening when she's with me.

Her hand drops from mine, and she jerks her chin toward the building. "Let's go."

I follow her inside, and she grabs a cart, but when she starts pushing it, I gently move her out of the way and push it instead.

When she gives me a funny look, I shrug. "Seems like a manly job, ya know?" I nudge my shoulder into her. "Remember my bod earlier, angel? I'm manly."

Rolling her eyes, she fights a smile. "If you say so, *manly man.*"

"Damn right I do." I nod.

As we walk down the first few aisles, we grab the necessities we know the house so desperately needs. And when we get to the cereal aisle, she gapes at the shelves before pointing, practically leaping up and down on her short little legs.

"Ooh, fall is here! You know why? Because look at that!" She points to the cereal with Frankenstein on the front. "Franken Berry cereal is my favorite."

I grin, jerking my chin toward it. "Go on, girl. Get you some."

When she steps closer, she looks at the other weird fucking ones next to it. One with a ghost and one with a vampire. "Which one should we get? They're all so good."

I smile as I take her in. Her cutoff jean shorts hug her legs as she shifts back and forth, trying to decide which one to get. Everything about her is sweet. Even being in her presence lightens the darkness in my soul.

That girl is sunshine. And I'm a black fucking cloud that could swallow her whole. She just doesn't know it yet.

Stepping around her, I grab one of each. "How about all three, Haley baby?" Tossing them in the cart, I wink. "YOLO, right?"

She looks from the cart to me before widening her eyes. "You don't understand. I have *zero* willpower when it comes to a few things in life." Holding her finger up, she starts counting. "Sitting pretty at number one? Nerds Clusters. Two, Milky Way bars, but it's fair to say that's tied with Hershey's Cookies 'N' Creme bars because they are literally better than sex." She blushes after the words slip out but carries on. "Three, pizza. From literally anywhere. Gas stations, frozen, or a fancy Italian place … I'll eat it. Four, smutty romance books with pretty covers. I love them. I have more paperbacks than I even know what to do with. Yet I can't stop purchasing more."

She's blabbering now, and I eat it up, wanting to learn more little facts about her.

"And last but certainly not least." She stops, pointing to the boxes. "Sugary, overprocessed cereal. Just like these ones."

I can't help but lean a little closer to her, smirking. "If you think a shitty ol' candy bar is better than sex, then you are clearly not having sex with the right guys, Haley baby."

"That's what you got? Out of that entire list of shit I just rattled off … that was your takeaway?" She moves her head from side to side. "You're such a dude."

"Well, yeah. My third leg doesn't lie." I keep my face straight.

Her cheeks redden a little, and she starts walking. "Don't let me forget to get some bottles of water. We're almost out."

"You got it, babe." I smile. "And I need deodorant, or I'll be fixing to smell like ass in another few days, and then I'll have to use yours."

"Don't you dare." She shoots me a warning look, pointing her finger.

As I push the cart next to her, I can't help but feel a sense of comfort. Something I don't usually feel. Ever.

I could get used to this.

I could get used to her.

HALEY

As Cade's playlist continues to play in the truck on the ride back to Brooks, I can't help but notice how many different types of music he listens to. Country switches to rock and then light metal before a little rap gets mixed in and even some pop tunes. Cade Huff has a lot of layers, it seems. But I get the feeling he won't let me be the one to unpeel them.

"So, tell me about this dancing thing y'all have going on," I say, glancing over at him, knowing I need to add something in there so I don't sound like I'm being nosy. "Are you going to wear tights or what?"

"Nut huggers?" he says, raising an eyebrow. "Why? Are you hoping I will so you can get a little peek?" He does a cheesy, seductive smirk, narrowing his eyes as he bobs his head up and down. "Ohh ... sweet, innocent Haley Thompson has seen me shirtless, and now, she wants me to wear tights so she can see my D. I see how it is."

"Um, no." I scrunch my nose up. "I don't think I'd ever want to see you in a set of tights. Sorry. But ... ew."

His eyebrows shoot up. "Woman, I'd be doing everyone in that building a favor if I wore nut huggers, showing a perfect outline of my dick. Don't even lie." He shakes his head. "But then I'd probably pop a hole in them because you know ... *so* big. And that'd make for an awkward night." He chuckles, amused with himself. "And it's going all right, I guess. The chick I'm dancing with is really fucking intense. And in case you haven't noticed, I'm just not that serious. Not about dancing anyway."

"You? Not serious?" I feign shock. "You don't say?" I smile at him, poking a finger into his side before I pull my hand back. "So, you're saying you clash?" I ask, trying to get a feel for what kind of relationship the two of them have. Because the thought of them having one at all bugs me. "Or ... no?"

"Oh, hell yes, we clash. We're like oil and water," he instantly rattles back, and I feel a pang of jealousy in my gut. "Or pineapple and pizza. Which is gross, by the way."

They probably have some sort of weird sexual tension between them. The kind I read about in my books. Everyone knows that those types of couples have the hottest sex.

I play with my necklace mindlessly, dragging in a quiet breath.

Before I can respond, he continues, "She's kind of a bitch, but I think it's because she probably has a shit ton of pressure on her shoulders." He shrugs, gripping the steering wheel a little tighter. "Any other chick would probably let me get away with fucking off during practice. Her? Forget it. She's more of a hard-ass than Coach is."

I shift my gaze to the road. "Wow, she sounds ... interesting." *And like I suspected ... exactly like a girl you'd find in an enemies-to-lovers book.*

31

"She is," he mutters. "That's for damn sure."

The way he talks about her sounds like he's almost … fascinated by her in some weird way while also being aggravated. And why wouldn't he be enthralled? He's an athlete. She's an athlete. A top-tier one at that. I, myself, am intrigued. But I'm also annoyed, thinking about how, if this were a book, he'd probably be sneaking her into the closet of the dance studio, doing dirty things to her fit, seamless body.

And now, I'm grinding my teeth, imagining punching a girl over a hypothetical situation.

People like Poppy and Cade are used to being the center of attention. The kind of people who, when they walk into a room, others take note of. I'm just me. I don't even know where I fit in or where my place is.

And Cade Huff? He fits in everywhere. And is loved by everyone. Of course he isn't into me. Even if I wish so badly that he were.

CADE

We get home and put away the groceries, and then I sneak away to my room for a little bit to take care of business. The business that will keep me from biting everyone's head off. Mostly Haley's because even the thought of hypothetically snapping at her makes my stomach turn.

My mind travels back to when Hunter told us about Haley's attack. I can't help but wonder if she is ever nervous or scared in day-to-day life now that something like that has happened to her. I mean, fuck, the girl was stalked and kidnapped just last year. She had a literal living fucking stalker. But she walks around, looking like sunshine, shining everywhere she goes. I don't understand it. How can someone be that good? That … strong?

Maybe it's an act. I mean, I, myself, play the part of the carefree, funny guy everyone wants to be friends with. I play it well too. But deep down, I can hardly stand myself for being the fuckup that I really am. She doesn't seem like she's acting though. She comes off as far too genuine for that.

Most of the guys on the team know that I've been to rehab before. I think for a lot of them, they probably think I was a kid who partied too much and my parents sent me to rehab. I doubt they know how deep I was into bad shit when my mom and dad made the choice to ship my ass away.

Now, my teammates just think I'm that dude on the team who drinks a bit too much, parties a little too hard on the weekends, and smokes some weed from time to time. They have no idea that I'm under the influence of something most of the time.

It's not like I'm stealing shit from my loved ones just to get money to feed my addiction. And I maintain a social life too. Somehow, I'm a good enough liar that my friends, family, and teammates overlook when I'm fucked up.

If I take too much and I'm drooling on myself, I'll claim I'm tired. And when I don't have it in time and my body begins to claim war on itself, making every cell inside of me ache, agitating me to no end, I tell them I'm having a bad day. For every question or suspicion, I have a lie to match. One that'll convince anyone that there is nothing—absolutely *nothing*—wrong with me. I'm fine. I've got it under control. It's them who should feel bad for second-guessing me in the first place. Don't they know that addicts hate being questioned?

So, I say I'm fine. I convince myself they are crazy for even asking. And sometimes, I even tell myself that's true. And a lot of the time, I believe it. But the days until I'm called into LaConte's office for a drug test are limited. And I know that.

Heading back down the stairs, I see Watson and Hunter sitting in the living room.

"You made it home," I say lazily, passing them by.

"Yeah, well … someone was too cool to join," Watson murmurs.

"I came back and hung out with Haley," I call back. "And before anyone asks, yes, my dick stayed inside my pants."

"Jesus," Hunter mutters.

Haley sits at the bar with a bowl filled to the brim with purple cereal and little marshmallows. She looks like a little kid about to dive in with the spoon in her hand.

Taking the seat next to her, I jerk my chin toward her snack, which is big enough to be an entire meal.

"Went with Boo Berries first, huh?" I frown, looking it all over. "I feel like when I was a kid, there were way more marshmallows than that. Cheap fuckers."

"I was thinking that same thing." Finishing her mouthful, she shrugs. "Still good though."

"Mom would shit if she saw all the cereal you bought," Hunter calls from the couch, clearly entertained. "I should send her a picture."

"Don't you dare. Or I'll tell the guys about that one time you p—"

"Finish that sentence, and you'll be homeless before you can take another bite of your nasty-ass cereal," Hunter warns. "Try me. I'll give your room to someone else."

33

"That's okay. Then, she can be my bed buddy." I wink before moving closer to her. "You're going to have to tell me the story at some point. You do realize that?"

Before she can respond, Hunter adds, "Don't even fucking think about it."

"Your mother doesn't like you guys to have sugar? Or what?" Watson asks, clearly confused. "My mom bakes cookies every damn day and thinks no meal is complete without dessert."

"Watson, your mother probably still has a breast pump machine, where she pumps you out some milk to go with those cookies," I say, looking into the living room at him. "No offense though."

"Fuck off," he utters, giving me the finger.

"Our parents hate any kind of dyes and overprocessed foods," she mutters. "Or fast food. Artificial sweeteners. Candy. You name it, and we probably couldn't have it, growing up."

"Don't worry, fellas. My sister made up for lost time. You should see how many times her ass went to McDonald's once she got her license." Hunter chuckles. "And if you get in her car, I promise you'll find some of those Nerds Clusters that are nothing but sugar. Or Sour Patch Kids. Any shit with any kind of dye? Sign her up."

Haley is completely and utterly unbothered by her brother as she continues eating. She simply shrugs and puts her lips in a flat line as she glances at me. "YOLO."

Stealing her spoon, I take a bite. "YO-fucking-LO, Haley baby."

"Gross," Hunter mutters. "I can see you sharing a spoon, you know. That's nasty. And your nickname for her is annoying. Haley baby? Are you, what, a seventy-five-year-old dude, sitting around a poker table, surrounded by strippers?"

My grin only spreads wider. "I fucking wish, Thompson! Now, that would be the dream. I have a whole new goal in life to strive for. And don't be jealous, big guy. I'd share a spoon with you too. You think I give a fuck?" I look at Haley. "So, I'm not going to lie, but Lucky Charms beats the hell out of this shit."

"I'll forgive you for saying that. But … no. Just no. The only good thing about Lucky Charms cereal is the charms. The actual cereal tastes like toilet paper."

I stare at her. "You eat toilet paper? That's kind of disgusting. But because you're cute, I guess I'll let it slide."

"You're irritating." She laughs before she slowly stands and heads to the sink. Once she's rinsed her spoon and bowl, she walks toward the love seat and plops down. "What are we watching, fellas?"

"Trying to figure it out," Hunter utters. "Watson's more indecisive than a fucking five-year-old child with ice cream flavors."

"Hales can decide." Watson shrugs, tossing the remote to Haley. "Just nothing where the dog dies."

"Word," I add. "If the dog dies, I'm out."

Chucking the remote at me, she grabs the pillow and lies down, a yawn ripping through her. "Cade can choose. As long as it isn't a documentary about anything medical, I don't care."

When Watson and I look at her funny, Hunter shrugs. "Thompson household things—you wouldn't understand."

"Huh. Well then ..." is all I say before I start my search.

It takes me a few minutes, but I wind up on something that everyone will enjoy. And if they don't, that's on them.

"*The* fucking *Notebook*?" Watson scoffs. "Are you serious right now, Huff?"

"Have you seen *The Notebook*, Gentry?" I ask, raising a brow at him.

"No. And I don't think today needs to be the day I do either."

"It's a good one. My mama's favorite." I wink. "So, sit back, shut up, get a tissue ready, and enjoy the fucking show."

I relax, getting comfortable. Fully ignoring the three sets of eyes staring at me in shock.

What can I say? I like what I like.

Haley snores softly, but I'm the only one close enough to hear it over the television. The girl didn't even make it to the part when Noah gets his woman back. Watson might have made fun of my choice in movie, but I don't think that fucker has even blinked the entire time.

Haley's lips are parted, and her hand is resting between her cheek and the couch. I wonder if she always sleeps like that. She looks so peaceful. A sort of peace I could only dream about, but I know I'll never reach it. Still, something about watching her ... I find a calmness just in that itself.

The movie ends, and it's only Watson, Haley, and me left. Hunter left halfway through to take a phone call and never returned. And even though Watson was engrossed in the entire thing, now that it's over, his eyes look heavy.

"Well," he says, yawning, "that was fucking depressing."

"Why? Now, they are both birds, probably shitting on people and living their best life." I stretch my arms before resting my head on my hand, winking at him. "If you're a bird, I'm a bird, Gentry."

"Shut up," he groans. "You're such a vagina sometimes, man." He yawns again, tilting his head toward Haley. "I guess we should wake her. Or … carry her? Or maybe we could leave her there? She looks comfortable."

"She can't sleep out here all night." I shake my head. Taking my phone out, I pretend like I'm scrolling and bored. "I'm not all that tired yet anyway. I'll move her in a bit if she doesn't wake up. No biggie."

He doesn't argue with that. Instead, he stands up and heads up the stairs. "Night, Hufferpuff. Have fun crying into your pillow, watching more shitty movies."

"You loved that movie, and you know it." I give him a cocky grin. "You candle-sniffing, Nicholas Sparks–loving bastard."

He ignores me, but gives his head a slight shake and heads to his room. Once he's gone, I set my phone down and look at her again. I don't want to just move her; I want to carry her to my bed and hold on to her like a damn comfort pillow. Keeping her close to me could chase away my nightmares … maybe.

I don't want to scare her though. Which is part of the reason I don't want to leave her out here alone. What if she wakes up and doesn't know where she is? That might freak her out. Then again, she's sound asleep, and considering her history, having a dude suddenly picking her up probably isn't the best idea either. But reluctantly, I stand and kneel down next to her.

Brushing a strand of hair out of her face, I get a better look at her. Admiring that handful of freckles sprinkled across her nose and cheeks. And her plump lips, which are a shade of deep pink, and I can't help but wonder what they taste like. Sweet, just like her, I imagine. Her lashes are thick and dark compared to her hair, which is a mix of golden blonde and almost light brown. I brush my thumb across the smallest beauty mark that rests above the left side of her lips, making her that much more stunning.

I take a mental picture of her right now even though it probably makes me a creep. Because, to be honest … I've never seen anything so beautiful in all my life.

An angel. But who was she sent here for? It sure as hell wasn't me.

Gradually sliding my hands under her back, I start to pull her to my chest when her eyes fly open, and she inhales so deeply that her throat squeaks. Pure panic covers her face until she sees it's just me.

"I'm sorry. I didn't mean to scare you," I whisper. "I just … I didn't want your back to hurt tomorrow from sleeping on this tiny couch." I feel her heart racing against my body. "You're safe," I tell her softly, but I don't know why I said it or what would make me comfortable enough to say something like that.

She studies me for a second before her eyes look sleepy again, and she yawns as she gives me a slight shake of her head. "It's fine," she whispers before wrapping her arms around my neck.

Hunter would love this.

Not.

Slowly, I carry her to her room and pull the comforter down as much as I can before laying her down and pulling it over her. Her arm flies over her head, and her head flops to the side, giving me a profile view of her pretty face. As much as I'd like to crawl in next to her, pulling her against me, I don't. Because I'm not what she needs. Hell, I'm not what anyone needs.

The way she was looking at me earlier, it was clear she thinks I'm a better man than I am. But that's just because she doesn't know any different. If only she knew the truth, she wouldn't be doing things like dancing against me or going to the grocery store with me. I know that much.

I'm not a good guy. Even if I wish I could be, just to be worthy of her.

She is the sun. And I'm just a storm moving through that could ruin her if I got too close.

I refuse to do that. She's too special for me to destroy her.

Haley

The lights are bright when I try to open my eyes. And the smell of mildew is strong when it hits my nostrils. It reminds me of my grandparents' basement, but much, much worse. This is the kind of scent that burns the back of your throat because it's so heavy.

I don't know where I am. I don't even remember how I got here. The last thing I recall is, I was leaving school. After that, it's all blank.

The sound of a door creaking open startles me. But no matter how much I try to focus my eyes on the moving blurb approaching me, I can't do it. My brain feels hazy, and if I wasn't scared, I'd probably fall back asleep.

"My sweet Haley," a voice coos, and I instantly feel sick. "I'm so happy to see your beautiful eyes open."

Rhett Dawson. The same guy I put a restraining order on just weeks prior because he had been stalking me excessively. Going so far as breaking into my house. While my family was asleep.

My skin crawls, but when I feel his fingertips on my hand, I try to pull my arm upward. I quickly realize that I'm fastened down. Which doesn't matter anyway because my body feels like it weighs a thousand pounds, like I've been drugged. And when I try to scream for help and nothing happens, I hear him laughing next to me before his lips kiss *my knuckles. Squeezing my eyes shut, I pray that this is a nightmare and I'm about to wake up.*

"You are mine, Haley." He drawls out my name so slowly, making my stomach turn more. "I think you just need to be reminded of that."

I feel his fingers graze my chin, moving down to my neck, and I lie there in complete fear. Unable to move. Or scream. Or do anything, knowing that my life is never going to be the same after this.

Before he can go further, I hear muffled yelling, and by the grace of God, he turns away from me and leaves the room. And shortly after, I hear the door clicking, indicating a lock being turned.

I'm going to die here. Wherever the hell this place might be. I'm going to die, and I haven't even done anything with my life yet. I don't even know who I am.

And even if I don't die, what if he rapes me? Then, will life even be worth living?

Tears stream down my face, soaking into my hair. I squeeze my eyes shut and pray for my big brother, Holden, to look down from heaven and help me.

My eyes fly open, and I drag my hand down my face. Thankful when sunlight peeks through the window, proving it's morning. When I have this nightmare in the middle of the night, I'm never able to fall back asleep. And then I walk around the next day, looking like a zombie who has been run over a few times.

An instant headache, mixed with my stomach churning, is not how I wanted to start my day.

The nightmare is nothing new. But from what my therapist has told me, it's normal and it might not go away. Which really, really sucks.

I don't walk around in constant fear every day of my life. However, am I cautious? Hell yes, I am. Although, this year at Brooks, I'm trying to get out of my comfort zone and do *college girl* shit. Because if I don't, then *he* wins.

But that day can never be erased. And sometimes, I swear I can hear the sound of the loud, squeaking boots he always wore behind me. Or his heavy breathing in my ear. Even though I know it's all in my head. And, yeah, I've had a few panic attacks since it happened.

Rhett was a guy from the same high school that I went to. People knew him as the kid who was weird and different. Sometimes, kids weren't that nice to him, and I hated that.

So, what was supposed to be only a compliment to make his day less crappy—something about his T-shirt being really cool—ended up with an obsession that almost cost me my life. I'd wanted to be nice. I hated how some of the guys at school would make him feel bad about himself. People could be so cruel, and I always tried to play a small part in spreading kindness. That was just who I was, just like Hunter always showed me. It gave me joy to see others smile.

Even now, even after he kidnapped me … I still feel bad for how he was treated in school. But had I known that my trying to help would lead to what happened, I would have just sat there in my seat and not tried to make his day better.

Rhett lives in a facility now. One for people with extreme mental illness. It turns out, when he did what he did to me, he had a lot of demons he was fighting, and he needed help. I don't wish any harm on him, but I hope I never have to see him again for the rest of my life. Even the thought of seeing him face-to-face sends chills down my spine and cripples me inside.

I don't go to therapy anymore. I did for six months after it happened because my parents made me. But it didn't seem to help me much. I guess I prefer to deal with things internally, which isn't always good. So, even though the nightmares still haunt me, I don't like to talk about the worst hours of my life when I was kept in his basement. Maybe it's too fresh. I mean, it was only a year ago. I don't know how long it takes the mind to heal from something like that, but even I know that it's longer than a measly year.

As I swing my legs off the bed and trudge toward the bathroom, I hear my brother and Watson talking outside their rooms.

"We need to go," Watson says, shaking his head. "I'm done waiting just because he can't get his ass up in the morning. It's becoming a fucking problem."

Hunter sighs. He's loyal to a fault. So, I'm sure leaving Cade here and going to practice would tear him up inside. That's just how he is. How he's always been.

Leaning against Cade's door, he smacks his palm against the wood at least five times. "Cade, get the fuck up! You're going to be late, and Coach will have your fucking ass."

"I'll be in the truck," Watson says, a stern look on his face. "I'll give him three minutes, and if his ass isn't in the vehicle, he can go by himself. Or not go. Either way, I don't fucking care," Watson mutters before taking off down the stairs.

"Cade, hurry up. I'm not doing this today," Hunter growls. "I don't have time for your shit."

It's not unusual for the guys to take separate vehicles to practice. But I think my brother knows that if he doesn't wake him up now, Cade will oversleep and miss the entire thing. And then Coach will likely bench him for the next game. Which isn't just bad for Cade. It'll hurt the team as a whole. They need him.

"Christ almighty, I'm coming, Thompson," Cade calls out lazily. "Calm your pickle. I'm fucking awake, goddammit. We'll make it in time for Watson to give Coach a big ol' smooch on his ass and a blow job if he's really lucky."

Seconds later, the door swings open, and out walks Cade. Though he's fully dressed, gear in hand, his hair is messier than usual, and his eyes look sleepy. Still ... he's stupidly handsome. Especially when he gives me his signature grin.

"Morning, Haley baby." He winks. "You're looking as beautiful as ever."

"Huff, shut up and get in the truck," my brother says, heading down the stairs. "See ya, Hales."

"Bye," I mutter, my eyes remaining on Cade because ... well, how can they not?

Cade rolls his eyes but smirks at me. "So dramatic," he retorts before following Hunter.

He might be a mess, but, dammit, he's hard not to adore.

CADE

As we head outside, I walk next to Hunter and pinch his nipple. "Y'all get too worked up, you and Gentry."

Shoving me away, he rubs his chest. "Stop fucking off. Watson's pissed at you. And I can't say I blame him either." He glares back at me, resting his hand on the truck door just as Watson lays on the horn. "Why the hell have you been sleeping in so much lately, Huff? I don't get it. This is go time. Not time to slack off."

"Oh, shut up," I say, pretending like nothing is off with me. "I'm up, aren't I? And with plenty of time to spare. I'm bright-eyed and bushy-tailed and ready to fucking roll. So, get off my nutsack, would ya?"

I climb into the back of Watson's truck. He doesn't look my way, much less speak to me. Watson is very much a type-A personality. And the one thing he can't stand is *almost* being late. I think he thinks that's just as bad as actually being late. Not being good with time is a thing Haley and I have in common. It's something I find downright adorable about her. The girl barely makes it on time anywhere. She's always rushing out the door with just minutes to spare before class starts.

I haven't always been the dude who sleeps in and shows up late. Time is just something that's been easy to lose track of lately. But when you play for a D1 college, that's not exactly a good quality to have. I understand why the boys are annoyed that I kept them waiting. But, goddamn, I wish they'd back off. I always show up even if I am sometimes racing the clock to get to where I'm going. I'm there when I need to be.

Watson and Hunter talk about our opponent for this weekend's games. I don't chime in because, honestly, I don't really care to talk about it. We'll show up and do what we need to do to bring home the win. But stressing about it now won't do a damn thing.

Besides ... it's just hockey. There's other shit going on in the world that matters more.

When that sour thought crosses my mind, I feel guilty. If Eli could be here right now, he'd be doing everything he could to prepare for our next game. He'd make me prepare, too, even though I'd bitch the entire time, just like I always used to.

Eli should be here, playing as a Wolf. He's the one who wanted it. And he's the one who deserved it. Not me.

I'm the main puppet in my very own show. Pretending I'm the furthest thing from what I actually am. But it's only a matter of time before people learn the truth. And my world will crumble beneath me.

I finish showering after practice and head to my locker to get dressed. Once I tug my clothes on, I look at my phone to find a text from Poppy.

Great.

She wants to practice and only has time within the next hour. As if I'm not already dead enough from Coach running us ragged, now, I have to go be a balle-fucking-rina on top of it. I could kick Brody O'Brien right in the nuts for making us do this fundraiser if it wasn't for such a good cause.

We haven't practiced nearly as often as some of the other groups. Fuck, especially as much as Hunter and his partner, Sutton. But I'm sensing there is more to them than just dance partners. More like ... a developing relationship or at least fuck buddies. Which would be hot since they claimed to hate each other not that long ago.

I wanted to tell Coach to shove this dancing shit up his ass when he first propositioned us weeks ago to do it. Because number one, most of us were already stupid busy between school, life, and hockey. But now, let's add something else we need to do.

Jesus Christ, when does it end?

But when he told us that we were dancing for the One Wish foundation, I couldn't say no. Brody had started this foundation for kids who couldn't afford to play sports or follow their dreams. It raises money for those who would likely never have the same opportunities as other kids do, simply because of what they were born into. And in doing all of this, Brody shared his story and all of his childhood shit with the world. He's a real man. One I look up to more than he'll ever know.

Even if he is making my life hell with this dancing shit.

Brody O'Brien took his crap situation and turned it into a positive. I took a bad situation, and then I made it a thousand times worse.

I never deserved to skate on the same ice as that motherfucker. Truth be told, not many do.

Texting her back, I let her know I'll meet her at our usual spot in forty-five minutes, and then I toss my phone back in my bag.

This wouldn't suck nearly as bad if my dance partner was someone else. Someone whose body I wanted to run my hands down.

Someone like Haley.

Haley

"Remind me again why we're here," I say to Remi as I shift on the metal bleachers, in hopes of awakening my ass that fell asleep ten minutes ago.

"Because I have an assignment. And my assignment is to interview the football players." She grins. "Which, by the way ... we still haven't talked about that dirty dancing you were doing with one of them a few weeks ago." She fans herself. "Hot."

I poke her side before leaning back on my elbows. Truthfully, I can't recall how hot the guy was or how good his dance moves were. The only part of that night worth remembering was when Cade cut in and danced with me. And that's annoying.

"His name is Nash Jones. Just in case you were wondering," she adds. "Just ... like ... FYI."

"I wasn't," I toss back. And I mean it. I haven't thought about the random dude I danced with. I wish I had been though because that would mean I hadn't been thinking about a certain roommate of mine. A roommate named Cade.

"Welp, that sucks because he just so happens to be one of the guys I need to interview. And it looks like they are all done with practice." Quickly standing, she grabs my arm and tugs me up. "Choppity-chop. Duty calls. Try to look friendly so they'll agree to my interview, would you?" Looking at my shirt, she squints her eyes the slightest bit. "Pull your shirt down a little. Show some of that cleavage I'm so jealous of. That'll for sure get me a full interview."

Looking down, I do the opposite and pull my shirt up higher. "What?! No way. Not a chance in hell."

"You're no fun." She pouts before heading toward the players.

Remi has dreams of going into sports broadcasting. Football being her main focus. The only information I know about sports is whatever my brother has told me. And if you asked me to name an athlete, I'd probably just rattle off Michael Jordan or Tom Brady because those are the only two names I've heard so many times that I know I wouldn't screw them up.

As I follow her down the ramp and to the entrance by the field, she waves to the dozens of men heading our way. She's not shy or embarrassed. Just the opposite as she marches toward them.

"Fellas, hey. My name is Remi, and I'm taking a class here at Brooks that requires me to interview some of the college's most-talked-about athletes. I was wondering if a few of you could hang back and answer some questions about the upcoming season." She awkwardly looks around the group of guys. "Specifically, Nash, Jace, and Tabor."

Nash throws a towel lazily over his shoulder, giving her a grin. "Sure. I'll do you one better. Why don't you and your friend join us for a drink and something to eat at Club 83 after we shower?" His eyes float to mine, and his smile grows. "You guys like it there, right?"

I blush, biting my bottom lip and averting my eyes from his. Obviously, he is toying with me because he and I were just dancing at Club 83 last week.

"Sounds perfect," Remi coos, fully in her *get what I want* mode. "Meet us there in, say, an hour?"

"Make it forty-five minutes," Tabor grumbles. "I'm hungry."

"Perfecto!" She doesn't hide her excitement. "See y'all soon."

As they all strut off, some looking back to give us one last smirk, I drive my finger into her side. "Thanks, asshole. I really wanted to hang out with a bunch of football players this afternoon."

"You're welcome," she tosses back lightly. "Anytime."

She is impossible.

CADE

I sit on my barstool after an hour-long practice with Poppy. I offered to bring her here to get a bite to eat. I know I haven't exactly made it easy, us being partners and all. And I feel like a dick. It's pretty clear she's got some shit going on personally, and if anyone understands struggling, it's me.

"Are you going to stare at that corner booth all night or …" she mutters, leaning closer. "I just spilled my life secrets, and you're just over here, completely ignoring me."

I turn back toward her, slowly turning my beer bottle around in front of me. "Sorry." I shrug. "And all you told me was that you grew up near campus and that your parents aren't around. That's all. It's not like you told me where you buried your bodies or anything."

She widens her eyes. "Keep screwing off during our practices, and you'll find out. Now … tell me the dirt," she says, taking a sip from her Sprite. "Is it the blonde or the brunette that's got your nuts in a bind?"

"Neither," I mutter, looking straight ahead before picking my beer up and bringing it to my lips.

"Oh, wow. I … uh, I didn't really see that coming. But it's totally cool! And I guess I shouldn't be surprised, considering your dance moves. Clearly, that should have been a giveaway. But why do you spend your time with every chick on campus if you're gay?"

I almost spit a mouthful of beer out, looking at her. "What?"

"You said you weren't looking at either of those girls. But since we got here, you've been glaring in that direction. Like, basically setting the place on fire with your eyes. So, if you aren't looking at them, I figure you've been looking at one of the football players." She leans forward, checking them out. "Not that I can blame you. Every one of them is fucking hot."

"I'm not looking at anyone," I grumble. "And I like women. If you want me to show you how much I like women, I can do that right now." I lean closer. "Quickie in the bathroom, Princess Poppy?"

Scrunching her nose up, she pushes me away. "Hell no."

I rear my head back. "Seriously? You really wouldn't fuck me right now?"

She snorts from laughing so hard. "No way! Sorry to bruise your ego, big guy, but I wouldn't touch you with a ten-foot pole. Are you attractive? Obviously. But you aren't my type."

"I am literally everyone's type," I say, looking at her like she has five heads. "Your loss."

When I glance in Haley's direction again, Poppy sighs. "All right, I'll give you two nights off from practicing our routine. *If* you tell me why you keep looking over there."

"Three nights off." I swing my gaze back to her. "And you have to let me choose a dance move to add into our routine."

"Three nights off, and you are *not* adding shit into our perfectly thought-out dance." She laughs. "So, tell me, Cade Huff, infamous bad boy of Brooks University, who are you looking at?"

Finishing my beer, I lift it toward the bartender so she knows I'm ready for another. And within seconds, it's replaced with a fresh one, and she gives me a sweet, sexy smile.

That girl blew me last year in the utility closet. Deep-throats like a fucking champ too.

"Haley Thompson," I say, dipping my head down slightly.

"Blonde or brunette, Huffypuffy? Don't leave me hanging here. I'm invested now."

"The blonde," I mutter. "The one in the green T-shirt with her hair in two French braids."

She leans around me, whistling low. "She's hot, I'll admit. But her last name, Thompson? Does that mean she's—"

"Hunter's little sister," I finish her sentence. "Yep."

"If it makes you feel any better, she's looking this way right now." She turns her attention back toward me. "I'd say she's feeling you too, big fella."

"I doubt that," I huff out even though I know she is. But I've been sending her mixed signals. Mostly because I don't have the willpower to fully push her away. "She seems like she's having a good time."

When I look at Poppy, she just smirks. "Wanna make a bet?"

And before I can answer, she leans forward, planting a kiss right on my lips. She smells like cinnamon. Spicy and bold. Nothing like the way Haley smells. And her lips feel all wrong. And when she flicks her tongue against mine, my dick feels nothing. Not an electric jolt or a small twitch. Nothing. Just a fucking dead, soft, hopeless zone.

Because of fucking Haley Thompson. That's why.

I pull back, not wanting to play this game. At the end of the day, I don't want to make Haley upset. Even if she probably doesn't give a fuck. I don't even want to take a chance.

Poppy gives me an amused, satisfied look. "Yep. She's pissed now." When I start to turn, she stops me. "Don't look at her. It'll look like you did that just to make her jealous."

"*I* didn't do anything," I say quickly. "That was all you."

After a few more minutes of us awkwardly sitting there and me trying my best not to look her way, Poppy mutters, "They are leaving."

Out of the corner of my eye, I see a group of people walking behind me. Turning slowly, I glance back just as she walks by. Right next to fucking Nash.

"Hey, Cade," her voice barely squeaks as soon as our eyes meet and she comes to a stop.

Holding my hand up, I give her a half-smile. "What's up, Haley baby?"

Jerking her thumb toward her friend, she shrugs. "Remi was interviewing some of the football players. I tagged along."

I open my mouth to answer, but Nash interrupts me before I get the words out. "Haley, you still game to go get ice cream?" The cocky smile on his lips makes me want to punch him right in the face as his eyes shift to mine. "Cade Huff, we meet again."

"Yep. And lucky for you, there's no music playing so I can't steal your dance partner," I mutter, looking back at Haley as I talk.

She awkwardly looks between both of us before she looks at Poppy. And when she does, she almost looks sad before plastering on a fake smile for

Nash. "Yeah. Yeah, let's go." She looks back at me, smiling as she holds her hand up. "Have a good night, Cade."

As they leave, walking toward the exit, I feel my heart sink. I know I'm too fucking damaged for her. But it sucks that I'll never even get a chance to try to be good enough for Haley.

Once they are gone, our center, Walker James, walks in and takes a seat next to Poppy, and I swear I feel the fucking anger radiating from her skin as she shoots him a harsh glare.

"There're, like, twenty other open seats, asshole." She waves her hand around the U-shaped bar. "Pick one."

The bartender slides him a beer, knowing his usual already.

Putting it to his lips, he gives her a cocky smirk. "Nah, think I'll sit right here. It's a bit chilly outside, and I figured Satan herself would put off some warmth."

"Careful. I might melt off some of those fancy clothes you're so fond of these days," she coos. "Cade, I'm out. I'll message you in a few days to find out a time to meet." She stands. "And, Walker … fuck off."

As she leaves, I glance at Walker with a confused look on my face, and he shrugs.

"Think she probably just wants my dick or something. You know how it is."

"Wow," I say and shake my head.

He's a cocky fucker—that's for sure. But he stepped into Cam Hardy's shoes, and those weren't easy soles to fill. But he's managed to do a good job so far.

Holding my hand up at the bartender, I order Walker and me a bunch of shots. Because if I have to see my girl leaving with someone else … I'm going to get fucked up to make it hurt a little less.

HALEY

I don't really know why I'm hanging out with Nash right now. I would have been just as happy going home, taking off my bra, pulling on some sweatpants, and diving into one of the new books I just got. Besides, Nash could be a freaking stalker, and here I am, setting myself up for another damn kidnapping.

Watching Poppy kiss Cade felt like a literal punch in the gut. Or maybe even a knife. *Definitely a knife.* A rusty one that'll probably give me some

LOST BOY

terrible disease. I stole glances their way all night. And for a little while, I really was starting to think they were just friends. And then she kissed him. And then I wanted to punch her. Me, Haley Thompson, the girl who wouldn't hurt a fly. My fist curled as I pictured popping her right in the nose. In my brain, it happened.

Only it didn't. And now, they are probably naked, having stupid attractive-people sex.

"Haley?" Nash's voice pulls me back to reality, though I still feel like I'm in a daze. "Flavor?"

"Oh, I'm sorry," I whisper and look at the case of ice cream. "Uh, how about a scoop of cookie dough?" I frown, not really sold on it, but feeling too put on the spot to think of what I really want. "Yep. Uh, that sounds good."

As we get our ice cream and walk outside on the lit sidewalks, I don't miss a few of the girls walking by checking Nash out. I don't blame them either. With his dirty-blond hair, sharp jawline, and boyish grin, it's hard not to look. And the fact that his muscles strain against his Brooks football shirt isn't terrible on the eyes either. I'm lucky that he asked me to be here with him. So, why do I wish I were at home instead?

"How do you know Cade Huff?" he asks as we walk along next to each other.

"Well, I live with him," I say. "And he's my brother's best friend and teammate."

His steps slow, and he frowns. "And your brother is ..."

"Hunter Thompson." I lick my ice cream, not missing as Nash's eyes dart to my lips and darken the slightest bit.

"Holy shit, for real?" he mutters, thankfully tearing his gaze from my mouth because it's freaking uncomfortable to be stared at while eating ice cream. "I had no idea." It's like everything I just said clicks because his eyebrows pull together slightly. "Wait, you live with Cade?"

"Cade, Watson, and Hunter." I nod. "For now anyway. Until my dorm situation is figured out. It was flooded a few weeks ago. But from what I've heard, they haven't even started renovating it."

"Huh, no shit?" he barely mumbles before he stops walking altogether and turns toward me. "Look, Haley, I've only hung out with you twice. And once was on the dance floor, and we didn't even get to talk. But Cade seems to just ... pop up everywhere. So, I gotta ask ... is there something between you two?" He pauses. "I just don't want to waste my time if I don't have a chance. Because I like you, Haley. And I like hanging out with you. But I'm not the type of guy to want in on a love triangle."

He flashes me that grin, and I truly believe if my mind wasn't so caught up in Cade, I'd probably be melting, like every other girl does.

"Even if you are gorgeous and super cool to hang out with."

49

You barely know me, is what I want to say.

He doesn't know that I sleep with my socks on at night. Or that I eat an excessive amount of sugar and that I currently have over two hundred thousand unread emails in my Gmail account and thirty-seven unread texts and twenty-nine voice mails. And that my phone is almost always dying because I don't plug it in long enough. I see twenty percent charged, and I consider that golden.

All the things about me that drive most people crazy, this guy has no clue about. Yet here he is, saying he likes me. He's being sweet and telling me I'm cool to hang out with. But I need to let go of the fantasy that Cade Huff and I could ever have some crazy love affair. He's never going to want me like that. And Nash is a catch by anyone's standards.

Knowing that I'm taking too long to answer his question, I smile. "No, there's nothing between us. Just friends."

Relief washes over his face, and the corner of his lips turns up when I pat his arm.

"I like hanging out with you too."

I'm not lying because there is nothing going on between Cade and me. I like him, and he likes kissing gorgeous ballerinas with perfect, long legs. It's time for me to let my crush go and move on.

"Good," he says softly. "That's really, really good."

And maybe he's right. Perhaps it will be good. Maybe it already is.

Everyone knows you never end up with the person you have a crush on. It's time for me to stop thinking the sun rises and sets on Cade Huff's left asscheek.

CADE

The music stops, and Poppy looks at me with a smile on her face. "Now, we're getting somewhere, Huff."

Grabbing my water bottle, I take a drink and wipe my mouth. "Call me butter, Princess Poppy. Because I'm on a roll." I give her a cocky look. "You'd better be careful, walking off the stage after we perform."

"Why?" she huffs out, knowing I'm about to throw some off-the-wall line at her—but she's getting used to it.

I shrug. "Because, when the women in there see my moves, their panties are gonna drop, and they'll probably throw them up onstage." I wink. "Be prepared—that's all I'm saying."

"You're too much," she deadpans. "Literally."

"My mama tells me I'm perfect," I drawl, and she pretends to gag.

We are a few weeks away from our performance, and if we don't win this shit, I'll be shocked. Our song is fucking awesome. It's upbeat, just like our routine. And I'll be competing against a bunch of dudes with two left feet when it comes time to dance. I have it in the bag. And my dance partner is wildly talented. And the more I get to know her, the more I feel like I understand her.

It's not that her parents are pressuring her to do good. It's that she *has* to do good because her parents aren't in the picture and she has little to no money to put herself through school. She is here strictly on a scholarship. Dancing is her lifeline and her way out of her past. Pain in the ass as she might be, I respect how cutthroat she is for it.

I have, however, heard of her giving Hunter's new girlfriend, Sutton, a hard time. And he's my boy. My brother. If someone is fucking with his girl, they are fucking with him too.

"So, I'm not trying to get all *Gossip Girl* with ya, but I have to know, what the fuck is the issue with you and Hunter's lady friend?" I put my back to the wall of the studio and sink down onto my ass. "Why are you being a mean girl? On Wednesdays, do you even wear pink?"

"Cade, sometimes, it's oddly creepy how many *chick flick* titles and references you know," she says, staring at me like I'm a freak.

Walking toward me, she wipes her forehead with the back of her hand before sitting down next to me. "Look, I've had to work my entire life just to make ends meet. I've gone to bed hungry. I've been scared to close my eyes because of who might break into my house, and I've danced until my feet bled just so I could be here." She shrugs her slender shoulders. "And Sutton Savage has the world at her fingertips. And all resources at the drop of a hat. She got into Juilliard—which, by the way, is impossible—and yet she left there to be here." She pulls her lips to the side in thought. "I don't respect that. And not to mention that Paige, Hunter's actual girlfriend, is one of my good friends."

"He and Paige broke up nearly two fucking years ago, Pop," I toss back. "And that girl's used my boy for a walking, talking dildo since the day she dumped his ass. She calls, and he goes running." I shrug. "I, for one, think it's fucking phenomenal that he's got himself a new lady."

She looks appalled, her mouth hanging open. "His family treated her like garbage!"

"So? He treated her like a queen. I saw it firsthand." I press the back of my head to the wall. "That's why I don't do relationships. No one is really ride or die. They can say it till they are blue in the face, but when it comes time to ride, no one wants to die."

Out of the corner of my eye, I see her staring at me for what seems like forever. Finally, she bursts into laughter, leaning against me.

"Cade Huff, you are so fucking weird." She settles down, inhaling. "So, what about you and Haley? Whatever happened with that?"

"Nothing," I answer quickly. "Never will either."

"Why is that?"

"Because, Poppy, I actually care about her. And you know what would happen if I let her get too close?" I turn toward her, narrowing my eyes. "I'd dim her shine—that's what. And I'm not fucking doing that. So, instead, I'll watch from afar. Just as long as that means I can watch her light burn bright."

The silence between us grows thicker and thicker before she eventually sighs.

"Damn," she whispers. "You really do care."

Yeah, I do. And it doesn't even fucking matter because she'll never be mine.

I pull into the driveway to find Haley is the only one home. Her car sits alone in her usual parking spot, and I wonder where everyone else is. The two of us … alone … in a house isn't good. Too fucking tempting really.

Walking into the house, I head upstairs to my room. Just as I pass the bathroom door, out strolls Haley with nothing on her body but a towel. With her head down and lost in her own world, she runs right into me.

I don't stop my body in time, and since I'm a helluva lot bigger than her, it's a damn bulldozer effect when our bodies collide. She falls backward, holding on to the towel for dear life so it doesn't completely slide off her and onto the floor. As I catch her in my arms, her towel slips down just enough to expose the top of her tits, causing a low groan to release from my throat.

As hard as it is to do, I peel my eyes away from her body and look at her face. Which really doesn't help me from drooling over her because she's so damn beautiful.

"Well, hi there." I grin, trying to pretend like her perfect, full tits aren't almost bursting out for the world to see.

"Hi," she squeaks, her voice barely audible.

I look at her face and notice her cheeks are red and almost chafed or something. Her eyes are bloodshot with bags under them. But before I can look any harder, she steps away from me, yanking her towel upward and tightening it around her. Her wet hair is slicked back, like she just combed it. And her skin is free of any makeup, leaving her in her most beautiful form. Bare. There're a lot of chicks who look hot in pictures or at parties with ten pounds of makeup on, but when they wash it off, they look like someone else. That's not Haley. She's a natural showstopper. And she'd take the breath out of any motherfucker's chest just by looking their way. But I can tell something's wrong even though she's trying to hide it.

I turn sideways and lean my shoulder and head against the wall, examining her. There's a depth of sadness in her eyes I've never seen before. She looks lost.

"You all right, gorgeous?"

She nods slowly, but I see her lips tremble.

"I'm fine," her voice croaks as she starts to turn.

Taking her wrist softly, I hold her in place before turning her toward me. "Haley, what's going on?" She doesn't answer, so I tilt her chin up. "You can talk to me, I promise."

She doesn't look convinced. A tear rolls down her cheek, and I brush it away with my thumb.

"It's okay; you can trust me," I whisper. "I swear it."

She chews her lip nervously as a few more tears spill from her pretty eyes. "I don't want to tell Hunter because I know he won't understand why I'm upset. But my mom called. She didn't want anyone to tell me before she could." Her lip quivers. "She said that"—she starts to cry harder—"Rhett … the guy who attacked me … he … killed himself. They found him in his room. He had gone home for the weekend to spend his birthday with his parents."

She shrinks into herself, her shoulders sagging. I scoop her up and carry her into her room, sitting down on the edge of the bed.

"Shh," I murmur against her hair. "It's okay."

"I know it's stupid that I'm crying. I mean, he stalked me, kidnapped me, and beat the shit out of me." She's so hysterical that her entire body shakes in my arms, so I tighten my hold. "But I still feel bad. I don't know why I feel bad. I'm so fucked up."

"You feel bad because you're a good person, Haley," I whisper, keeping her head tucked against my chest. "Whatever you are feeling is okay. If you're relieved, that's fine. If you're happy, that's fine. If you're sad and you need a shoulder to cry on, that's fine. If you need to break some shit, I'm game. Whatever you need, Haley, I'll be here for you." I kiss the top of her head, her hair tickling my lips. "I'm not going anywhere."

I know in this moment, it seems like I'm saving her. But the truth is … she's the one saving me.

Because getting high isn't even on my mind right now. Neither is that next pill. Or even having a drink. I'm just thinking about what I can do to help her pain.

For once in my life, it's not about me. I'm thinking about her. And how I'd give anything to always be the person who gets to dry her tears.

I never thought I'd be the hero in any story. But holding her like this sure makes me wish I could be.

Haley

I pull my Brooks U crewneck sweatshirt over my head before twisting my still-semi-damp hair into a bun.

After Cade held me for a while, I figured I should probably get some actual clothes on in case anyone else came home. Cade has never really struck me as the guy I would want in my corner when shit hit the fan, but it turns out … he's perfect for the job.

I yank on a pair of black leggings before I slip on my Birkenstocks. Grabbing my phone and tucking it into my back pocket, I know I need to get out of the house. I don't know where I'm going, but I just can't be here.

I know it makes no sense that I'm sad. I guess, deep down, I feel this guilt now that Rhett is dead. I worry that his obsession with me, landing him in a psychiatric facility, was somehow the driving force behind him committing suicide. Despite the obvious—that he had issues—he was still someone's son. And brother. And grandson. Probably cousin too. People are missing him right now. Even if he is a monster in my particular story. To them, they likely have so many fond memories, and now, that's all they will ever have. Memories.

I pull my door open to find Cade leaning lazily against his bedroom door, looking down at his phone. When he hears me coming out, he looks up and grins.

"Haley baby, whaddya say you and I get out of the house for the rest of the day? Blow this Popsicle stand?"

He flashes me a light, carefree grin. One that makes him look five years younger, I swear. Every now and then, there's a look of pain in his eyes or maybe sorrow. But when he looks at me like that, there's not a cloud in sight. He just looks happy. And when Cade looks happy, it makes my heart squeeze in my chest.

"I say … hell yes." I nod. "Let's do it."

Walking toward me, he holds his arm out like we're headed to a grand ball or something, and I giggle, looping my arm in his as we head down the stairs.

Right now, it doesn't matter that Nash texted me earlier and asked if I wanted to grab a bite to eat. Or that I have a mountain of homework to do. And honestly, when I glance over at Cade and he smiles down at me, showing his subtle dimple, all the stuff with Rhett doesn't even matter. All that matters is that Cade Huff is here to save the day.

We continue to drive, chatting about nothing in particular, yet it's so comfortable between us, like neither of us has to talk if we don't want to. Which is rare for me because I'm a nervous chatterbox who feels the need to fill the void of silence with random words strung together to make sentences. It's not like that right now. I'm just ... content.

I snack on my bag of crack—also known as Nerds Clusters.

A few minutes into our ride, Cade went into a store before returning with a large bag of them as well as a Hershey's Cookies 'N' Creme and a Milky Way.

He just handed them to me, and when I looked at him, a big grin on my face, he winked and said, "Figured, on a day like today, you would want number one and two on the list of things you said you could never give up."

What he doesn't understand is that I have no willpower when it comes to these things. Even if I make myself sick, eating them all at once. I'll do it with no regrets.

"Here we are," he says, pulling into a parking spot. "Let's go make your day better. Want to?"

He pushes his door open and climbs out, and I quickly do the same. As I walk next to Cade, I look up at the ginormous building. And when I see it's a bookstore, I swear that the sun shines brighter on it and heavenly music starts to play.

"You brought me to a bookstore?" I say, tucking my arm around his and moving in closer. "Like ... for real?"

He shrugs like it's no big deal, smiling at me. "I remember what you said. That you couldn't stop buying books, no matter what." He pauses. "*Smutty* books, if I remember correctly. So, in other words, you read porn." He nudges me playfully. "I figured it was a safe choice when trying to cheer up my Haley baby."

"It was," I whisper. "But this doesn't seem like your type of place."

He stops, pretending to be offended. "You don't think I can read?" Before I can answer, he smirks. "Kidding. Of course I can, but I don't like to. But guess what they probably do have here. Dirty magazines—that's what."

When my mouth hangs open, he leans a little closer to me. "I'm just playing. Now, let's go get our nerd on. Or should I say, freak on? Since, apparently, that's what you're into."

He holds the door open for me, letting me walk inside first. It just feels right. Everything about this—us—feels just as it should. But maybe that's not a good thing. Perhaps he doesn't feel the same way I do.

Either way, today, I've learned something. Cade Huff has a side to him that not many people get to see. I consider myself lucky that he's shown it to me.

CADE

I watch her with pure fascination as she picks up yet another book, running her hand over the cover slowly before flipping it over to see the back. Books give her joy—that's pretty obvious. I wouldn't say hockey gives me joy—that isn't it. It gives me purpose. And it's a place where I am free to take out my aggression. I've always had a darkness lurking inside me, secretly hiding. Some rage or fury. I think we all do. And hockey is a place for me to get that out in a productive way. But lately, it seems more like a job.

The only peace I seem to find these days is when I'm putting a smile on Haley Thompson's lips. And that's the truth.

Getting high or fucked up certainly doesn't give me any joy or bring me happiness. When I first tried drinking and drugs, it numbed some of the shit I didn't want to feel. Like the pain of missing Eli. And the memory of him taking his last breath in my arms, my shirt soaked in his blood. Or the guilt that consumes every cell in my body, reminding me that my big mouth had gotten him shot. I needed a way to live with myself. And pills, unfortunately, became my way. Now ... well, now, my brain is just fucking wired to need them.

But she takes away my pain. I just don't know if she's strong enough to handle it.

By now, Haley has five books stacked in her arms. I've only been in her room briefly, but I didn't see any books in there, aside from the ones on her nightstand. So, I don't know where the hell she keeps them.

"Hey, where do you keep these books anyway?" I ask. "I've never seen them in your room."

She sighs, kneeling down to look at another one. "They are in the closet for now. I don't have a bookcase. I did at my parents' house. But the dorm was too small for that. So, they are all boxed up." Her face lights up, and she pushes up to stand. "One day, I'll have them all on full display on a big bookcase. It'll be light blue."

"Light blue?" I rear my head back. "Can't say I've ever seen a blue bookcase." I laugh. "Who am I kidding? I'm no bookcase expert."

She looks down at her books and smiles. "I love the color blue. Especially light blue. And when I was a kid, I always wanted a baby-blue bookcase, but my mom said no. It didn't go with our ... *decor*. So, anyway, my brother Holden always promised me that, someday, he'd build me one.

He said he'd learn how." Her smile disappears. "He didn't get a chance to, but someday, I will have one. And maybe even a little reading nook area."

"Yeah, you will. I know it," I say softly.

Because I'm going to make sure of it.

Looking at a book with a weird cover that has cartoon characters on it with no faces, I pick it up. "What do you like about them? If you don't mind me asking."

"Books?" she says, heading down another aisle. "I love getting lost in a whole other world. The problems aren't my own, but I feel them at the same magnitude as if they were." She inhales. "But you know what I love most about books? That the impossible can happen. The most unlikely couple can get their happy ending. An evil villain can become someone's hero. And the underdog can come out on top." She shrugs, holding her books tight to her chest. "Anything can happen in the world of fiction. And that's what makes it so special."

I stare at her, completely entranced before I eventually clear my throat. "What about the books without a happy ending? You don't read those?"

"Well, I try my best not to read them. I'm a *happily ever after* girl at heart. And when it doesn't end that way, I'm furious." She breathes out a laugh. "The few times I accidentally read a book with a sad ending, I made up a second version of them in my head. One where everything was happy and perfect by the last and final page."

"You're an optimist." I say it like a statement, not a question.

"I suppose I am." She nods. "I'm not ignorant, thinking there's nothing wrong with the world. It's easy to look around and see that there's darkness. But I truly believe that every person on this earth has some good inside them. It just takes the right somebody to find it."

As she starts looking again, I stuff my hand in my pocket and shift on my feet. But when my fingertips touch the little plastic baggie I shoved in there before we left, I'm reminded that I'll never be more than an addict. And addicts don't get girls like Haley Thompson.

She's smart. She's funny and kind. She's perfect. She's looking at me right now like I hung the moon just by bringing her here today. If only she knew the truth, she'd run away and never look back. I'm not ready for her to do that. I'm not ready to let her go.

"All right, so you ate enough sugar in the car to probably qualify for a diabetes screening, we got our dirty nerdy on at the bookstore, and now ... we're about to eat some pizza." I wave toward Main Street in Topsam—a town forty-five minutes from Brooks. "Just in this one area alone, there are three pizza joints. All of them sell pizza by the slice." I raise an eyebrow, giving her an inquisitive look. "Whatcha say, my dirty book lover? Try 'em all and find the best one?"

The area between her brows crinkles as she stares at me, her mouth hanging open subtly. "You remembered everything I said from my list of things I can't live without?" she whispers, completely surprised. "Seriously?"

"I did," I say like it's no big deal. "I didn't bother stopping for sugary cereal because, well, one, we have a shit ton at home. And, two, I was actually afraid you'd end up in a sugar coma, and I'm not all that good with medical shit. Not like you anyway. Coming from a family of doctors and going to be one yourself."

"I came from a family of them, yes. But I don't know about that last part." She sighs before looking toward one of the pizza places. "I can't believe you remembered everything I told you."

She gazes up at me and gives me that look—like I hung the moon or painted the stars in the sky. I'm not worthy of it, but I'll bask in it anyway because it makes me feel so fucking good inside.

"I remember everything when it comes to you," I utter, and in this moment, I swear that if I pulled her in to kiss her, it would be the most natural thing in the whole damn world. But instead, I reach out and dab the tip of her nose with my finger. "So? What do you say? Pizza or bust?"

"Pizza or bust," she says, nodding slowly. "You're just full of surprises, Cade Huff."

"Yeah, no kidding," I mutter. Because to be honest, I'm surprised with myself.

Swinging my arms, I smack my palms together. Then, I throw my arm around her shoulders and drag her against me. "Let's do it! My money is on Rosalie's Pizza being the best."

Gazing up at me, she raises an eyebrow. "I'm guessing Brewer's will be the best. Care to make this bet interesting?"

"I'm listening," I drawl.

"If Brewer's is the best, you have to give up something you love for two weeks. If Rosalie's is the best, I have to give up something."

I don't even have to think of what I'd want her to give up. It's easy. "Candy. Of any sort. If you lose, none of that sugary shit for you."

She widens her eyes. "You are cruel. But fine." She looks deep in thought for a moment before a light bulb goes on. "Sex. If I win, you have to stop being a man-whore for two weeks."

I frown, rearing my head back. "Who says I'm a man-whore? Have you seen me bring anyone home since you moved in with us?"

"No. But I hear things." She laughs lightly, but I can tell she's feeling awkward. "But if you and Poppy are dating, obviously, you can hook up with her. I just meant ... you know, word around campus is that you like to sleep around. *All* of the hockey guys do. So, you know, I was talking about that." She exhales slowly, putting her hand over her eyes. "I'm going to stop talking now."

"I am *not* dating Poppy." I snort. "Hell fucking no."

"Oh," she says softly. "I just ... I thought ..."

"She kissed me to be funny. We sure as shit aren't dating," I tell her. "But I'll take your bet, Haley baby. You're on."

Satisfied with my answer, she smiles. "Okay, you're on."

We head toward competitor number one, Rosalie's.

"Poor fucking Reggie's Pizza didn't even make our bet. Fucker probably will be the best one."

"Guess we shall see," she singsongs. "Let's go stuff our faces. I'm starving."

"Yeah, me too," I mutter, knowing that what I'm starving for isn't food.

Haley

In the end, neither of us won. Reggie's was, hands down, the best pizza I'd ever had in my life. And when we both bit into it, we looked at each other because we knew it beat the other two. By a long shot.

Which means ... he can still have sex with whoever he wants. Which is annoying.

But on the bright side, I don't have to give my candy up for a month. Thankfully.

We walk along the sidewalk, our hands almost touching as we trudge next to each other.

"I'm so full," I whine. "Why did you think this was a good idea?"

"Babe, I feel the same. But when I bet you to eat two more slices at Reggie's, I didn't think you'd actually do it."

"I grew up with two brothers. I hate turning down a bet." I grimace, rubbing my stomach. "It seemed like a great idea at the time. Plus, you told me I couldn't do it." I groan, feeling like crap for stuffing myself so full. "Now, I know I should have just left after one slice. Considering they were the size of my head."

He glances at me before messing the top of my hair up with his hand. "I'll admit, I'm pretty impressed. I've never seen a chick eat that much." He chuckles. "Hell, half the chicks I know would have just eaten some lettuce. They'd be over there, actin' like a damn rabbit."

"I sort of wish I were like that. But what can I say? I love food way too much. Food and books are life," I say, absolutely meaning it.

"And sweatpants." He grins. "Don't forget how much you love those."

"Um, yes. And I'm not ashamed either," I deadpan just as my phone chimes in my pocket. Taking it out, I see a message from Nash.

Nash ... who I ditched today to hang out with Cade.

"That your boyfriend?" Cade nudges me, grinning, but there's a hint of some other emotion on his face. "Soft Hands Nash?"

Rolling my eyes at him, I sigh. "Yes, it's Nash."

His jaw tightens, like he wasn't expecting it to actually be him. "Are you guys dating or ..."

"No, we are not dating." I shake my head. "We've hardly even hung out." I look at him, gauging his reaction. "But he's really nice."

"That's good," he mutters, nodding slowly.

The energy between us shifts, becoming thick and awkward, and I curse my phone for ruining the vibe we had moments before Nash texted me.

"What do you think Hunter will say when he finds out we've been hanging out today?" I ask, changing the subject.

He shrugs his shoulders, seeming more closed off. "Don't really know, I guess."

"Well, no matter what he says, thank you, Cade. A day that started off crappy ended up being really good. *Really* good." I give him a smile, trying to pull him back to me. "I had the best time."

"Me too, Haley baby." He nods. "Me too."

I wish I could make this day last forever. Keeping us here, Cade and me, in this little bubble of happiness. But every perfect day comes to an end. And sadly, the end is almost here for ours. And I just wonder how he'll act tomorrow.

He's not dependable because I never know which Cade I'm going to get when I walk through the door. But one thing I'm realizing is ... when I need him, he's here.

CADE

Interviews are running really fucking late, and I go a little crazier with every minute that passes as I wait for them to call me up. I'd leave, but Coach warned us that we can't until we talk to the press. We just won our game against Florida, and it was a big W for us. The guys are all happy, and that makes me glad to see.

But my knee started to throb in period two and seems to be getting worse by the second. I'm agitated as hell right now. A dose used to get me through the games and then the interviews, but lately, I've been reaching for my stash much more frequently these days. And even when I take a bit more, it doesn't feel nearly as good. It's no longer a choice, but just something I have to do to feel normal and to not get sick from depriving my body of it. That really fucking sucks because it's like racing against the clock all the time, and I can't relax. I'm trapped in a nightmare, only I'm wide awake.

I know I'll get everything under control though. Once the hockey season is over, I'll lock myself in my room for a week and go through withdrawal. I'll be fine. I've done it before; I can do it again. I just need to get through the season for my guys. I've let so many people down in my life. I don't want to add them to that list of names. Especially when they've all worked so hard to get this far. They don't need my lowlife ass fucking it up now.

Besides, I really don't want them to look at me as anything other than Cade Huff, a defenseman who has their backs and goes hard for his team.

But I'd be lying to myself if I said I'm not struggling to keep my head above water right now. And to add to it, sleeping has become a real bitch. I can't fall asleep. And when I do finally fall asleep, I can't stay asleep. And before I know it, it's time to wake up for practice. I'm starting to wear thin. My body, mind, everything. I'm getting through the days, doing what needs to be done, but barely.

It's been a week since I spent the afternoon trying to make Haley's day better. I've seen her at the house and talked to her a little here and there, but I've been too preoccupied with my own shit to give her too much attention.

And, somehow, her brother hasn't found out we hung out that day, and I don't feel like telling him. Because if I do, I'll have to listen to him bitch at me too. And I get it. I understand why Hunter wants to keep me away from his sweet, innocent sister. But, fuck, it's hard to obey that rule. She's the only thing lately that makes me feel semi-normal. She's the one thing that brings me peace.

I wish I could be better for her. I wish I could at least be a consistent friend and someone she could count on to be there. Haley is one of those people who gives more than she'll ever take. I'm not built like that. At least, I never thought I was until she came along.

A few nights ago, I saw Nash pick her up from the house. From my window, I watched his truck pull in before she walked out and climbed up into the passenger seat. He drives a fucking Ford. She's the type of girl who should be sitting pretty in a Chevy. I didn't look long enough to see if they kissed when she got in. I couldn't. Because I knew if I saw that, I'd lose my mind.

I think Haley could be my lifeline. I look at her, and it's like looking at a flotation device in a pool. I want to grab her and hope that she'll save me from drowning. But at the end of the day, it's not her job to save me. It's my own. And let's face it … I'm not fucking strong enough. And I'm not about to burden her with my weaknesses.

In the midst of my thoughts, I'm called over for an interview, and right when I sit down, I know I'm going to rush through it because, to be honest, I can't stand the thought of being here for another twenty fucking minutes.

HALEY

The Wolves won their game. They'd had some sloppy moments, but overall, they did good. Cade seemed like he was struggling. As I watched him on the ice, it seemed as though he was lost out there. He'd missed things he normally doesn't, and he wasn't himself. But he's been standoffish with me all week, and I can't tell if it's just him being him. Or if something is going on or if I did something to upset him.

Either way, when Nash asked me to hang out a few nights ago, even adding that it could be just as friends, I accepted. Because if I put all of my eggs in the Cade Huff basket … they'd fall through the bottom and crack. That basket has holes in it and is far from trustworthy.

My brother strolls out, heading toward the exit, and I shoot up from my seat to rush over to hug him. Our parents have never really believed in his dream to play hockey, so they don't come to his games. I wish they would; they'd be blown away by how awesome he is out there.

"Good job, big bro!" I throw my arms around him. "You were great."

"Thanks," he says, giving me a squeeze before releasing me. "Thanks for coming."

"No place I'd rather be." I mess his hair up. "But when you play for the pros, you'd better give me box seats, bitch."

He laughs, nodding. "Yeah, yeah. Sure."

I can tell he's sad about something, but I don't know what it is. It's been a while since I've seen him with Sutton. I know they were only fake dating, but I know my brother's heart, and it was absolutely more to him than just pretending.

"Hey, are you all right?" I ask, knowing he won't want to burden me with whatever is on his mind. "You seem off."

"I'm good," he says, keeping his voice low. "Do you need a ride? I'm going to head out."

"No. I'm all set." I shake my head. "I'll see you at home later."

I expect him to ask if I'm waiting for someone, but he doesn't. Probably because whatever is going on with him has him fully consumed. Which is good because I don't want to admit to him that I'm waiting for Cade to tell him good game.

Hunter heads outside, and a few minutes later, I spot Cade walking toward me. He's walking fast, and even though a few people are trying to get his attention, he blows past them, never giving them a second look.

"Hey," I say, holding my hand up, moving closer to him. "Congratulations on your win."

"Thanks," he says, looking toward me, but not really at me. He gives me a tight-lipped smile before dragging a hand over the top of his head. "Look, I can't really talk, sorry. I have something to get to."

My smile falls, but I try to hide it by plastering on a bigger one, which I'm sure makes me look like a crazy person. "Oh, yeah. No problem. I was just getting ready to head out anyway."

"Sweet." He nods, continuing to move toward the door.

I expect him to ask me if I need a ride. Something. Anything to show he gives a shit that I'm here.

Instead, he just holds his hand up. "See you later."

I watch him head outside into the parking lot and to his truck, and even though I have no right to be mad, I'm fuming.

How can the same guy who gave me the most perfect day act like this a week later?

And this right here is a reminder of why it's all right for me to continue hanging out with Nash without feeling guilty. Because unlike Cade, he doesn't make me feel like I'm a damn nuisance half the time. I've kept Nash at arm's length and made myself too available to Cade. No more though. He's made it real clear just by his actions that he doesn't feel the same way about me as I do him.

Cade gives a little, and then he takes a lot. Over and over. He's hot, and then he's icy cold. It's exhausting and confusing. And I'm done with it. I'm done with him.

I had no intentions of coming to a party at the football house after tonight's hockey game. But when Nash texted me minutes after Cade was a complete douchebag with a capital D, I thought, *Why the hell not?*

I asked Remi to join, and, bam, here we are.

I stumble slightly but continue to let my hips roll and my head bob to the music. I've let myself get too drunk, and that's pretty stupid of me. *What kind of person who has been kidnapped lets their guard down enough to get this drunk at a party?* Me, apparently. But when I got here, I was still irritated with Cade, and I needed to let off some steam. And so, here I am, drunk as a skunk.

So far, I've spent the past hour alternating between dancing with Remi or Nash. I'm not sure if I like Nash—like, *really* like him. Or if I'm testing the waters, hoping I'll stop thinking about Cade and picturing him naked. Either way, hanging out with a hot dude like Nash seems like a solid place to start.

"Maybe you should switch to water," Nash says softly in my ear before pulling back and giving me a small shrug. "Just so that you don't feel like shit tomorrow." He cringes. "Or you know … puke. That's never fun." He swipes his thumb over my chin. "You're too pretty for puking."

Since I got here, I've only seen him drink one beer. And even though we've danced, he's not acting like a wild animal, like some of the other dudes around here. He's completely sober.

"You're cute," I say, reaching up and touching his hair. "I like you."

"That's good." He laughs, grinning down at me. "I like you too. Which is why I don't want you to get alcohol poisoning. And judging by your size and how much you've had to drink, it's a strong possibility that's where you're headed."

I spot Remi behind him, dancing with a bunch of girls as she tips her head back and laughs. "That's my best friend!" I call out. "She's the best. Isn't she the best? I love her."

"She is," Nash mutters, looking over the top of my head. "Let's go get you some water."

"If by water you mean another drink … then yes! Lead the way." I squeeze his hand. "Has anyone ever told you your hands are soooo soft?" I break into a fit of giggles, like an idiot. "Like Charmin soft."

He gives me a slightly frustrated look. "Did you just compare my hands to toilet paper?"

I shrug my shoulders. "Evvveryone has to use TP sometimes. Nothin' to be 'shamed of, Nashy Washy."

He continues to hold my hand, leading us toward the kitchen. He doesn't need to weave a path; people just make space for him, just like they do every other football or hockey player at Brooks. I roll my eyes to myself. He'll never have to go through that awkward *excuse me, can I sneak past you* conversation.

I sway to the music as he reaches in the fridge before grabbing a bottle of water and twisting the top off. But just as I take it from him, bringing it to my lips, it's yanked away from me. And when I realize what's going on, I see Cade standing between Nash and me. Blocking me, almost like a shield. His shoulders tense as he glares down at me.

"Don't drink shit that random people give you, Haley baby," he growls, tilting his head forward. "Ever."

His eyes are bloodshot, and his voice sounds different. He's drunk—there's no mistaking that—and he's really, really pissing me off.

"My name is *Haley*!" I hiss, jabbing a finger into his hard abdomen. "Not Haley baby. Just Haley to you. Asshole!"

"You'll always be Haley baby to me," he says, his gaze flicking to my lips. "And you can't go walking around these parties, trusting everyone." His gaze hardens. "Something could happen to you."

Maybe it should make me soften that he cares, but it only fuels my irritation further. Standing taller, I continue to jab my fingertip into his body. "What I do is none of your business, Cade! I'm not your problem!"

His face dips lower, moving closer to mine as he glares into my eyes. "Maybe not. But maybe I wish you were," he mutters, low enough for only me to hear. "Maybe you wish you could be too."

"No," I growl. "I don't."

"I think you're lying, angel. I think you want to be my problem," he says matter-of-factly. "And I'm really, *really* close to making you my fucking problem."

"Huff, what the fuck?!" Nash calls from behind him.

Growing angry again, Cade swings around to face Nash. Keeping me securely tucked behind his body. Reaching behind himself with one hand, he grazes my hip, sending a lightning bolt shooting through my entire body. Jolting me like I'm being electrocuted from his touch.

"I'm not a random person, Huff. Hales and I are friends."

"She's just Haley to you, no cute fucking nicknames, Nash," Cade growls.

"I'll call her whatever I want, Huff," Nash drawls just as I peek around Cade's side. He steps closer, his eyes glaring into Cade's. "Besides, from what I can see, you're too fucked up most of the time to know what she needs. I wouldn't trust whatever you fucking give her—that's for sure."

"Shut the fuck up, pretty boy, before I break those extra-soft hands of yours and let the hockey team use them for shit paper," Cade taunts him, leaning in closer. "And she doesn't want you anyway. That's probably why she had to get hammered. To tolerate your ass."

"Cade!" I hiss, stepping to the side of him. "You are so out of line."

"I ought to put you in your place right now, puck boy," Nash says with a cocky tone. "Haley doesn't need you here."

"You can try, but then I'll have to embarrass you in front of Haley. Who you are fucking obsessed with even though she doesn't want you," Cade chimes in, and I don't have to look at his face to know he's smirking. "Besides, you might rip that Abercrombie & Fitch shirt your mama bought you. That'd be a shame, huh? Did she buy that for you when your balls finally dropped last week?"

"Haley, let's get out of here," Nash says, his eyes remaining on Cade's. "This clown is ruining the night."

I glance nervously up at Cade, only able to see the side of his face. But even from his profile, I can tell he's fuming, fueled with red-hot anger. I continue to stare at him. Maybe I'm hoping he'll tell me not to go. In some way, that would prove that what I'm feeling between us isn't all in my head. That when his hand touched me, maybe, just maybe … he felt the electricity the way I did.

Turning toward me, he leans down closer to my ear. "Don't take drinks from just anyone, *Haley*. Watson's here. If you need him, he'll be around. Be careful."

As he takes a step away, I involuntarily, stupidly, pathetically grab his arm. "Where are you going?"

"Home," he mutters, never looking at me. "Nash is right. You don't need me here." His shoulders sag slightly, and he sighs. "Just remember what I said. Do not take drinks from random people." He cranes his neck and jerks his head toward Nash. "This guy? He's not good enough for you, Haley. None of the assholes in here are."

When he struts off, I glare up at Nash, who looks smug, like he's won something. Like I'm a prize and it's all a stupid game.

Stepping around him, I grab the unopened bottle of vodka and twist the cap. Putting some in a plastic cup, I tip it back, letting it burn the whole way down.

Tilting my chin up at Nash, I narrow my eyes. "I am *not* your property. And how you just acted? Well, I find it excruciatingly unattractive. So, I'm going to go now. And you aren't going to follow me."

As I turn, he catches my hand softly. "Hales, wait."

"No," is all I offer him, but he forces me to look at him.

"What is the deal with you and Huff?" He's frustrated now. "You said nothing. But what I just saw? That sure as shit was something."

"There's nothing going on between us. But if there were, it's really none of your business!" I hiss because I'm too drunk to not act like a raging idiot. "You and I are friends. You don't get to know every detail of my life!"

Walking out of the kitchen, I spot Cade heading outside, and I chase him down just as he makes it out onto the front lawn.

"Hey!" I holler, charging toward him as he turns around.

"Haley, what the fuck are—"

Unable to help myself as the madness inside of me boils uncontrollably, I shove his chest. "You listen to me! I didn't get drunk because I can't stand Nash! I'm drunk because you keep stringing me along. Giving me a little hope before yanking it away!" I shove him again. "You took me to a bookstore, Cade! A bookstore! And now, here we are, a week later, and you didn't even want to speak to me after the game. What the fuck is that?!"

"*Haley* ..." He says my name like a warning. Almost like ... *give it up and walk away.*

But I'm too drunk to listen. Or maybe too pissed off to care.

"Go back inside," he mutters. "Now."

I've always been Miss Calm, Cool, and Collected. Yet here I am, losing my mind over Cade Huff in plain sight.

"No," I say through gritted teeth. "I was having fun with Nash. My night went from being crappy because of you, by the way, to decent because of him. And you couldn't stand it, could you?" I shake my head. "You just had to swoop in and ruin it for me. Do you hate me that much that you couldn't let me have one measly night of fun?" I exhale slowly. "You know what? I am going to go back inside, and I'm going to find a guy to take me home." I glare, acting like a complete child, knowing this is toxic behavior but so desperate for him to see me. "Someone who doesn't treat me like I'm an infectious disease half the time, like you do!"

As I start to turn, his hand catches my wrist, and he pulls me toward him. "Do you think I want to be fucking chasing you around at a party, sick to my stomach as I watch you look at Nash the way you should be looking at me?" he growls. "No, Haley. I'd give anything to not fucking care what you're doing or who you're doing it with." He gets closer, angry, hot energy rolling off his body.

"If you care, then why do you push me away?" I whimper. "Can't you see I want you to care?"

"You only think that because you don't really know me." His voice is gritty and raw. "If you knew the fucking truth, you wouldn't be running after me right now. I promise you that, Haley." He laughs bitterly, but it dies quickly. "You wouldn't look at me the way you do either."

I stare up at him. "I don't understand."

"And you never will either." He drops my wrist. "I'm not the type of guy you want to be chasing. It won't end well for you." He takes a step back. "What happened in there with me and Nash? That was a mistake. Forget it."

Turning away from me, he stalks off. Every fiber in my being wants to chase him—again. But my brain tells me not to be that pathetic. So, instead, I gather myself up, walk back inside, and find Watson.

Because I'm ready to go the hell home.

After looking around for a few minutes, I find Watson in a group of guys and immediately beeline it for him.

"Would you mind, um … taking me home?" I say quickly. "Please."

Stepping away from the group, he bends down and puts his hands on my shoulders. "Yeah. Sure, sure. Let's go. Are you all right though? Did something happen?"

I shake my head. "No. I'm just really tired, and I drank too much."

He throws his huge arm around me. "Let's go, Hales. Let's get you home."

As we head out, we walk by Remi, and I take her hand. "I'm super tired. Watson is going to take me home. Do you need a ride? He won't mind."

"If you're all right, I think I'll stay." She glances at the group she has been dancing with before turning her attention back to me. "But if you need me, I can totally go home too."

I give her a reassuring smile, though I'm sure it's lopsided and goofy because of how fuzzy my brain feels. "Stay. Have fun. But please, if you need a ride, call." I laugh and give her a hug. "I mean, I personally can't drive you tonight. But I know Watson would."

"Thanks, babe. Love you," she says, smiling as I release her.

"Love you more." I turn back toward Watson.

And everything starts to spin. And my head feels fuzzier than ever.

I guess that last shot wasn't the best idea after all.

CADE

Even in my drunken, high stupor, I'm fucking fuming as I walk along the sidewalk, heading home. I didn't want to leave her there. I wanted to kiss her. I wanted to tell her why I act the way I do when it comes to her. The fucking girl makes me feel things I never have, and it's making me insane.

I made that scene with Nash, but truth be told, he's not a bad guy. I know he wouldn't hurt her; it's the other ones there I worry about. And despite the fact that she's been hurt before, she seems to trust so easily. And she shouldn't.

Humans are just monsters in disguise. Take me, for example. She looks at me like I'm a good person. When I can't stand her presence half the time because I need to get high and she's in my way. The only reason why I even came tonight is because I'd heard she was there. I was scared. I never want her to get hurt. But I'm also a jealous fuck when it comes to that girl.

I should have just left her alone. I mean, Nash is a better man than I am. She should be there with him. And I should go the fuck home. Which is where I'm headed. And for all I know, she's dancing with him again. Smiling at him like he's the best thing since sliced fucking bread or some shit.

I went to the party tonight to keep an eye on her. But before walking in there, I swore to myself that I wouldn't go over to her. Not tonight. I'd let her live her life. Because so many other times since she moved in, I have swooped in when she didn't need me to. I didn't want to do that. But then I saw her with a bottle of water in her hand. And I didn't see who had given it to her. And then, before I could stop myself, I was headed toward her. And when I saw her look up, flashing him her beautiful, angelic smile, I lost my cool. Selfishly, I fucking hated it. I love when she looks at me like that even if I'm not worth it.

Just like always, my mind wanders back to the night Eli died. A night when I had run my mouth to the wrong people and it cost my best friend his life. Maybe that's why I walked away tonight. I don't like putting anyone in a situation with the potential of conflict. Unless it's on the ice, of course.

I hear a truck coming behind me, and I stuff my hands in my pockets and keep my head down. When I hear it slow down, I peer over at it and sigh.

"Get in, Huff," Watson says, his truck coming to a stop along the curb. "And don't try to pull some shit and take off. I'm in no mood to chase you."

Rolling my eyes toward the dark, starry sky, I turn toward the truck to find Haley in the front seat, pouting. And when I climb in the back, she cranes her neck and shoots me a glare.

"Well, this is cozy. *Not*," she sasses before turning the music up loud and yelling over the sound. "First, you ruin my night, and now, you've interrupted my jam sesh!"

"What a shame that is," Watson grunts, clearly annoyed with whatever is going on in his truck right now.

As fucked as my mind is, even I can't help but focus on her as she flails around in her seat, belting out the words completely off-key. She turns in her seat, pointing her finger closer to Watson's face, completely popping his bubble by invading his personal space, but watching him grow more annoyed is totally worth it.

Haley's always so soft-spoken and sweet. I like seeing her like this even though I know better than anyone that getting too drunk to escape whatever hell you're going through inside won't make it better. That still doesn't stop me from doing it though. But I want more for her than that. I don't want her to have to numb her reality. I want her to fucking love it.

When we pull into the driveway of the house, Watson looks back at me. "I have to go somewhere. Can you make sure she makes it inside?"

Before I can answer, she unbuckles and jabs a fingertip into his forearm. "What are you saying, *jerky jerk*?" she slurs. "That I need a babysitter?! Because I don't!" She quickly turns to look at me. "Especially not this guy! The guuuy who just ruined my night!"

Watson sighs. "Huff, what the fuck is she talking about?"

"Who knows?" I shrug. "Does she even know? I mean, I'm going to say no, Gentry. She just called you *jerky jerk*, so I dare say she's a mess. Besides, do you trust her judgment? She dances with football players."

"Hot football players, asshole! And I was going to kiss him too! If you hadn't shown up!" she continues to sass. "Maybe even sleep with him! Who knows, you butthead?"

I ball my hands into fists, my fingertips digging into my palms as I grind my back teeth together. I don't want to fucking hear that she wants to sleep with Nash. I don't want to hear her talk about any fucking man who isn't me.

As much as my own mind is spinning from the alcohol and everything else I've mixed with it, I'm in complete control. My tolerance for all things meant to fuck you up is pretty damn high. Not like that's a good thing.

Climbing out of the back, I close the door before opening hers. "Come on, Haley baby. Let's go inside."

"Why should I?" She squints her eyes at me. "You ruined my whooole night!"

LOST BOY

"I didn't," I mutter. "That wasn't going anywhere, and you know it."

"What the fuck are you guys talking about?" Watson huffs.

"Her and Nash. That shit ain't going anywhere. She's not into him," I say, shrugging. "So, if anything, I saved you, babe. You can thank me later."

She slides to the end of the seat, glaring up at me. "Oh, I am into him all right! I'm *so* into him!" Her voice is growly and deeper than usual.

Her hair is wild, and her makeup is smudged. She's a beautiful mess. But right now, she's *really* pissing me off.

Quickly sliding my hands around her, I toss her over my shoulder before she even has time to realize it. But when she does, she starts kicking and hitting me, and I'm pretty thankful Hunter isn't home tonight.

"You sure you've got her?" Watson asks, looking concerned. "I can come in."

"I'm good," I say nonchalantly. "She'll be snoring and drooling on her pillow in no time."

"Yeah, and she'd better be alone," Watson warns, tilting his chin up. "Or Hunter will kill you."

"Do you think I'm looking to be puked on tonight?" I drawl. "Have a good night, Watty. Remember, don't be silly; wrap your willy. The world ain't ready for little Watsons running around, following the rules and shit."

I step back and close the door, all while I have a tiny beast on my shoulder, who is kicking and screaming like a crazy person. Throwing an absolute fit.

"Damn, woman." I laugh, walking into the house and kicking the door shut. "You're strong for being, like, five foot nothing."

As we head upstairs, I breathe her in for a few more seconds, knowing that's all I'll ever get when it comes to her. A few seconds. That's all.

Pushing her door open, I walk inside before dropping her on her bed. I make it to the door when she throws herself in front of me, pushing her back to the door and closing it.

Her finger pokes into my chest as she glares up. "I am five foot two, asshole!"

I smirk down at her, unable to stop myself because she's so fucking cute.

I bob my head up and down slowly. "My bad. Trust me, I'll be the first to admit … every inch counts."

"Yeah, well, that's because you probably have a tiny penis to go with your tiny heart. And—"

I stop her mouth with my finger, putting it to her lips.

"Gotta stop you right there." I glare at her. "I'm far from tiny—I promise you that, angel."

"You're annoying," she hisses. "And that's not once, but twice that you've shown up when I was with Nash." She steps closer, close enough that her tits almost push against me. "How would you like it if I showed up and cockblocked you? Huh? What if I showed up when you were with your precious Poppy and did that?"

"Go for it. You'd be doing me a favor." I shrug. "Besides, his cock wasn't going anywhere near you, sweet thing," I say arrogantly. "So, there was nothing to block."

"Oh, it might have." She stands taller. "Maybe I wanted his *cock* near me. Maybe I wanted him inside of me. Did you ever think of that before you went and messed it—"

"Shut up," I snarl.

My lips are on hers before I can stop myself, mostly because I don't want to hear her mouthy words. She doesn't kiss me back, but instead, she shoves me.

"You didn't want him. Stop fucking lying to yourself and me."

"You can't do that!" She hits my chest. "You can't do shit like kiss me!"

"I had to shut you up before you said more stupid shit. And let me ask you, is that why you're here instead of there?" I growl, narrowing my eyes at her. "Is that why you took off right after I did?" Slowly, I give her a small smirk. "That's what I thought, Haley. You danced with him for an hour. And it took me a matter of minutes to show up, ruin your night, and have you following me home. Nash is no one to you. And we both know it."

"I did not follow you!" she jeers, anger radiating from her petite body. "Get over yourself!"

"You don't think I feel the way your body melts against me every time I touch you?" I mutter. "You don't want Nash, Haley. Part of me wishes you did, but you don't."

She stares up at me, nostrils flaring. "I … I don't know what you mean."

It takes me a second, but eventually, I blink a few times and will myself back to reality. My head is still spinning, and I'm too wasted to be saying these things to her. Mostly because if I wasn't this hammered … I wouldn't say any of them at all.

As I start to step around her, she puts her hand on my abdomen. "Why do you keep getting in my way? Every time I'm having fun, you appear. Like fucking Houdini." Her eyes fill with tears. "It's hard to stop wanting you when you won't leave me be."

I try to think of something, anything, that won't blow my cover. I can't say what I'm actually thinking.

Because I want you, Haley. I've wanted you since the second you walked into this fucking house.

"Because I want to protect you," I say, emotionless. "That's all."

"And I think that's bullshit," she whispers. "I think you feel it too. That feeling when we touch."

"Nope." I shake my head. "I don't feel anything when it comes to you or us, Haley."

Her eyes seem to haze over as she pulls her hand back, only to move it lower and slide it under my shirt. And when she does … I'm fucking weak in the knees.

She continues to move it upward before stopping on my chest. "If you feel nothing, why is your heart beating so fast?"

I don't answer. I just stand there, staring at her. I know I need to leave her room. Nothing good can come from me being here. But, goddamn it, she makes it hard to walk away from her.

"You feel it too." She slurs the words, and I know she's still drunk. "I know you do."

Placing my hand over hers, I try to shove hers away. "You're drunk," I tell her.

"Who cares?" she rasps. "We've been skating around each other for weeks. I know what I want. It's you. Right now."

I quickly shake my head. "Haley, no. This isn't what you need. I'm not what you need."

Moving her free hand to my side, she skates both hands down until they stop at the waistband of my jeans. Staring up at me, her eyes are filled with hunger. "I don't remember saying I needed you. I said I wanted you." She dips her fingers under my waistband. "And I do. I want you so bad that I'm physically aching right now."

"We have to live together. Your brother, he'd fucking kill me," I say, trying to convince myself more than her. "We shouldn't."

"I know we shouldn't. But sometimes, the things we shouldn't do … feel the best," she whispers before taking my hand in hers and moving it to her chest. "Feel my heart, Cade? It's racing because, right now … I want you."

I feel myself giving in. I know this feeling all too well. With every drink, every joint, and every pill … there's a moment, a split second, where I know I'll do whatever I have to do to get it. And despite my greatest efforts to push her away … my selfishness is going to win. Just like it always does.

"And what do you want from me, Haley?"

"I want a night to forget all the reasons we shouldn't be attracted to each other." She keeps her voice low. "One night where we give in to what we want."

"It'd only be for tonight, Haley," I quip back. "That's all I can give you."

"Fine," she says, moving her hands to her own shirt before peeling it from her body. "But if you're going to cockblock my night, the least you can do is make up for it."

"You weren't. Going. To. Fuck. Him," I say through gritted teeth. "Stop saying that."

"Does it make you mad, Cade, when you think about another man fucking me?" she coos, and her voice doesn't even sound like the Haley I know. This Haley sounds confident and desperate.

75

"Yes," I growl. My jaw tenses so tightly that it hurts.

I know firsthand that if you put a drink in front of an alcoholic, they will probably want to chug it. If you put a pill in front of an addict, they'll likely want to snort it. And if you put a shirtless Haley Thompson in front of me, begging for me to have sex with her ... I'm going to want to fuck her.

It's just simple facts. And you can't fight logic.

"Then, what are you going to do about it?" she whispers, giving me *fuck me* eyes, making me weak in the knees.

"You need to be sure," my voice barely croaks. "And if we do this ... no one can know, and it can't happen again."

"Kiss me, Cade. Stop treating me like I'm this innocent, breakable thing. I want the whole Cade Huff experience."

"Cade Huff experience?" I narrow my eyes. "What the fuck is that?"

"Don't treat me like an innocent little girl. Treat me the same way you treat all of your other hookups," she says, looking up with her bloodshot eyes. "Fuck me, Cade. Don't make me beg. Just fuck me already."

I swallow, sucking in a breath. Feeling the blood rush to my cock, I know right then I'm not telling her no. I mean, when an angel like her demands to be fucked, I'm going to give her every inch of my aching cock until she comes so hard on it that she screams my name. End of story.

CADE

When I wake up, my head is pounding. I have no idea if it's because my body is in need of something or if it's because I mixed pills with drinking last night. Either way, when my vision clears and I look around, I realize I'm in Haley's bed. Everything in my mind is fuzzy, but when I turn to look at her, a lot of memories flood my brain, hitting me all at once, like a ton of fucking bricks.

Me kissing my way down her stomach as I peeled her shorts off.

Her hands in my hair as I pushed my tongue deeper inside of her. Her tightening her thighs around my neck as she came in my mouth, crying out my name.

Me burying my cock inside of her, not even sure I could fit because she was so fucking tight.

As I squeeze my eyes shut, I remember the way her lips parted and her eyes fluttered when she came. Her back arched while she lost control, giving herself all to me. Some details might be missing or blurry, but I know for sure that I ate her like my last meal right before we had sex.

But you can't have sex with girls like Haley without consequences. She isn't like that. She's going to get attached. Hell, she already was attached—I could tell by the way she looked at me.

There's only one thing I can do right now—get out of here before she wakes up and pretend it never happened. Because it can't happen again even if I want it to. The closer she gets to me, the more she'll learn how truly, deeply fucked up I really am.

Everyone has a few demons, but I'm fucking filled with them. And angels like her aren't built for disasters like me.

I don't want to be the demise of Haley Thompson. But if I let her get too close to me, that's exactly what is going to happen.

Haley

The second I wake up, I yank my comforter over my face to shield my eyes from the unwelcoming sunlight that's overflowing into the room through the window. I groan before a yawn rips through me, and I stretch just as a painful stabbing sensation hits me right in my temples.

"Shit," I mutter, my voice hoarse.

I try to form a thought, but everything is foggy. However, the soreness between my legs somehow sharpens my memory, and unless I had the world's greatest dream, it seems I hooked up with Cade last night.

But as I pull my covers down, looking at the empty side of my bed, I wonder, *Where the hell did he go?*

Did he take off right after it happened?

Because I only remember bits and pieces of the entire thing.

Him going down on me. Him yanking his jeans down before climbing over me as I begged him to—I cringe—*fuck me.*

I vaguely remember my orgasm because I recall thinking about how I've been missing out, never before having such an intense orgasm until now. But I don't know what happened after that.

Did we cuddle? Did he run away? Did he just slip out to make coffee and he plans to come right back to bed?

And mostly ... does this change anything between us? Or did he really mean it when he said it could only be one night?

All questions I don't have an answer for.

After lying here for another ten minutes, I decide to go take a shower. I have homework to do today, and I also need to get groceries at some point. So, tossing my blankets from my body, I trudge toward the bathroom.

Seeing no sign of Cade anywhere.

LOST BOY

I sit at the counter with my giant bowl of sugary cereal. Poking my spoon at it, but not shoveling it in like I normally do. Because no matter how hard I try, I can't stop thinking about last night. Details slowly make their way into my mind one at a time as flashbacks of Cade appear like a slideshow. His touch, his kiss, and the way he looked at me. When I see these flashbacks, they don't seem like a typical hookup. The way his eyes burned into mine is far from just ordinary. But he left. And that speaks volumes about how much he doesn't feel the same.

My brother's first down the stairs, and I wonder when he even got home. He holds his hand up and waves as he trudges toward the refrigerator and pulls out a bottle of water. I don't bother asking where he was last night because I don't want to tell him where I was either.

"Sup?" he says, tipping the bottle up and downing the entire thing.

"Not much, just having breakfast before I bust into some homework." I pause. "I'm heading to the grocery store later. Can you think of anything you need?"

"Can you grab me some chips?" Watson calls, appearing out of nowhere. "Oh, and I'll give you money for a steak. I'm craving one bad."

"I'll chip in too." Hunter nods in agreement. "T-bone, please."

"Rib eye for me." Watson grins, turning his head toward Cade as he rounds the corner from the stairs, strutting into the kitchen. "Cade, what kind of steak do you want? Haley's going to the store," Watson says, and I hear the excitement in his voice. "We're grilling and chilling tonight."

I turn to glance at Cade, but he looks anywhere but at me. Avoiding my gaze like it could kill him dead in his steps or something.

"Oh shit. I, uh … have to rehearse with Poppy tonight. Sorry, fellas." He clears his throat nervously. "Sorry, Haley."

Just him calling me *Haley* and not his usual, obnoxious *Haley baby* instantly proves to me that he's dodging me and trying to act indifferent.

"We're all rehearsing tonight," my brother says, frowning. "Can't you just practice with Poppy before dinner?"

I watch Cade scramble to come up with an excuse, but eventually, he shrugs. "I told Poppy we'd go to dinner after. So, you know, I'd kind of feel like a dick if I canceled on her."

I visibly flinch just as the words leave his lips, and my heart sinks. We had sex hours ago, and now, he's taking another woman to dinner.

How could I have been so dumb?

Why would he like me? He could have anyone he wants.

"Ooh, you and Poppy?" Watson smirks, cupping his chin with his fingers and nodding slowly. "She's hot. I can't lie."

"And super bitchy," Hunter grunts, and I want to high-five him, but I refrain. "Personally, I don't like her. At all." Just when I think I couldn't agree with my brother more, he adds, "But maybe she can whoop your unruly ass into shape. Who knows?"

"For real, I'd be fucking scared of her if she were my girl." Watson laughs. "Attaboy, Cade."

As they all carry on, it's like I'm not even here. I want to get up and go to my room, but I can't because then I'll look pathetic. So, instead, I sit here. I sit here and try not to cry.

When it comes to Cade, I truly feel like an infatuated girl who has her first crush. That crush you can't have for whatever reason, yet you can't get them off your mind. The frustration bubbles inside of me, and I wish he'd just look my way. Just throw me one single measly bone.

God, I'm pathetic.

"I'm leaving early for the stadium," Watson says, pulling his sneakers on. "Gotta go see Ryann first."

"Same." Hunter nods in agreement. "Well, I don't need to go see Ryann, but I have to go somewhere else."

"I'll meet you guys over there. Just need to grab something from my room, and then I'm headed out too," Cade says before jogging up the stairs.

"Later, Hales." Watson waves.

"See ya." Hunter tips his chin up before they both disappear out the door.

I get up and head to the sink to rinse my bowl. Now that everyone is gone, maybe Cade will acknowledge last night when he comes back down. But that hope quickly dies when he returns to the kitchen, walks past me to grab a Gatorade from the refrigerator, and heads toward the door.

I take a few steps after him, mustering up every ounce of confidence I have inside of me to address him. "Cade?"

"Yeah?" Slowly, he turns. "What's up?"

Part of me doesn't want to give him the satisfaction of bringing up last night. I mean, it's clear he doesn't want to acknowledge it, so I shouldn't either. But then the other part of me—the angrier side—wants to know why the hell he's acting this way.

"Are we going to talk about last night at all?" I ask, leaning my hip against the countertop. "Or … just skate around it and pretend it didn't happen?"

He gets a weird look on his face and squints his eyes the slightest bit. "Last night?" He tilts his head. "What, uh, are you talking about?" He widens his eyes. "Did I say something? Fuck, sorry if I was inappropriate. I was really drunk."

I don't know whether to be heartbroken, relieved, or offended. But the pain shooting through my chest chooses for me.

"You really don't remember?" I fold my arms over my chest. "At all?"

He shrugs his shoulders. "I was pretty fucked up. The last thing I remember is getting in Watson's truck. Did I say something? Did I ... *do* something?"

Looking at his face for any sign he's bluffing and finding none, I sigh. "No, you were fine. Don't worry about it."

Turning quickly, I go to my room before the tears behind my eyes start pouring out. But as soon as I close my door, that's exactly what they do. And I collapse on my bed, sobbing like the loser that I am.

The loser Cade Huff has made me.

CADE

Before practice, I drive toward the familiar place just outside of town. I met Van a few months back. He's as good as any drug dealer can be, I suppose. We are far from friends, but he hooks me up with what I need and doesn't ask questions.

The image of Haley's face assaults my mind, and I feel a throbbing pain radiate through my chest, crippling my entire body. She was already quiet and acting differently after I pretended I didn't remember our night together. But when I said I was going to dinner with Poppy, her entire body sank. And then I had to relive that same look after I acted like I had no idea what she was talking about when she brought up last night. What a joke that was. I remember everything.

I can recall the way her pretty pink nipples hardened when I started kissing down her stomach. Or how hard she pulled my hair or how she fastened her legs around my neck like my tongue couldn't get deep enough for her. She was so eager for more.

I remember how her hair smelled, how her skin tasted, and how her lips molded to mine. I didn't lie about one thing. I was fucked up. But no amount of drugs or alcohol would make me forget being with her.

Was it dumb, pretending like I forgot? Probably. But being with her had been a mistake. Giving in to her had been wrong. Because even at my best, she'd still deserve more. So, I guess, in some fucked up way, it seemed like the only thing I could do was act like it never happened. I did it because I care about her.

It was for her own good, and one day, she'll understand that. When she's married with kids. A house with a front porch swing and a white picket fence. All the things that I can't be for her, she'll have that down the road.

And where the fuck will that leave me?

I had no plans with Poppy after rehearsing tonight. But when the guys were poking and prodding, I got nervous and blurted the dinner thing out. I hadn't thought of how it would make Haley feel. And that look on her face, the sheer pain I saw, it'll haunt me forever. But I couldn't stand the thought of eating dinner together tonight and not being able to reach across the table and touch her. I need to keep my distance, or I'll do something stupid. *Again.*

Pulling in front of the old, run-down trailer, I throw my truck in park and climb out. I hate coming here. I have always hated coming here. But the thing about drugs? They don't give you a choice. When it comes to getting your hands on them, hate it or not, you'll do whatever you have to do.

There are a few other vehicles in the driveway, which always freaks me out. I'm on the local college hockey team. If word gets around that I'm a druggie, it's not going to look good on the school. Or me.

I push my hat down lower on my forehead and pull my hood over it in hopes of not being recognized. The people inside are likely too fucked up to care anyway—I hope.

Pushing the door open, I don't see Van right away. Instead, my eyes land directly on a couple in the corner as they shoot up together. The girl is young and pretty. If she was older than a freshman in college, I'd be surprised. She doesn't fit the typical look of a junkie. Then again, who does? She's dressed nicely, and it makes me wonder if this journey with drugs is new for her and if she went right to the hard shit to start with. I wish I could tell her to get out while she still can. Her boyfriend, on the other hand, looks like he's much more experienced. His hair is greasy and unkempt, his clothes look worn, and his eyes look … lost. My stomach turns as I think about how it only takes one person, one moment, one bad decision to wind up in a place like this, putting poison in your body like you're invincible and that it can't kill you at any time.

I've never tried heroin. Not only am I terrified of needles, but I also genuinely don't want to die—even though I put a lot of shit in my body that certainly isn't prolonging my life any. Mostly though, I know I've already put my mom through enough, and I don't want to hurt her any worse than I already have. Heroin is too risky. I've heard of far too many people overdosing because their shit had been cut with fentanyl. No thanks.

When I look at the couple, in a way, it makes me think I'm less of a druggie than they are. But am I really? I'm here too, aren't I?

My skin crawls as I watch the couple completely zone out. I wonder where her parents think she is right now. Does she have siblings? Did she have big dreams? Where are those dreams now? It's not like there's a time machine that can take her back to before she tried drugs for the first time and magically make her normal again. If there were, I'd get in it and push a button to take me back to when Eli was still alive. And I wouldn't be here in this dumpy place right now, watching this girl lose herself.

"Cade, my man," Van says, walking out of his bedroom. "Was wondering when you were going to come see me."

Reluctantly, I tear my eyes from the girl, knowing I can't help her. She's not my problem. "Hey, I can't stay long. Do you have my shit?"

Lighting a cigarette, he inhales sharply before blowing the smoke out. All while he continues to stare me down with those beady eyes. His hair is a mess, and he's much skinnier than he was when we first met. I guess that's what happens though; the deeper you get into addiction, the less everything else in the world—like personal hygiene and nutrition—matters.

"Why the rush, big, bad Cade Huff?" His eyes squint as he takes another drag, letting the cigarette hang from his mouth.

"Because I've got to get to the arena—that's why." I move around on my feet.

I do need to get to the arena—that's true—but I also really need more pills before I leave. And I don't have time for his shit. Typically, he gives me what I need and sends me on my way. But the past few times, he's been acting weird.

"I got a question for you. What the fuck are you going to do when the pros call you?" He smirks, showing his nasty teeth, and I can't imagine ever giving up on myself that much to let my hygiene go down the drain. "You really think the NHL wants a junkie?"

"I'm not a junkie," I growl.

"Just because you ain't got a needle hanging out of your arm doesn't make you any less of a junkie than the rest of us." He waves to himself and the couple, who now look asleep. "At the end of the day, *brother*, drugs run our lives. You. Me. Them." He points to the couch where the guy and girl lie. "So, quit actin' like you're better than anyone. You ain't." He eyes me over, still smirking. "You ain't shit. It's only a matter of time before this high isn't enough. And then, I promise, you will have a needle in your arm too. Won't be so big and bad then, will you?"

"If you can't sell me what I need, I'll go," I mutter, growing more annoyed by the minute.

"Oh, I got what you need, boy," he says, looking me up and down. "Just gotta remind you who you are. Which is a fucking drug addict."

As he walks away to get my shit, I take the money from my pocket, knowing I'm running low on funds and I'll have to dip into the emergency account my parents set up for me. And when I do, they'll know something's up. I'll come up with a story, an excuse. I always do.

I wait anxiously for him to hand over my drugs. And this right here is why I lied this morning when I told Haley I didn't remember last night.

I don't belong in Haley's world. And she sure as hell doesn't belong in mine.

Haley

Sitting across from me at the diner, Remi eyes me over. She stares at me curiously, and I'm scared to death of what's going to come out of her mouth next. We've known each other for so long that I swear she knows me as well as I know myself. This is the first time I've seen her since my *sex with Cade* debacle, and all it's going to take for me to spill my guts about the whole thing is for her to suspect something.

"You look weird," she says, narrowing her eyes. "Why do you look weird?"

Stuffing a pancake into my mouth, I nervously shrug. "Me? Weird? I'm not weird." I swallow the excessive amount of food before chugging some now-lukewarm coffee. "You're weird. Not me."

The staredown continues before that look flashes in her eyes. The look that says ... *You have a secret, and I'm sure as hell going to find out what it is.*

"You slept with Nash!" she whisper-yells. "You got it on like Donkey Kong with football boy!"

I gawk at her. "What? No, I did not sleep with Nash. I haven't even kissed Nash." I grimace. "I don't want to either."

"Why? He's so hot." She looks disappointed. Then, her eyes widen, and she smiles from ear to ear. "Cade! You slept with Cade! I can't believe I didn't figure it out sooner since, hello, he took you to a bookstore and on a pizza testing date!" She's practically bouncing in her seat. "Hanging out with Nash *and* rolling around in the sheets with Cade? Who are you, and what have you done with mousy, sweet, and innocent Haley Thompson?"

"I haven't even confirmed if I did it, Sherlock Holmes," I sass. "I might not have slept with anyone!"

"But you did," she says, calling my bluff. "So, don't even lie."

Pushing my plate to the side, I shield my face with my hands. "I did," I mutter. "After that party at the football house, I had sex with Cade Huff—among other things."

"I knew it!" she squeals, and I'm so glad we are in a corner booth all by ourselves so that no one is staring our way. "Tell. Me. Everything."

Slowly, I bring my hands down. My cheeks are on fire. "Well, for starters … he doesn't even remember it." I pout. "I'm *that* forgettable."

All the excitement leaves her face. "Oh shit," she mumbles. "That's, uh … wow."

"Tell me about it!" I grouch. "There I was, drunk off my ass, and I still know it was the best sex I've ever had. Meanwhile, *town bicycle, lady killer* Cade Huff can't remember it. The asshole." I drag my hand over my face. "Seriously?"

"Fuck him," she says, trying to lighten my mood. "And who knows? Maybe Nash will be even better."

"I'm not going to just go jump on Nash's dick because Cade is too much of a jerk to remember having sex with me," I huff out, shaking my head. "It is what it is, right?"

"Right," she says before cringing. "Oh crap. You have to go watch the fundraiser this weekend though. The one the Brooks hockey team and dancers are doing together."

Damn my brother for giving me a ticket to that. And damn me because I felt too bad to say no.

"Do you *have* to remind me?" I groan. "I can't wait to watch him and Poppy fondle each other onstage."

"Well, I've heard Poppy is a complete bitch. *So* not like that little pink troll from the movie." She shrugs nonchalantly. "His loss, babe."

I exhale slowly. Resting my elbow on the table, I cradle my cheek in my palm. "Yeah," I barely squeak. "His loss."

CADE

It's our last dance practice before the big event, and I think we're ready. Or as ready as we'll ever be. Poppy and I are just finishing up. And as I grab my sneakers and start putting them on, she steps in front of me.

"Hey, Cade?" Poppy's voice is much softer than it usually is. "Can I ask you something?"

"You can, but I might not answer." I wink. "This isn't Truth or Dare. So, technically …"

Shooting me a glare, she comes closer to me, dropping her voice to a whisper. "I know you and I aren't super close. And if it wasn't for this fundraiser, we probably would have gone through our whole lives without speaking. But I just … please don't get mad."

As she pauses, my entire body grows on edge. Because I know I don't want to hear what she's about to say. When someone uses the words *don't get mad* … it's never good.

"If you need someone to talk to, I'm here. About Haley. Or … other stuff." She looks down for a second before standing taller. "My brother is an addict and—"

"Whoa, girl," I say, stopping her. "I don't know what you're trying to imply, but pump the fucking brakes."

"There're just a lot of signs, you know? That you're … using drugs," she whispers. "You're always late. You're moody. I swear you've lost a little weight since we started dancing together." She stops, swallowing. "But mostly … I saw your truck at Van's last week. He's a bad dude, Cade. I really hope you're not getting tangled up with him."

"How about you just worry about getting this dance the fuck over with and don't worry about me?" I glower before standing abruptly and towering over her. "I'm not your brother, Poppy. Don't ever say shit like that again to me either. If you do, you'll be dancing by yourself at the fundraiser. That's a promise."

And then I leave, never looking back.

Where does she get off, making assumptions about me? What I do and whose house I'm at is none of her fucking business. Besides, I'm fine.

I walk up the stairs and into my room. The sight on the living room couch made my day suck just a tiny bit less, surprisingly.

While living with Haley, I have learned something. There is nothing more beautiful than her in her baggy sweatpants and ratty high school T-shirt, her hair pulled up in a messy bun or ponytail. It's a sight I hope to see every single day. But I've only been graced with it a handful of times—when I really needed it. Today was one of those days.

I really don't know how she comes from the same family as Hunter. Or how her parents made her when they are the most type-A people you could ever meet. Her socks never match, she makes a mess every time she bakes or cooks something, and she's extremely forgetful. Oh, and she mysteriously has candy with her at all times. I do not get how she is a Thompson.

She also leaves a trail of things everywhere she goes. A hairbrush. School papers. A bottle of water. A book. Oh, and she always loses the remote minutes after it's given to her.

Hurricane Haley has become my favorite thing in life.

But she can't knowingly be my favorite thing. No, I have to adore her from a distance—far enough away that she won't see me and catch on. That is the only way to keep her safe from me.

I say hi when I see her. I ask her how her day is going, but I keep it light. It's been nearly a week since we hooked up, and it still consumes so much of my brain.

In a few days, I have to perform with Poppy, and that's annoying because she's suddenly onto me, suspecting I'm a druggie. I'm not like Van. I'm fine. And even if I'm not, it's not her concern. We aren't even friends.

I collapse on my bed, knowing I have to go to hockey practice in a few short hours and I'm already fucking dragging.

All I want to do right now is get this performance over with. Get it behind me and get Poppy and her concerns out of my life.

Haley

Hunter was given a few tickets so family could attend tonight's show, and when he offered me one, I took it without question. I knew our parents likely wouldn't come watch it. With their work, it's always hard for them to come to events like this. And they typically don't show much support for anything to do with hockey.

I really didn't want to come either. Sure, I think it's for an amazing cause, supporting Brody O'Brien's One Wish foundation to help less fortunate kids play sports and get a chance to do extracurricular activities. I love all of that. But watching Cade and Poppy prance around on the stage together like they are some couple on *Dancing with the Stars*? No thanks. Hard pass. I might actually chew the inside of my cheek off.

But here I am, like the good sister I am. I wanted Hunter to have someone in the stands. I wanted Sutton to have someone too. So, I came. And I dressed up. Wearing a fancy, body-hugging little black dress, covered in sequins and leaving little to the imagination. Some might say it's a revenge dress. And those people … would absolutely be right. But who am I kidding, trying to show off my body to a man who's dancing with a girl as stacked as Poppy?

Watson is currently onstage, dancing with a girl named Ryann, and I honestly don't think I've ever seen Watson be so gentle and sweet. His eyes never leave her, not for the whole performance. He's been disappearing a lot lately, and now, I'm wondering if that pretty little thing is the reason why.

Every performance is great. Some funny. Some more romantic. But when Poppy and Cade are presented, I'm a little relieved that it's an upbeat song and not a slow, sensual one.

"What a Night" by Flo Rida plays, and I can't even lie—Cade and Poppy are phenomenal. The playful music, followed by their moves onstage, has the entire room smiling and dancing around in their seats.

He grins, captivating every face in the crowd, and I feel a pang in my chest. It happens every time I look at him, ever since I first moved into the house.

As I watch their performance end, I come to grips with something. I'm in love with that boy. And he barely knows I exist.

It is time for me to find another place to live. I can't be around him any longer.

CADE

After our performance, we get some waters and watch Hunter and Sutton go onstage.

Personally, I think we killed it. Of course, if we hadn't smoothed everything over at rehearsal last night, we probably would have sucked. And by smoothed everything over, I mean, I apologized for being a dick, and she agreed to not speculate when it came to my life.

I jerk my chin toward Hunter and Sutton. "I can't lie—they are good," I say, tilting my chin up and grinning at Poppy. "Do you still think I'm the worst dance partner?"

"I don't think I ever said that," she says, rolling her eyes before holding her fist up. "You did good, Huff. I'm proud of you."

"Thanks." I wink, bumping my fist against hers. "I had a damn good dancing partner who made me look better."

Hunter and Sutton end their performance with a big move just before the curtain drops.

I look over at Poppy. "That was some *Dirty Dancing* shit right there. They might have it in the bag."

Lost Boy

"It was all right, I guess," Poppy utters, but I know she's just salty because it was phenomenal, and we both know it.

Within moments, the next performance begins, and I vaguely hear Poppy saying something to me. But my eyes are fixated behind her—on a scene in the small room backstage, where Haley is crying against Watson's chest and the others there look painfully somber.

"What's going on?" I whisper partly to myself and partly to Poppy.

Turning, she follows my gaze before we both start walking that way. "I don't know. We'd better find out though."

After we walk in, I close the door behind us because the show is still going on. My eyes go straight to Haley, who takes my breath away just from her beauty. Her tight, sparkly black dress forms to her body like it was made just for her. Her shoulder-length hair is pulled halfway up with a few pieces loose in the front. Even while she's crying, she's so beautiful.

"What's going on?" I say to no one in particular, just whoever will answer first.

"Sutton had an asthma attack after her and Hunter's performance," Watson answers, grimacing. "She's not doing good, man. She ... she fucking stopped breathing."

"Shit," I utter, watching Haley as she squeezes her eyes shut while Watson keeps her close to him.

"That's ... awful," Poppy's voice barely squeaks, and a dancer named Lana whirls her head toward her.

"I'm sure you think it's *awful,* Poppy. You've been rotten to her for weeks. No, since she got to Brooks, you've done everything you can to make her life hell."

Poppy's face pales, and she seems to shrink into herself. "I know I have," she whispers. "But I don't want anything bad to happen to her. You have to know that, Lana."

Lana, Poppy, Sutton, and Ryann—Watson's dance partner—all live together. I've known for a while that Poppy doesn't like Sutton, but I've gotten to know her well enough to know that deep down, she'd never wish harm on her. Or on anyone.

"I'm going to go find Ryann," Poppy mumbles, peeking up at me.

At the mention of Ryann's name, Watson locks eyes with me and glances to Haley, and I know he wants me to take over and hold her instead so he can go to Ryann. It's pretty obvious he likes the girl.

Haley must sense what he's doing because she steps back, wrapping her arms around herself before wiping her eyes. "Go check on Ryann. She and Sutton have gotten really close." She sniffles. "She needs you right now."

Giving her one last squeeze, he dips his head closer. "She'll be fine, Haley. Sutton is going to be fine."

91

Haley's eyebrows pull together, and she nods slowly. "I hope so," her voice croaks.

When Watson leaves, I put my hand on her back. "Do you want to sit down?"

Her head moves side to side quickly, and she doesn't look at me.

"Okay. Do you want me to take you home?"

"No," she snaps. "I don't need anything from you, Cade." She looks up, her eyes filled with tears. "Just leave me be, would you? For once, can you just do that?"

I feel like I've been kicked in the chest, but I eventually nod my head once. "Yeah. Fine. Anything you want."

"Good," she hisses before walking away from me.

I've made her hate me. And I guess that's what I wanted, but, fuck, it doesn't make it hurt less.

Haley

I drive toward the hospital. And for the first time in nine days, I pull in a calm breath and let it out. Because I just got the phone call from my brother that Sutton woke up.

As kids, Sutton and I were so close. But after our families had a falling-out, we sort of parted ways. I've never stopped loving her as a friend though.

I could see how much pain Hunter was in while she was in a coma after her asthma attack. I just wanted her to open her beautiful eyes and wake up. And finally ... she has.

Though I've been so consumed with everything going on with Sutton, I haven't missed the little gifts being left outside my bedroom door during the past week—like random candy and other treats I love. And since Watson doesn't know my favorite things and has been too busy with Ryann, I know who's been leaving them. Cade.

Being near Cade hurts me but makes me feel good too. It hurts because I'm only allowed to get so close to him. But, sometimes, being in his presence feels like a gift. Something about him brings me comfort.

I'd planned to find a place to move to, but after Sutton's stint in the hospital, that plan went on the back burner for a bit. Now that she's better, it's time for me to start searching.

Pulling my car into a parking spot, I glance up at the brick building and smile. Today, when I visit Sutton, I won't just be talking to her while she's being kept alive by tubes and machines. Today, I'll get to actually talk to my friend. And she's going to be just fine.

On the ride home, I feel lighter. I turn the music up a little louder than usual and let it filter through my car. I even put the window down halfway.

Sutton couldn't talk too much during my visit because her throat was sore from over a week of intubation. But we got to visit for most of the afternoon, and it felt a lot like old times. Only now, she and my brother are in love instead of enemies. Who am I kidding? I think they have always been in love and just didn't realize it.

Pulling into my parking spot, I notice that only Cade's truck is home. I debate for a moment that maybe I should leave until Watson or Hunter come home, but then I realize I'm being silly, and I get my ass out of the car and head inside.

Once I get into the house, my eyes sweep the room, but I don't see him anywhere downstairs. He must be in his room, which is fine by me because I don't want to see him anyway. Not really.

The first thing I want to do is take my jeans off and put on sweatpants, so I head up the stairs, glancing down at my phone as I push the door open.

When I look up, my jaw drops, and my heart stops as I stare at my wall. A wall that had absolutely nothing on it now has a beautiful baby-blue three-bay bookcase. There aren't any books in it, but my boxes of books are sitting next to them. It's the most gorgeous sight I've ever seen, but it also infuriates me.

Marching across the hallway, I pound on Cade's closed door.

Within moments, he opens it, shirtless and in sweatpants. I try to keep my eyes on his and not let them float downward. Which I fail to do ... miserably.

I wave my arm toward my open bedroom door. "What the hell is that, Cade?"

"What is what?" He leans against the door, his eyes burning into mine.

"The bookcase. No, the *blue* bookcase!" I shake my head. "You're the only person I've ever told about wanting a baby-blue bookcase. Well, you and Remi. And she isn't the type of chick to build a damn bookcase. Especially not one this size."

"Who says I'm the type of guy to do it then?" He shrugs. "I might not even own any tools. Hell, I might not even know how to measure."

"So, you didn't do it then?" I raise an eyebrow, folding my arms over my chest.

"No, I did," he answers lightly. "You're welcome, by the way."

"Why?"

"Because you've had a rough week. I figured it would make you happy." Holding his hands out, he widens his eyes. "Excuse me for trying to do something to make you smile, grumpzilla."

"I *love* when you do nice things, Cade! But guess what comes after your nice shit. Not-so-nice shit. Every single time." I stomp my foot. "You keep dangling that carrot in front of me. Almost making me feel like ..." I pause, gripping the back of my neck with my hand. "You know what? Never mind."

As I start to turn, he catches my hand and spins me toward him and crowds me against his doorframe. One hand rests above my head, and the other moves to my cheek. "Almost making you feel like what, angel?"

I look up at him, embarrassed to say what I'm about to say. "Like I have a shot," I whisper, barely hearing myself. "Like maybe, just maybe, you might care."

He dips his head closer, making my brain feel fuzzy and my skin prickle. The power he holds over me from the slightest touch is pathetic.

"I might have a shitty way of showing it, but I promise you ... I care more than I've ever cared before, Haley." His hand continues to cup my face as his eyes look into mine. "I care so much that it makes me crazy sometimes."

"How can you say that?" I squeak, my voice growing hoarse. "You don't even remember ..." I stop, feeling tears stinging my eyes before one escapes.

He brushes my cheek, wiping the tear away. "I remember everything," he rasps. "Always have."

"Y-you do?" I utter, frowning. "But you said—"

"I know what I said. I'm no good for you. I've got demons, Haley. Ones that you aren't equipped to battle. Nor should you have to." His nostrils flare with emotion, and he shakes his head the slightest bit. "You're too fucking perfect to be ruined by me. I can't do it. I'd never forgive myself."

"I'm not perfect, Cade," I protest, standing a little taller. "And I don't believe you. Why can't you let me decide what's good for me and what isn't?"

"Because you'll make the wrong decision," he mutters. "And I can't give you the choice. I'm not strong enough to walk away from you."

"But I want you," I cry out. "How can you not see that?"

"I *do* see it, Haley. I see the way you look at me. The way you smile just for me." He slides his hand lower, running the pad of his thumb along my jawline. "But the truth is, if you knew me—the real me—you wouldn't look at me that way. And the thought of you looking at me any other way than the way you are right now ... fucking kills me." His eyes dance between mine. "If I let you in, you'll see what I really am. And I'm not letting that happen.

95

Because I like that you still think of me as a good guy. Selfishly, I can't let that go."

"Why did you build me the bookcase?" I breathe out.

His lips hovering over mine weakens me, like a hurricane passing over cold water, slowly breaking apart, losing its control. Losing itself.

This thing between me and Cade, it's hopeless. Still, here I am, unable to walk away.

"Because you said you wanted them," he says matter-of-factly. Like that reason should make perfect sense. "So I wanted you to have them."

Another tear falls from my eye, dripping down my cheek. "You remember that night? You really remember being together?"

"I remember every part of it." His deep voice cracks. "I couldn't forget it if I wanted to, Haley. And trust me, I've tried."

"Cade," I whimper desperately, barely recognizing the agony in my voice. "Kiss me. Please."

"I can't be everything you deserve, Haley. I need you to tell me you know that."

"I'm not asking for anything. I get it—you don't want me that way. Please, Cade, just kiss—" I don't finish my sentence because his lips are on mine, giving me life. Making everything perfect yet confusing, all at once.

It's a disaster. This thing between us. But I'll worry about the mess after everything is said and done.

He kisses me, sliding his hand to the back of my neck. He lifts me up, wrapping my legs around his waist and pushing my back against the doorframe.

It feels like my soul leaves my body. Like I'm watching this moment happen to someone else.

His mouth tastes minty, like spearmint gum, as his tongue slips against mine the smallest bit, teasing me and making me want more. I grind against him, wanting him so bad that my core aches.

When he rears back slightly, I panic that he is changing his mind. That he's going to run away. Again.

"Tell me what you want, Haley."

I press my lips to his once more before pulling back and looking him in the eye. "I want to be as close to you as I can get."

"Last time ... you were drunk. Are you sure this is what you want now that you're"—he pauses, seeming to grow nervous—"sober?"

"Yes," I say instantly. "*Especially* now that I'm sober."

He carries me into his room and sets me down on his bed. And as he stands before me, I can see a bulge growing under his sweatpants. The air becomes thicker, and breathing becomes harder as I draw in a few shaky breaths.

LOST BOY

"Need to redo the other night," he says softly, but his voice is gruff. "I need to make it better for you."

"It was perfect," I whisper just as he tugs my shirt and bra over my head and pushes me back until my spine is flat on the bed.

Moving his hands down my body, he pulls my jeans and panties off and dips his fingers inside of me. "Christ, angel. You're already so ready for me," he mutters before hooking his hands on the backs of my legs and pushing my knees upward. "Have you thought of me, Haley? Have you thought about when I ate you until you came on my tongue?"

"Yes," I breathe out. "Yes, I have."

"You tasted as sweet as you are, baby. And I've had a craving for you since that night." Crawling forward, he dips his face between my legs and drags his tongue inside of me. "So fucking sweet," he groans. "Hard to eat anything else these days without wishing it were this perfect pussy."

My hands tangle in his hair, and my back arches. I moan uncontrollably as I watch his mouth work against me. He gazes up, his eyes darkening as he widens his tongue and dives in again.

"Getting you nice and ready to take my cock, sweetheart."

He slides his hand under his chin, rubbing his fingers through my wetness before dragging one down until he reaches my ass. Slowly, he works it inside of me, and I moan, biting down on my bottom lip.

His finger stays lubricated, and his movement becomes faster. But his mouth never leaves my body. I tighten my thighs around his neck, throwing my head back against the bed. Every sensation hits me at once, and I come undone. My head feels dizzy as my orgasm hits me like a high-speed train, and I cry out, my entire body shaking, especially my legs.

Releasing my legs, he reaches up and fondles my breast before leaning down and flicking his tongue against my nipple. I might have just come, but I'm already ready for more, and my nipples harden from his touch.

He pulls his sweatpants and boxers down and palms himself, gliding his hand back and forth. A whimper slips from my lips from the sight, and he smirks.

"Dirty girl, you like watching me play with my hard cock, don't you?"

Shyly, I nod.

"Get on your knees and crawl to me, angel. Crawl until my cock slides between your plump lips."

Sitting up, I get on my knees and do what he said without question. Crawling toward him, I open my mouth and gaze up at him as the tip of his cock grazes my lips and his hard length slides against my tongue.

His eyes are hooded as his hips jerk forward, pushing him deeper into my mouth.

"Suck," he growls. "You were mouthy when you came into my room after you saw your bookcase. Let me wash that pretty wet mouth out with my cum."

I drag him deeper. Tilting my chin upward at him, I begin bobbing my mouth harder, taking more of him each time. He grabs a fistful of my hair and tightens his grip, pulling it backward enough to make my head sting. It's borderline painful, but it only intensifies the ache between my legs.

I hollow my cheeks out around him, gazing up at him with the desire to make him feel good. My reward is when he groans, telling me he's enjoying himself. But I also feel a deep-rooted yearning to show him that I can be whatever he needs. Just because I'm sweet doesn't mean I can't get a little dirty sometimes. Especially for a guy as hot as Cade.

"Fuck. Your mouth feels too good. I'm going to blow my load down your throat and watch you lick me clean." He barely gets the words out before his eyes roll and his hips jerk.

I hold strong, keeping my lips firmly around his cock, when I feel the warm liquid hit the back of my throat. It's something I've never liked to do when giving oral sex, but suddenly, I do it like a pro.

Swallowing, I drag my tongue up and down his length once more before releasing him and wiping my mouth.

Not expecting him to recover quickly, I awkwardly start to grab for the covers to pull them over my bare, exposed body when he collapses on the bed. But not before reaching in his nightstand and tearing open a foil packet.

"Come here." He motions his finger toward me before rolling the condom over his length, which is still very much rock hard. "Bring your sexy ass over here. Come ride my dick and make me come again. I want to see those tits bounce." He smirks, his eyes growing playful. "You can yell at me about how I piss you off while you fuck me, if you want. Truth be told, angel … I think you're sexy as hell when you're pissed."

For a split second, nerves build inside of me at the thought of him seeing me completely naked at that angle. I've seen the girls who chase him. He's used to supermodel-looking chicks. I'm curvy and, dare I say, stubby. But one look at his glistening cock, which is anxiously waiting for me to climb aboard, and my nerves vanish as quickly as they came. Replaced with a desperate need inside of me. A need that is already craving another orgasm from this man.

I climb over him, and he grips my hips and lowers me onto him, filling me more than I even knew was possible. The sting from his sheer size is quickly numbed as I begin rolling my hips. Any nervousness is gone, and suddenly, I don't give a shit what I look like as I move up and down on him, riding him as hard as my body will let me.

His palms come down on my asscheeks—hard—and a slapping sound rings through the air on contact. He clutches my ass, digging his fingertips into it, and sits up slightly to rest his head against the headboard.

"Dirty little angel, fucking my dick just like I asked you to." He reaches his hand up my back and gives my hair a yank. "I can't decide if you look prettier with your lips wrapped around my cock or while you're riding me as you try to make yourself come."

I slow, leaning down to kiss him before slipping my tongue inside of his mouth. "And I can't decide if you look hotter right now or when your face is between my thighs," I coo against his mouth before nipping his bottom lip, surprising us both with my filthy words.

At first, there's no hiding the shocked look on his face. But then he just looks painfully turned on as his pupils dilate, taking up most of the blue in his eyes.

"Angel, I'd eat every meal between your legs if I could," he breathes out as I start to move on him again. "Sweetest slice of heaven I ever have tasted."

I reach behind me, cupping his balls in my hand and massaging them while my hips continue to roll against his body. I'm so close, but I want him to finish at the same time.

"Fuck," he hisses just as the tingling in my body begins, and I fall over the ledge, letting go. "Squeeze me, angel. Drip down my cock and soak my sheets," he growls, slapping my ass. "Coming with you." He barely croaks the words out before his body begins to shudder against mine, a chain of curses coming from his lips.

He leans up and kisses me, and my body collapses against his. Dragging air into our lungs, we breathe like wild animals on a hunt for our prey. His fingertips strum up my back, and he kisses my shoulder blade.

"What are you doing to me, angel?" he rasps.

"Same thing you're doing to me," I answer, feeling more confused than ever.

CADE

This isn't really how I expected my day to go, to be honest.

We're lying together in my bed. Haley's head against my chest with her ear on my heart. A calmness washes over my body that I haven't felt in so damn long. I'm so tired. I'm tired of fucking up. And I'm tired of having no control over my life. Right here, in this moment, I know I could be happy with her. I wouldn't need the drugs. Or the alcohol. I could be content if I never touched another pill. As long as I had her, I'd be all set.

"Thank you for my bookcase," she says softly. "I can't even put into words how much I love it."

I run my fingers against her bare back, trying to stay with her for as long as I can even though I know, soon, my body is going to tell me it's time to bolt. "You are very welcome. I'll help you put your books away. I just figured you had certain places for each one. I didn't want to put them in the wrong order and risk you beating me up." I look down, wiggling my eyebrows. "On second thought, you're mighty fine when there's smoke coming from your ears. Maybe I should piss you off more often."

"Don't even think about it," she murmurs. "You really are something, Cade Huff. You know that?"

She cranes her neck up to look at me. A look that scares me as much as it heals me. I eat it up. I love it. But building a bookcase doesn't make me worthy of it. I know that much.

"It was nothing. Just wanted to do something nice for you." I smile down at her.

My own money was wearing thin. But the fact that I spent a good deal of what was left on the materials for the bookcase and not drugs? It speaks volumes to how much she means to me. But just because I had the willpower to put her first this one time doesn't mean I will have it all the time.

"It's far from nothing," she whispers, her voice growing thicker. "It's … everything."

I look at the ceiling for a second, not really knowing what to say.

Now that I know how much the bookcase I made means to her, I realize I've only set myself up for failure. Because that isn't usually me. I'm not that guy. And now, she'll want more. She'll think I can give her more.

I can't promise anything to her. I know I can't.

But I know one thing: I want her. I want her more than I've ever wanted anything in my entire life.

More than hockey. More than drugs. More than sobriety.

But I can't fully have her until I get my life in order. And I don't know when that'll be. It wouldn't be fair to keep a girl like her waiting. What a selfish bastard it would make me to try.

I could tell her the truth. I could admit out loud the reasons why I'm not prepared to be the man she needs and deserves. I could say it right now. Maybe it would free me. But if it freed me, it would imprison her. Because from that point forward, I know she would worry. And the look she's giving me right now? Forget it. She'd look at me differently. I fucking hate the thought of that alone.

"I don't really know what I'm doing, Haley." I swallow back a lump of emotion. "All I know is … I can't stay away from you."

LOST BOY

"Me neither," she whispers so softly that I hardly hear her. She presses her lips to my abdomen. "When my world goes to shit, you're always here." I feel her shrug against me. "And that's got to count for something ... right?"

I blow out a breath softly, barely nodding. "Yeah, I guess it does."

But what will happen when her world goes to shit because of me? Who's going to save her then?

CADE

After practice, I rush home and head upstairs. Locking the door to the bathroom, I take the clear baggie out of my pocket and get what I need out of it. Pulling the drawer open, I reach around till I find the mirror I hid back there. I quiet that voice in my brain that's telling me to give it the drugs it needs. I'm just a passenger in my own life.

Once I'm done snorting the crushed pill, I pick the mirror up to clean it and catch sight of myself. My eyes are bloodshot. I'm not skinny enough for people who don't know me to notice, but I've lost enough weight that when my parents come to visit in a few weeks, they'll know right away that something is up. A small, lingering amount of white shit sits under my nose, and I quickly wipe it off before stuffing the baggie into my pocket.

Loser, I say to myself. *You don't deserve that girl in the room next door who looks at you like you hung the fucking moon. You don't even deserve to breathe the same air as her.*

I don't shut the voice off in my head because I know it's right. Haley Thompson is perfection. And I'm just the fraud who led her to believe I'm not an absolute piece of shit when that's exactly what I am.

You're slipping at practice. The guys are starting to notice something's going on with you.

I hold the mirror in the sink, washing it and willing my thoughts to shut the fuck up. Guilt consumes every fiber of my being. Along with that feeling of dread because I know my time is running out. I'm not going to be able to fool everyone for much longer.

Reaching into the shower, I crank the knob as hot as it'll go and strip my clothes off, leaving them in a pile. I hold my hand under the spray, and it almost burns my fingertips, but I waste no time climbing in.

Not being strong enough to get through the day sober is a whole other type of hell no one talks about. And while I know I chose to use those first few times ... it wasn't really a choice after that. It became a necessity.

I'm constantly looking at the time. It's not that I can't wait for my next high; it's that my body is trained to already be thinking of it. It doesn't matter that it's only been a few hours. I'm ready to do it all over again. Or my mind and body are.

When Haley and I hooked up the other day and I came harder than I ever had before, I helped her put her books away. I loved watching her as she put each one in a certain spot, and then she would change it at least five times.

That day, I felt something in my soul come alive again. And I figured something out as I stared at her while she was in deep concentration, scowling with that crease between her brow as she looked from shelf to shelf. I knew right then that I loved her. That I was in love with her.

That night, I told myself that I needed to get my act together. I couldn't be an active addict while being with a girl like her. And since I had the next day off from practice and all things hockey, I figured I'd skip classes, claiming I didn't feel good. And I really wouldn't since I'd be starving my body of the one thing it thought it needed, starting the withdrawal process.

By the next day, I had never been so sick in my life. Well, besides the last time I had gone through withdrawal. Haley came in to check on me, but I told her I didn't want her to catch what I had. And I sent her away.

She returned a few hours later with ginger ale, Gatorade, ibuprofen, and a cool washcloth for my forehead. Curling up to me, she held my aching body, taking the washcloth away as I started to shiver. When I tried to tell her to leave, that I didn't want her to get sick, she simply put her hand on my forehead and gave me a faint smile.

And she said, "I'm not going anywhere."

For the next few hours, I ran to the bathroom, puked I didn't know how many times, wanted to scream in agony as every single joint, muscle, ligament, and cell ached to a level I'd never felt before. And by nine o'clock that night, Haley had fallen asleep, and I gave in to the monster inside my head and went to Van's house for more drugs. I had hockey the next morning, and I couldn't show up the way I was.

I let the shower spray down my body, scorching my skin as I think back to when all that happened last week. If I had just stayed strong, would I have been feeling normal by now? Or would I have still been in pure hell? I suppose it'd have been no worse than the hell I'm in right now. I can't stand to look at myself in a mirror, so how the hell will she look at me when she learns the truth?

I love her, and that should be enough for me to get myself straight. I shouldn't be looking at her like a burden for coming between me and getting high. But sometimes, that's how I see her. I can't help it. I don't think any amount of love would change that.

Love can't fix everything. And it sure as hell can't fix me.

The calmest seas can be turned upside down by the strongest storm.

Haley is like a serene sea. And I'm the storm.

In the end, everything in my path will be wrecked.

I have no right to ruin Haley. No right at all.

She's too perfect to be taken out by my wrath.

Haley

I look out the window, fiddling with my necklace. The clouds are dark, and the wind is picking up. Typically, thunderstorms are more of a spring and summer thing. Yet here we are. About to get hit with one.

"So, look ... I'm supposed to go over to Sutton's tonight and help her move a few things around," Hunter says, coming behind me. "But I can stay here. Or you can come with me." He pauses, and I know he's looking out the window too. "I know how much you hate storms."

"I'll be fine," I say, turning toward him. "I'm inside ... right? And it'll probably pass quickly."

He eyes me over, seeing if I mean it. My brother is that guy. The one who wants to be there for everyone even if it's hard.

"Promise," I add, flashing him a half-smile.

"I'll be here for our little sis," Watson says, coming next to me and throwing his arm around my shoulders. "I'll keep ya safe."

"I don't know if that makes me feel any better," Hunter says, narrowing his eyes.

"I'll be here too," I hear Cade say as he strolls downstairs, his hair wet from his shower. "I've got nowhere to be."

I don't know why Hunter doesn't hate storms the way I do. He was there when my hatred for lightning began. Our mom was driving us home from school, and lightning struck a tree. It landed directly on my mom's car, trapping us in there for hours. Since then, I've really, *really* hated storms.

Hunter has been so preoccupied with Sutton since she got home from the hospital that he surprisingly hasn't caught on that Cade and I have been spending more time together than usual. Watson's definitely noticed, but for some reason, he hasn't really brought it up. But that's probably because he's with Ryann during all his free time.

"As long as you guys are sure." Hunter's eyes sweep over all of us. "And if you guys end up leaving, you need to take her with you," he warns them. "And you can drop her off at Sutton's to be with me. Okay?"

"You got it, Hunty," Cade chimes. "Go get you some hot thunderstorm sex."

"Ew," I groan. "I'm right here."

"My bad." He shrugs but gives me a mischievous smirk.

If anything could take my mind off an impending storm ... it would be me and Cade, naked.

As Hunter pulls his hood up to shield himself from the wind, Cade holds his hand up and waves. "Take 'er easy, my friend. And if she's easy, take 'er twice."

Hunter rolls his eyes and heads outside. Meanwhile, Cade cracks up, thinking he's hilarious.

As another gust of wind hits the window, I look at Watson and shrug. "Guess all those candles your mama gave you might come in handy after all, huh?"

"Why's that?" He frowns, releasing me.

"Because if we lose power, I'm about to turn this place into Yankee Candle—that's why."

He laughs. "Nice."

Cade elbows my side. "Sounds romantic."

"Well, while we still have power, I'll make popcorn," Watson says, heading toward the kitchen.

"And I'll find a movie." Cade throws his arm around me and drags me to the couch with him. "Know any good pornos?" And then he puts his mouth to my ear. "Or we could just go make our own."

I swat at him, but my neck burns hot, and my core aches with need. I love Watson and all, but suddenly, I wish he'd leave too.

Intense flashes of lightning are followed by a boom so powerful that I'm worried the house might actually fall apart. I try to focus on the screen as *Sweet Home Alabama* plays, but it's hard. The guys were nice enough to let me pick the movie since they knew I was going to be a little bitch about the weather. Then again, I know Cade loves this movie. He's a *chick flick* sort of dude.

Watson's phone beeps, and when he looks at the screen, he stands quickly. "Fuck, I gotta go. I'll ... be back. Maybe." He looks at his phone again before slipping his sneakers on. "To be honest, I probably won't be back till really late, maybe even not until the morning." He looks from me to Cade. "You're going to stay, right? If not, I can take you with me, Haley."

I start to open my mouth to assure him I'm fine, but Cade beats me to it.

"I'm not going anywhere," he says, glancing over at me. "We're good. But seriously, be careful out there. It's fucking nuts."

An odd expression passes across Watson's face, but he eventually gives us a faint nod before heading outside.

Doing my best to relax back into the couch, I chew my nails aggressively. And just as the movie is almost to one of my favorite parts, the power goes out.

"Well then," Cade utters. Like he suddenly remembers I hate storms, he pulls me against him. "You all right?"

"I'm fine," my voice squeaks just as a flash of lightning lights up the room before another loud roar makes me jump. "Holy balls, that was so freaking loud." My voice trembles.

I really, really hate thunderstorms.

Standing up, he lifts me into his arms before walking into the kitchen and setting my ass on the countertop. Using the flashlight on his phone, he reaches in the cabinet where Watson keeps his stash of infamous candles and takes out an armful of them. Returning to the same cabinet, he reaches around until he finds a lighter.

One by one, he lights the candles before a small laugh comes from his lips. "It'll be smellin' like apple pie, vanilla cupcake, lemon bread, and pumpkin spice up in here in no time."

He isn't kidding either because within moments, an array of sweet scents hits my nostrils, and I don't know whether I like it or if it's too much.

When another round of lightning and thunder hits, I'm chewing my nails so hard that I'm surprised they aren't bleeding. Slowly walking toward me, he wedges himself between my legs and buries his face in my neck. He smells so good. Like pine with a little cologne. Nothing too heavy that would give me a headache, thank God.

He must feel my body shaking in fear because he nuzzles his face against the flesh of my neck before kissing there. His mouth works against my neck, and even though I'm still tense, with him kissing me this way, I almost forget about the storm outside.

Until it strikes again. This time, he cups my cheek before his lips attack mine.

Feeling his erection grow between my legs strikes a match inside of me, leaving me needing more. I kiss him back, and our tongues tease each other, making me remember what it felt like to have his face between my legs. And how much I'd like to do the same to him.

Peeling my shirt off, followed by my bra, he leans down, taking my nipple into his mouth and licking. I moan, thrusting my hips upward, hoping he'll take the hint.

"Patience, my greedy girl," he utters, and with the light from the candles, I see his smirk. "You know I'm going to give you my cock. But not so fast."

Slowly, he pushes me back until my spine is flat against the countertop. He cups my neck with his hand and then drags it between my breasts, down my stomach, and stops at the top of my sweatpants. Giving them a yank, he pulls them down and grins. "No panties today? It's like you were waiting for me to fuck you, weren't you, dirty girl?"

"Yes," my voice croaks.

When he rubs his thumb over my clit, I let out a muffled groan, and then he brings it to my mouth and drags it across my parted lips.

"That's how wet you are, baby. You're fucking soaked. I wanted to fuck you, but now … well, now, I'm just starving. And your pussy is what's on the menu tonight."

Lightning flashes, but suddenly, I don't care. Cade leans down and brings a nipple into his mouth, biting the slightest bit before dragging his tongue to the other one.

Gazing up at me, he runs his tongue down my abdomen, leaving a trail of wetness behind as he works his way downward. The hard countertop is far from comfortable, but I don't care. And as he buries his face between my thighs, his tongue swiping over me, making me moan, I'm not really concerned with how uncomfortable my body is.

"Look at you, dripping all over this countertop for me," he groans against my flesh just as thunder roars through the house, damn near shaking the walls, and my body jerks.

Craning his head up, he looks at me and replaces his tongue with a finger before working it in and out of me. "Don't focus on the storm, baby. Focus on me devouring you. Focus on the fact that you're going to soak my tongue and cry out my name."

As his tongue dives into me again, my thighs tighten around his neck, and I thread my fingers through his short hair as he licks me harder, widening his tongue and putting me over the edge.

Reaching up with both hands, he grips my sides before pushing me up and down against his mouth. My orgasm starts to build, taking over my entire body.

As I continue rocking against his tongue, I moan, biting down on my lip so hard that I'm surprised I don't taste blood.

"That's right; squeeze my fucking tongue, angel," he growls. "Who's making you come this hard? Say my fucking name."

"Cade," I cry out, gripping his hair tighter as I thrust myself harder against his mouth. "Fuck, Cade. Oh … my … God."

"That's right; *I* am. No one can eat your pussy like this, baby." He sucks gently, flicking his tongue against me as I tremble, a wave of relaxation washing over my body. "So fucking sweet, angel. So. Fucking. Sweet."

My vision goes dark for a few seconds before I finally come back down to planet Earth, suddenly aware of the storm outside again.

"I've eaten a lot of meals in this kitchen, but between your legs … that's my new favorite." He drags in a breath. "Now, be a good girl and open up those plump lips, angel baby. You're about to choke on my cock because I'm fixing to fuck that pretty face of yours."

Climbing onto the countertop, he straddles my body until his dick is literally grazing my lips. Slowly, I open my mouth, and before I realize it, I'm darting my tongue out to swipe it across the tip of his swollen cock. Just that little action earns me a hiss. And when I open wider, inviting him to do as he pleases, he thrusts his length into my mouth. I can't take all of it—he's far too big. But what I can take instantly has me gagging as he hits the back of my throat before pulling back and sliding out of my mouth.

"Go ahead and gag on me, angel. It only gets my dick harder," he growls, blue eyes glistening in the moonlight. He slowly plunges himself back in. "Fuck, you look so beautiful with my cock between your lips."

He moves his hips back and forth, staring at my mouth as he slides in and out, his eyes glazed over. "Holy fuck, angel. Seeing your lips wrapped around me is enough to send my cum straight down your throat right now."

I tilt my chin up, deciding to take that challenge. I move him in and out of my mouth faster and harder. He reaches his hand between my head and the countertop and takes a fistful of my hair and tightens his hold. Letting him slide all the way out, I run my mouth down, dragging my tongue over his balls and making him moan in pleasure.

When I work my mouth back to his cock, I curve my tongue under it and move my head back and forth.

"I'm going to come down your throat," he chokes out. "If you don't want me——"

I don't even let him finish his sentence before I wrap my lips around him tighter, raking my tongue along his hardness. He must like how it feels because within seconds, his hips are jerking, and his entire body is trembling as he fills my throat with himself, not holding back anything.

Pulling out, he drags his knuckles across my cheek before running his thumb across my lips. "Such a good fucking girl, angel."

By now, the worst of the storm has passed, leaving only the wind and rain. And truthfully, storms no longer seem that scary. Because now, I have a new memory to connect storms with.

And I also might never look at this kitchen the same.

When he climbs off of me, I watch him fish something out of the pocket of his pants that are pooled on the floor. Standing up, he pulls me forward and sits me upright before kissing me hard as he tangles his hand in my hair.

"I told you I was going to fuck you, and I am." His voice is gruff and desperate as he pulls me toward him, forcing me to wrap my legs around his waist.

He walks us toward the window. The rain pelts against the glass, making it nearly impossible to see out of. Dropping me to my feet, he quickly spins me around, pushing me forward against the window.

"I'm going to fuck you right here for the whole neighborhood to see, angel." He gives my ass a slap and then another before I hear a foil packet being opened. "Goddamn, Haley. I can't get enough of you. And I'll show anyone walking by that this pussy, this ass"—he wraps his fingers around my neck before dragging them upward and putting his thumb into my mouth— "and this mouth … are mine. I might not be able to keep you, but I'll ruin you for anyone else."

I suck his thumb into my mouth, swirling my tongue around his flesh, and I love the sound of his hiss. With my breasts pressed against the cool, foggy glass, he plunges himself inside of me, making me whimper.

His hips thrust against my ass as he pumps in and out of me. He buries his face between my shoulder blades, biting down on my skin.

"You feel so fucking good," he growls, reaching around and sliding his thumb along my clit, making circles and driving me wild. "First, I'm going to make you come. And then I'm going to blow my load all over this perfect ass."

"Cade," I whimper, feeling my orgasm building so fast that I know it's going to hit me like a freaking tidal wave. "Oh … Ca—"

He slows the slightest bit, moving in and out at a pace that lets me relish every second of this orgasm, making it last and not rushing it.

"That's right; squeeze around me, my angel. Drip down my cock, just like I'm going to drip all over your ass."

With my palm flat against the glass, a few more involuntary moans rip through me before he pulls out, and seconds later, I feel his cum on my asscheeks.

He drags in a few shaky breaths, keeping his face against my back, and his stubble tickles my skin. "I can't stay away from you, Haley," he rasps. "You make it fucking impossible."

I don't answer. Because … I can't stay away from him either.

CADE

Haley's body snuggles against mine as the sound of her breathing evens out, proving that she's asleep. This should be enough. I should stay my ass in this bed, holding her against me. Because she's the only thing that brings me peace.

Looking down at her, I brush the loose strands of hair off her face. She's a living, breathing angel. And I just want to be the man she deserves. But how can I be that when I can't even stand to be lying here right now?

She is everything I never knew I needed. But still, it isn't enough to keep me in this bed. Because my mind is racing and I need to calm it down.

After admiring her for a few minutes longer, I slowly slide my body out from under hers and get out of bed. I sneak to my dresser and grab that familiar baggie. And then tiptoe to the bathroom, pushing the door shut behind me.

No one is home besides us. I guess they stayed with their girls after all. They can do shit like that because they are normal. Well, sort of.

I hold up the baggie of pills, but before I get a chance to take what I need out, the door pushes the rest of the way open, and Haley is standing there, her eyebrows pulled together as she stares at the bag in my hand.

Her honey-blonde hair is a mess of waves, and there isn't a trace of makeup on her face. I wish I had memorized everything about her face leading up to this moment. Before I ruined it.

Now, she's looking at me like *that*.

"Cade?" she whispers after rubbing her sleepy eyes, waking up real fast. "What … what are you doing?"

Quickly, I attempt to pretend like everything is normal and plaster on a careless grin. "I just needed to take some ibuprofen because my knee hurts."

I try to reach for her playfully, but she steps back.

"Hey, what's wrong?"

I reach for her again, but she takes another step away.

"I don't think that's ibuprofen, Cade." The words spill from her lips as she grabs my hand, looking down. "These look like OxyContin. If you're going to lie, at least make it believable. My entire *family* is made up of doctors. I know what certain pills look like."

I could tell her the truth. That I have a problem and I need help. I know her enough by now to know that she'd hug me, and though she'd be disappointed and never look at me the same, she wouldn't be mad. All I have to do is say the words. And tell her I'm sorry.

But fuck that. Who is she to call me out this way? Besides, if I admit anything, she'll expect me to get help. And we're in the middle of the fucking hockey season. Of course I can't do that right now. I don't have time. But she wouldn't understand that. I know she wouldn't.

"Look, Haley," I say, shrugging lazily to downplay how worked up I really am right now. I'm a master of my own craft. Lying and covering shit up. "I know you think you know what's going on, but you don't have a clue. The truth is, my knee is fucked, and I have to take these to sleep." I even throw in one last thing to sell her on it all. "The doctor prescribed them. Don't think he would have if it was a big deal."

The words come out so easily. They always do when I need to cover my ass.

"Then, why aren't they in a prescription bottle?" she whispers so low that I barely hear her. "Why are they in a baggie?"

"Because I don't want to carry around a bottle of pills and have the guys think I'm in pain while I'm on the ice," I toss back like it's nothing. But it's another lie. "Figured leaving them in a bag in a safe place was my best bet." I soften my face, flashing her a reassuring smile. "Why are you so worked up, angel? Can't you see there's nothing to worry about?"

Our staredown continues before eventually, her brows pull together, and she looks at me with sad, heartbreaking eyes. I hate those eyes. I fucking despise them.

"Cade, I want to help you, but you can't lie to me."

"I'm not lying," I say quickly. Her words struck a nerve, angering me. "And I don't remember asking for your help ... so?"

"Why wouldn't you have just told me sooner then? If it really is about pain, why keep it a secret?" Her eyes narrow, and her arms fold over her chest. "Just seems weird—that's all."

"I don't know," I answer. "Guess I just didn't see a reason to. A lot of athletes need pain management."

She isn't buying what I'm saying, and that's something I'm not really used to. With my parents, I can convince them I'm fine, and typically, they believe me. But the way Haley is looking at me, I can tell she sees right through me. She knows I'm filling her with bullshit right now. Blowing smoke up her ass to cover my own.

That's what drugs do. They make you a selfish fucking prick. This is why I didn't want to let her get close to me. I didn't want to be responsible for putting that look on her face because she cares too much.

We're not getting anywhere right now, just going in circles.

"Let's go to bed," I say, pulling her against me and kissing her forehead. "Okay?"

Her body is cold and stiff against mine. Nothing like how she usually feels. And most of all ... I feel her emotionally pulling away, out of my reach.

I'm losing her, so I squeeze her tighter. "Okay, Haley?" With every second that passes, it seems like the wedge between us grows, and I feel the panic in my gut. "Angel ... please?" I rasp, just wanting to hold her so I can forget that she probably knows the truth now.

Just as I feel my world falling apart, she finally nods. Maybe it's because she believes me. Or perhaps she thinks she can fix me. Whatever it is, I'm grateful for it.

"Okay," she whispers.

I don't want to be this guy anymore. I want to be the man worthy of standing next to her. But I have no fucking idea how to get there.

Haley

Cade sleeps against me. Though he's sound asleep, his arms remain tightly around me, holding me close to his body. Our bodies might be touching, but I still feel like we're a thousand miles away from each other. Everything I thought I believed, I'm questioning it now.

I want to trust him when he says that the pills are only for pain management for his knee. But how can I when he's never even complained in front of me that his knee hurts? I feel like, since we've gotten closer, there have been so many signs indicating something is wrong. Ones that I missed. Or maybe overlooked because I'd so badly just wanted him to notice me that when he finally did, I didn't want to see his flaws or the signs that he was pulling back when I was diving deeper, falling for him to the point of no return.

I don't want to look at him differently. I don't want to, but I do. How can I not when I just walked in on him getting ready to take pills from a bag in the middle of the night? And he has so many characteristics of an addict. I can't help that my mind is going there. He's so hot and cold. He's moody. He is always cutting it close to getting to practice on time. And he randomly disappears and doesn't come home when Watson and Hunter do after practice.

It isn't fair of me to make assumptions with such little evidence. I'm letting my mind paint a picture that might not be completely true. So, I'll dig deeper, and I'll keep my guard up.

I tilt my head upward to get a good look at him—when he isn't hiding behind his charming jokes or dimpled grin. The sadness on his face is more obvious now than it's ever been. And the way his lips curve down, forming a frown, as he sleeps is something I've never seen before. I missed it. I ignored so many things because I was too busy chasing him. I never stopped to see him. Struggles and all.

My poor, lost boy. How did I not notice how much pain you were in before now? And why did it take me finding you in the bathroom with a baggie of pills to see you clearly?

This whole time, I've felt like he didn't see me. Maybe I'm the one who had my eyes closed.

13

CADE

We head back into the arena, and the team prepares for our final period of the game. I move across the ice sluggishly, getting ready to do my part—the bare minimum, nothing extra.

Hockey is something I'm beginning to resent, and I never really thought I'd feel this way. There was a time in my life when hockey was everything. Now, it seems to be the opposite.

"Huff, are you fucking out here, or are you back home, jerking off?" Watson growls, skating next to me. "This is a big game for us. Get your shit together."

"If I was stroking my chicken, you'd know it," I toss back. "The whole arena would. Because, you know, it's fucking massive." I smirk. "Hell, aliens in outer space would probably even know."

Shoving me lightly, he gives me a hard look. "Get it together, Cade. Right now, everyone is doing their best. Besides you. I've seen your best. This isn't it. It's far fucking from it." He sighs. "I don't know what's been going on with you lately, but whatever it is—too much partying, weed, women—just get it together." He jerks his chin toward the team. "At least do it for them."

Once he leaves, Hunter appears. Hunter is never quick to anger. Instead, he tries to be the voice of reason most of the time. I can already guess what will come out of his mouth before he even speaks.

"What's going on, big fella?" He tips his chin up at the clock. "And why the fuck are we tied up right now?"

"Well, because we scored two and they scored two," I say sarcastically. "Geesh, Thompson. You sure you're going to be a doctor? I thought docs were good at math."

Getting closer, he tips his helmet toward mine. "Are you good, man? Because I'm fucking worried about you. You've been late to shit. You're not around half the time. And you're moody as fuck."

"So, my world doesn't begin and end with hockey," I mutter with a shrug. "Excuse the fuck out of me."

"It did up until this fucking season," he says through gritted teeth. "When you were twice the player you are right now."

Skating away from him, I give him a cocky smirk. "What can I say? I guess I'm just not as fucking awesome as you, Thompson."

I thank God when the game is about to start back up so that I can be left alone. If I've sucked tonight, I don't know what to tell them. I'm doing the best I can.

"Huff, I think your eyes look swelled up under that helmet," Terrance Geel, my opponent and the biggest dude on the ice, says, giving me a smirk. "Must be from all that crying after losing last night's game, huh?"

"You're right. They are swollen." I nod. "But it's because your mama's damn titties were bouncing so hard and they kept smacking me in the face last night." Timing it just right, I elbow his side lightly. "You should see how swollen her lips are from sucking my—"

Before I can finish my sentence, the puck goes into play. I don't really want to be out here, if I'm being honest. But I would chop my own dick into pieces before I gave the guys the satisfaction that they were right and that I sucked. There's still another period left. I can show them they are wrong.

Besides, if they've noticed something is up, LaConte probably has too. I need to remind him I'm fine.

My head is soaked with sweat as I play as hard as I can, telling myself that it's just a little longer and I'll be free to go the hell home. I ignore the pain in my knee, letting it fuel me more.

With less than two minutes on the clock, we're still tied. And there's no way I'm staying here for overtime. Fuck. That.

Skating toward Terrance just as he skates across the blue line, I smash my body against his and offset him just enough for me to gain control of the puck. As I head toward the opposing team's goalie, I see Link and Walker, but neither of them is open. I play defense. It's what I'm good at. But right now ... I'm looking to score. Because I haven't brought my best game lately and I guess I have some making up to do.

That excitement grows in my chest as I close in on their goalie, reminding me that despite how messed up my life is right now, somewhere deep, deep down ... I do love this game.

I score, and the crowd goes wild, knowing this game is likely ours. But for once, I don't feel Eli with me. And it's probably because even he's stopped believing in me. Why wouldn't he? I'm a fucking mess.

He's dead, and I'm here. And I don't know why God would ever make it like that.

HALEY

I sit next to Sutton, my eyes glued on Cade as the clock winds down to zero.

"Whatever Hunter said to Cade must have worked," Sutton says next to me. "He sucked, and now, he's actually doing good. I mean ... he just scored a goal."

I don't know what my brother said to Cade, but it seemed to light a fire under his ass. Before Hunter went over to him, he was incredibly sloppy on the ice. Moving around like a zombie. Now, it's like he got a second wind.

I think back to the other night in the bathroom. I never noticed until now that he looks a little skinnier than he did when I first moved in. I didn't connect all the things that show he's been struggling with something. His hot and cold act when it comes to me, his never being on time for anything, and his being out late and sleeping in late.

A shiver runs down my spine as worry strikes deep inside of me. I might be the only one who knows that Cade is having a hard time. And now ... it might be up to me to make sure he's okay.

The game comes to an end, and despite Brooks losing last night's game, they take home the win tonight. The team cheers, skating toward each other and gripping Cade's mask, smacking him on the back because he scored the winning goal. His eyes find mine, and even though he smiles, my heart still aches. Because until the last few minutes of the game, he wasn't mentally on that ice. I want to help him, but I know it'll just cause a fight between us.

I can't try to save him. Because if I push too hard, he'll hate me.

But him hating me sounds a lot better than me losing him altogether.

Cade

I finish showering in record time. And thank God I'm one of the first to do interviews, so I get out of there earlier than some of the others. But if I know Haley, she'll be waiting for me and Hunter by the exit. And I don't have time to talk to her right now because I need to go to Van's.

Just as I thought, Haley is sitting on a bench next to the door. And when she spots me, she smiles. But it isn't her usual smile. The one I know I'm not worthy of. There's a hint of sadness in it, just like there has been since the night of the storm. I ruined it. From that moment forward, she hasn't looked at me like I am perfect, and she probably won't ever again. But here she is, waiting for me because she fucking feels bad.

I need her to move on with her life and forget about me. One day, she won't even remember me because she'll be so happy. I wish I could say the same about myself, but who am I kidding? She'll always be the one who got away. No, the one I pushed away to save her from me.

"Hey," I say, nodding.

She stands. "Hi. I rode here with Sutton, but she has plans with my brother. Can I catch a ride with you?"

Turning my head to look around, I blow out a breath and run my hand over my head. "Watson should be coming by soon. Maybe he could give you a ride?" I look at her, touching her cheek with my fingertips, feeling her soft skin. "Sorry, babe. I just have a few places I need to go—that's all."

"I'll go with you then," she says, her voice as soft as silk and so sweet. "I don't mind a bit. I can even sit in the truck while you go wherever you need to."

"Uh, well … it'll take a while. I think—"

"Cade!" a voice yells behind me, and when I turn, it's Poppy. "Cade! I need to talk to you."

"Nice," Haley mutters. "Really nice."

When Poppy looks at Haley, I can tell she's nervous. "Um, can I talk to Cade for a second? Alone?"

"Whatever," Haley mumbles and walks toward where Sutton is hugging Hunter.

Once she's gone, I look at Poppy. "Well? What is it?" I tilt my head toward Haley. "I was already putting myself on her shit list for the night. This should go over real well."

"Van is dead," she whispers so faintly that I hardly hear her.

And then I think that maybe I didn't hear her right. But when she repeats it, I know I did.

"How do you know?" I frown. "How do you even know Van?"

I'm so confused. I know she knew of him because she saw my truck there once and gave me a hard time. But how would she know he was dead before me? I have no idea.

"Because he's my brother," her voice squeaks. "And I know you're one of his customers, so I wanted to get to you before you went to his place, looking for whatever it is you go there for. He overdosed earlier today." Her tough exterior cracks the slightest bit. "He's gone, Cade."

"Fuck," I say, dragging my hand through my hair. "I'm ... I'm so sorry. I had no idea that he was your brother."

"How could you? I don't exactly shout it loud and proud." She shrugs, but I can tell she's barely hanging on. "Anyway, I came here as soon as I knew because police have been at his place all afternoon." She looks at me, shaking her head. "You can't go back there, Cade. You don't need your name being dragged into the mess he created."

"Holy shit." I swallow.

And when I wrap my arms around her, I'm not thinking that Haley is probably watching. In that second, I just know my friend needs me.

"Don't be like Van, Cade." She sniffles. "He and I ... that's all we knew, growing up. He never really stood a chance at wanting anything more." She trembles against me. "You have the world at your fingertips. A loving family. A girl who is clearly in love with you. And more talent in your pinkie than most people have in their entire body. Stop wasting your life, getting high, and just face your shit. Or one day, your parents could be getting the same call I had to get."

I should be thinking about the words she said. I should be thinking about the girl who cares about me, who is watching me hug another girl with no explanation. But I'm not thinking about either of those things.

I'm thinking about the fact that I'm out of drugs. And if I don't get them soon, I'm going to get really, really sick.

My life is a fucking mess. And I've somehow pulled that sweet angel into it.

HALEY

Thank God that Sutton and Hunter offered to bring me home before they went off to Club 83 to celebrate his win. Because after Poppy and Cade hugged for a few minutes, he released her and then left. Never even looking back at me.

The pain in my chest radiated through my entire body, slicing deep and growing with every step he took away from me, like I wasn't even there. Like those times we'd spent together, which meant everything to me, were nothing to him. And I had to stand there and pretend it was no big deal. Because my brother has no idea that Cade and I have gotten close. He just thought I'd asked Cade for a ride and he said he couldn't.

He didn't know that I was dying inside. Or that I was in love with his best friend.

So many times, Cade has done this to me. Yet I'm always eager to give him the chance to do it again. I don't know if I'll ever learn when it comes to that man.

"Looks like Cade is home," Hunter says, noticing his truck in the driveway. "I wonder why he said he couldn't give you a ride home."

"Hard to say," I huff out before climbing out of the truck. "Thanks for the ride. Be safe and have fun," I say, monotone. I don't have it in me to be sweet or charming. I'm in a terrible mood, and I should lock my grumpy ass in my room with pizza, ice cream, and Dr. Pepper.

"Do you want us to come in for a bit?" Hunter says. "Don't want you to feel like we're ditching you."

"Yeah," Sutton says, agreeing. "I'd rather hang out with you anyway, to be honest."

"What's that, Little Bird?" Hunter shoots her a glare but grins.

I inwardly roll my eyes at their adorableness. "I'm fine. I'm just going to go up to bed." I attempt to reassure them with a smile, but it's a lousy one at best. "Night, lovebirds."

I close the door, and as I head inside the house, I don't know what to expect. For all I know, Cade could be upstairs with Poppy, having stupid hot-people sex. Maybe he was fooling me all along. Maybe I was just a challenge to him. Who knows?

When I hear a ruckus upstairs, my stomach turns. Even if I saw him having sex with another girl, I think I would still have this deep-rooted love for him. I know that's sick. He holds a power over me. One I've never felt before with another human.

The nerves build as I walk up the stairs. And when I hear him swearing, along with footsteps in his room, I decide to chance seeing whatever I'm about to, and I push the door open.

LOST BOY

What I actually see hurts more than I think seeing him with another woman would have. As I take in the sight of him pulling his drawers out and throwing clothes on the bed, making a complete disaster of his entire room, tears fill my eyes.

"Cade," I whisper, my voice breaking. "Wh-what are you doing?"

It's like I'm not even here as he continues searching for what I already know he's looking for. Pills. Or maybe a money stash to buy them. But just seeing how rabid he is acting, I know it's one or the other. And it rips my heart from my chest to watch this unfold before me.

One of Brooks' most beloved guys. A good friend with a charming smile. Broken.

Setting my shoulders back, I inhale, closing my eyes for a split second to tell myself to be brave. And then I walk in front of him. His hand drags through his hair, and his face is angrier than I've ever seen it. His soft blue eyes are gone. Replaced with a darkness I never thought he was capable of holding.

"Cade, talk to me." I choke back the tears. "Tell me what you need."

Using his arm, he gently shoves me to the side before reaching for the final untouched drawer in his dresser. And when I try to grab his arm, he yanks it back, causing me to fall against the wall.

"Fuck, I'm sorry," he says, coming to me and lifting me back onto my feet. "I'm so sorry," he says again.

This time, I can tell he's on the brink of a meltdown.

"I'm so fucking sorry, Haley." His voice shakes as he continues to whisper how sorry he is. "I'm sorry," he sobs, clawing at my shirt.

He sits on the edge of his bed and pulls my body between his legs. As I stand there, he pushes his head against my stomach. Long, shaky, heartbreaking cries come from his lips, and I cry right along with him. Gone is the scary defenseman who takes no shit. Replaced with a sad, scared, lost boy. One I don't think I can save.

"I don't want to live this way," he weeps. "Eli would be so fucking ashamed of me."

When I was a kid, if I ever got the stomach flu, my mom would run her fingers through my hair, and no matter how awful I felt, it'd somehow help.

I delicately run my fingers through his hair, trying to comfort him even though I'm sure it's hopeless. "Who's Eli, Cade?" I ask softly. "It's okay; you can tell me anything, I promise."

He's so quiet, aside from the sounds of his cries. "Eli was my best friend. And he's dead because of me." He shakes harder. His hands grab at my back, clawing at my shirt to bring me closer. "I can't take the pain, Haley. I can't fucking take it anymore."

There are so many things I want to ask. But in this moment, I just want to let him know I'm here and that he can trust me. If I push too hard, I'll scare him away. I don't want to do that. Sadness fills my entire body like poison as he trembles against me in pain. A pain so deep that I know I can't take it away, no matter how much I wish I could.

"Let me help you," I whisper, gently running my fingers from his hair to his neck. "I want to help you, Cade."

"You can't help me. You're too fucking perfect for me. I'll ruin you, just like I'm ruined." His voice turns to more of a grumble. "You should just leave me be. I'm a waste of fucking space, Haley. It's never going to work"—his voice cracks—"with you and me."

"You aren't a waste of space." I sniffle, realizing that there's no time like the present to tell him how I feel.

Maybe if he knows the depth of my feelings, he'll see that I want to help him through this.

"Cade … I love you." I lean down, kissing the top of his head. "I don't care if you think you're ruined or a waste of space. I love you anyway. Just let me in. Let me love you."

"You don't mean that," he says, burying his head into my shirt further. "You can't love me, Haley. You read stories. Fairy tales. Ones where the guy saves the girl." Finally, he looks up at me, his whole face soaked with tears. "I can't save you. Fuck, all I do is cause you pain."

He's nearly hysterical now, and I don't know what to do or how to calm him down. I know he's having a breakdown, but then I think back to him talking to Poppy after the game and can't help but wonder if that has anything to do with him falling apart right now.

"What happened with you and Poppy tonight, Cade?" I whisper. "Does that have anything to do with how upset you are?"

He breathes against me, quiet for a moment. "Her brother died," his voice croaks. "He overdosed."

My heart sinks, but when he looks up at me and says, "Her brother was my dealer," I feel like I'm going to throw up.

I feel awful for shooting her daggers when she was obviously in so much pain. But I'm also sick, thinking about how, whatever Cade is doing, he's in deep enough that he knows people who are overdosing on drugs.

How the hell did I miss this? How have his friends, teammates, and family missed this?

It's been weeks since our first hookup, but even before we had sex, we were getting closer. He was probably high every time we hung out, kissed, or had sex. And I never even knew it. I was so wrapped up in wanting the boy that I didn't realize the boy needed my help.

"I don't want to drag you down with me, Haley." His hands move up and down my back. "You could go anywhere, do anything, have *anyone* you wanted."

"And what I want is you. You are who I want." I hold onto him. "Just lie down with me, okay?"

If I can just get him to fall asleep, maybe tomorrow, I can talk some sense into him and convince him that he needs help. At the very least, he needs to tell Coach LaConte. He can't fight this battle alone even if he thinks he can.

Gently, I reach down and peel his shirt off and kiss his shoulder. Crouching down, I pull down his pants, taking one leg out at a time, leaving him in his boxers. It isn't about sex right now. It's about taking care of him when he needs me to.

Slowly, he moves upward to the top of the bed and lies down. And once I've taken my own jeans off, I climb into bed, and I wrap my entire body around him.

His heart pounds against my ear, and his body trembles against my own.

And right now, I know one thing to be true: I'll do anything to save this boy. Even if it kills me.

We need rest right now. Tomorrow, we can deal with everything else.

Tomorrow will be better.

Once again, I wake up in a cold bed, all alone. And right away, I know in my gut that he isn't just downstairs, getting coffee or taking a shower. He left the house. I just know it.

I didn't allow myself to fall asleep last night until I knew he was sound asleep. Yet still, he snuck out. And I'm sure it was to get pills.

My stomach turns, and I can't tell if it's from being worked up over everything with Cade or if I'm getting the stomach flu. But I chalk it up to being from stress. Stress induced by Cade Huff.

Grabbing my phone from his nightstand, I quickly hit his contact, but the call goes straight to voice mail. I get out of bed, peering out the window to find no one else home. I know the guys have the day off from hockey, so it isn't like he's going to come home just to get ready for practice.

Quickly bolting into the bathroom, I brush my teeth and pee before I head into my own room. I throw on a pair of black leggings and a Brooks hoodie and slide on my sandals. Taking off down the stairs, I run outside, beelining it for my car.

I'm going to find him. I have to find him.

For hours, I drive around. I go anywhere and everywhere I can think of. Searching for Cade, not knowing if he even wants to be found. Or at least found by me. And then after that, I drive some more.

I've tried to call Cade a total of thirty-eight times today. And I've lost count of the number of text messages I sent him. All of which have gone unanswered.

My biggest fear is that he's dead. Or hurt and no one can get to him because, besides me and apparently Poppy ... nobody even knows he's in trouble. The stress of that makes me feel like I'm drowning, being pulled under by a current and unable to see clearly.

My stomach churns, and I feel like I might be sick. I haven't eaten anything today because honestly, I have no appetite. And besides, how the hell am I supposed to think about eating when I have no idea where Cade is?

A few months ago, life was simple. Boring even. And now, I'm in love with someone who I'm beginning to realize I can't save. Even if it's killing me to admit that, even to myself.

You can't help someone who refuses to let you.

If something happened to him, I'd be the last to find out because who the hell would think I was anyone important enough in Cade's life to call me? I'm just his dirty little secret. And the one he knows will be there when he falls apart. Because I always am. Maybe I always will be.

As a last-ditch effort to find him, I head to Poppy's house, knowing she lives in the dancers' house with Sutton and a few other girls. Maybe he went to her to grieve with her over the man who had overdosed. I might not find him there, but it's worth a shot. I just need to see him with my own two eyes and know that he is okay.

Parking in front of the house, I quickly climb out of my car and immediately see Poppy on the porch swing with a mug of coffee, her feet dangling.

Her eyes find mine, and my heart clenches with the sadness that lives inside of them. I know firsthand what it's like to lose a brother. The pain never goes away. It just feels dull sometimes.

I learned from Sutton that Poppy is a freshman here at Brooks. But given what an asset she is to the dance program, the school allowed her to live in this house off campus.

"Looking for Cade?" she mutters, leaning her head back.

I nod, chewing my bottom lip nervously. Another wave of nausea hits, but I force myself to ignore it. "Yeah. Have you seen or talked to him?"

When she shakes her head, I sigh.

"Damn it," I whisper. "Poppy, I'm really sorry about your brother. And I'm ... I'm really sorry for being so cold to you last night."

"I don't blame you. I know how it looked," she breathes out. "And thanks. Me too. But I kind of figured it would happen eventually. He'd been on that same bad path for years now." She pauses, setting her mug next to her and knitting her fingers together. "I know it sounds dramatic, but the truth is ... Cade could end up facing the same fate, Haley. He'll go to bigger and worse drugs. They always do." Her eyes bore into mine. "I've been around him enough lately to know that if anyone can save him ... it's you."

"I can't save him, Poppy." My voice breaks, and a lump instantly forms in my throat now that I've admitted that out loud. "He won't let me." I sniffle. "I love him more than he'll ever love me."

"That's because right now, he has to put drugs before anything and anyone else. And it'll only get worse if he doesn't get the help he needs. I promise you that." She gives me a sad smile. "Sometimes, people just need the right person to let them know that no matter what, they'll be there. I see the way Cade watches you. Looks at you and smiles at you." She blows out a tiny laugh. "And I listen to him yak about you during dance practice. You're the one who can save him. The *only* one. You just need to believe that." She stops, looking down at her hands. "Drugs have a way of taking a person and stripping them of who they really are. It starts little by little. But then"—she shakes her head—"it's all at once. Cade is a rare gem. I don't want to see him get lost."

"Me neither," I croak, swiping a tear away. "I should go. I need to find him." I give her a sad look. "Again, I'm really, really sorry about your brother."

She waves to me as I head toward my car, getting inside and quickly backing out. But I only make it a mile down the road before the turning inside my stomach worsens. And after trying to fight it for a few minutes, I eventually give up and pull over to the side of the road. Pushing my door open just in time to throw up on the dirt, I groan, squeezing my eyes shut. I have always hated throwing up. In fact, I'm sort of a baby about it.

Nothing is left in my stomach, yet I continue to heave. And once I finally get myself under control, I close the door and beat my fist against the steering wheel, crying in my empty car.

Where are you, Cade? Why can't you just come home?

I'm scared. And when I get scared, I become mad. But acting like a lunatic, hitting my car? I'll blame that on PMS. My period must be coming soon. That has to be why I'm acting so crazy right now. Hormones.

My thoughts catch up with me, and I frown. *When was the last time I had my period?*

I look through old text messages because I know I sent Remi a message the last time I had it, telling her how awful it was and how I couldn't stop eating nasty Cosmic Brownies and crunchy Cheetos.

Finally, I find the text. And when I look at the date, I suddenly feel dizzy. And nauseous again. Because that date ... well, it was over six weeks ago.

Which means my period is two weeks late.

125

Shit.

And I thought my life was falling apart five minutes ago ... but nothing compares to this moment right now.

I park in front of Remi's dorm and text her that I'm here. Within minutes, she's sprinting toward the car through the pouring rain.

Quickly getting in, she wipes the water from her face. "You said it was urgent?"

"I think I'm pregnant," I blurt out before I start crying again. "What if I'm pregnant? Oh my God, Remi. I can't be. I just can't."

"Whoa. What?" Her face pales before she pushes her door open again. "Switch seats. I'm driving."

"What?" I sniffle. "Where?"

"Walgreens," she mutters. "Switch sides. Now."

I don't argue. I just climb across the console and get in the passenger seat before buckling my seat belt.

As she starts driving, my mind races. I can't be pregnant. There's no way. Every time we've been together, we've been safe.

But that first night ... I was drunk. He was drunk. And probably high. I don't even remember if he put a condom on or not.

Oh my God, how could I have been so stupid?

"Pull over," I cry out, clutching my stomach with my hand. "Now!"

As she pulls onto the side of the road, I throw the door open and lean my head out. I dry-heave some more, and I begin to wonder if maybe actually throwing something up would be easier than this shit.

After a few minutes, I wipe away the tears that poured from my eyes and shut the door. "Tell me something. Anything."

"Um ..." she utters as she pulls back onto the road. "Well ... oh, oh, I know! I'm newly single. So, yeah. That's fun. Right?"

"What?!" I bark out, turning toward her. "What are you talking about? What happened with you and—"

She interrupts me before I can get his name out, "He cheated on me. With a freaking model who probably has fake tits and a flawless, perfect face. I found out, like ... ten minutes before you called."

This only makes me cry harder, and I put my hand on her shoulder.

"Remi, I'm so sorry." I shake my head. "I'm the worst friend ever."

"Actually, kind of the best because, number one, I'm too distracted with the fact that you're possibly knocked up to be sad. And, two, now that I'm single, we can just raise the baby together. I'd make a pretty good dad, if I do say so myself."

"Remi!" I snap, swatting her leg. "Shut up!"

"Too soon?" she whispers with a shrug. "My bad."

"Do you want to talk about it?" I ask her, keeping my voice soft.

"Not yet," she answers before giving me a sad smile.

"Okay." I nod.

And we're both quiet for the rest of the drive. I don't think either of us knows what to say. Her relationship just ended. And I'm about to find out if my life as I know it is officially over.

And maybe Cade's too.

I stare down at the two pink lines, and I can't even get myself to cry a single tear. I just feel numb. My body, my mind ... everything. Remi talks a mile a minute, but I don't know what she's saying. It's all background noise, like my head is underwater and I can only hear muffled sounds.

I feel like I'm watching someone else's life unfold. Because there's no way in hell this could be happening to me. I'm safe. And not an idiot. Yet here I am, knocked up by the most unreliable man on the planet. He couldn't even be there as a friend. How the hell is he going to be there for a baby?

Our baby.

Finally, I shake my head and force myself to focus as I look up at Remi. The lights in the bathroom are too bright. The walls, too white. And her voice, too damn loud.

"What am I going to do?" I rasp when the emotions finally flood in. "I'm not ready to be a mom." I cover my face with my hands and sob. "And he can't even take care of himself. He's going to go off the deep end when he finds out." I sniffle. "I can't be the reason why he spirals further than he already has."

On the way home from the store, I spilled my guts to Remi on how I learned that Cade is using drugs. And that I was scared he was in deeper than anyone else knew or even suspected. I know it wasn't my place to tell anyone, but given the circumstances of today ... I couldn't help myself. Besides, Remi is my oldest, most loyal friend. I trust her more than I trust anyone else in this world.

She leans down and wraps her arms around me. "It's going to be okay," she whispers. "I know it doesn't seem like it right now, but it will." When she pulls back, her eyes look into mine. "One day, you'll look back and wonder why you ever felt like the world was ending. I promise, Haley, one day, this will be the best thing that's ever happened to you."

"How?" I cry harder. "I live in a house with a bunch of hockey players. I still have years left of college. The baby's father is MIA and could be in a gutter for all I know, and my parents—" My eyes widen, and I feel sick. I have been so preoccupied with worrying about Cade that I haven't even thought of my parents. Or Hunter. "Oh God, Remi. My parents are going to kill me."

"They will be upset at first, but they will come around," she says, assuring me. "They love you. They want what's best for you. But that doesn't mean they won't love this baby too."

"I'm so afraid," I whisper, my voice cracking as my lip trembles. "I was stalked and kidnapped, and I wasn't nearly as afraid as I am right now." I look at her. "And the truth is, thinking about having a baby isn't what's making me so scared. It's thinking that I might push Cade over the edge when he finds out." I swallow. "I love him, Remi. I love him more than I've ever loved someone in my life. And I can't be the reason why he doesn't get better."

Her hand brushes hair off my face, and she gives me a small, weak smile. "You won't be. But you know what?"

"What?" I sniff.

"You might be the reason why he *does* get better." She inhales. "This baby might be the reason."

I burst into tears, burying my face into her shoulder.

God, I really, really hope she's right.

14

Haley

I lie in my bed, hugging my pillow against my stomach. My eyes are swollen after I cried myself to sleep last night. Remi had stayed with me, rubbing my back and trying to make me feel better. But this morning, she had swim practice, and now, I'm alone.

Remi is the only person I want near me when I am this distraught. Remi or Cade, but since he wasn't an option, Remi it was.

I heard him come home in the early morning hours, but I didn't bother to go out and confront him. I didn't know what I'd even say. All I know is, it's not just me anymore. There's a person growing inside of me, and me making myself sick all day and night, worrying whether or not Cade has overdosed somewhere, isn't healthy. I can't do it, no matter how much I love him.

He might hate me for what I'm about to do, but I don't care. If it keeps him here on this earth, so be it. He can hate me forever. I just can't bear the thought of him dying.

Getting out of bed, I pull a sweatshirt on over my tank top and head downstairs. It's quiet down here, which only makes everything feel worse.

As more tears spill from my eyes, I can't help but wonder, *How much can one person cry before they run out of tears?*

I curl up on the couch and try to calm myself down. When you're so anxious that your heart feels like it's in your throat and your stomach actually hurts … that's when you know things are bad. Very, very bad.

A few minutes later, my brother comes down the stairs, and I tell myself right then, before I tell him what's going on, I need to talk to Cade.

"What's wrong?" he asks when he takes one look at my face. "What the fuck happened?"

"I'm fine, really." I try to offer him a smile, but it's useless. "I didn't know you were home. I thought you were with Sutton."

"I was earlier, but I had to leave to come here for my practice stuff." His eyes narrow at me. "Are you going to tell me what's going on or what?"

"Please, Hunter," I say, my throat closing up from the lump in it. "Leave it alone for now. I'll talk to you soon enough."

He gives me a hard glare but eventually nods. "Fine. But promise me that if you need me, you'll tell me. All right?"

I wipe my eyes. "I will. Promise."

Watson walks into the room, his duffel bag slung on his shoulder. "You ready?" He looks around. "Where's Cade?"

"Fuck if I know." Hunter shrugs before looking at me. "Have you seen him today?"

I put my hands over my face to stop them from seeing me break down. "I don't want to say anything. He'll never forgive me."

"Forgive you?" Watson says, confused. "What the fuck are you talking about, Haley?"

I peer at him and then my brother through my fingers. "I think he's passed out in his room." My lip quivers, and I bite it to stop it. "I think he needs help, Hunter. I think … he's been taking drugs."

"Fuck," Hunter mutters, dragging his hand through his hair.

Both guys drop their bags and head toward the stairs, and I scurry off the couch to follow them.

"Please, don't tell him I said anything," I cry. "He'll hate me so much."

My brother pushes the door to Cade's room open, and Cade stirs a little, only to fall back asleep.

Watson takes a few large strides before stopping next to the bed and yanking the blankets off Cade. "Wake the fuck up, Huff! We have practice. And after practice, we're going to figure out a plan for you to get your fucking life together."

"Fuck off," Cade groans, pulling a pillow over his head.

"No, fuck you," Watson barks before grabbing his arm and flipping him onto his back. "Get the fuck up, Cade! We're on a team. Together. You don't fucking get high or drunk and sleep all fucking day."

Cade gets up on his feet and grabs Watson's shirt. "Fuck you, Gentry! Goody Two-shoes Gentry." As he shoves Watson, veins pop out of his neck. "Get off my dick, pussy boy."

Watson pulls him into a headlock before they crash into the dresser, and I can't help the sobs erupting from my mouth at the heartbreaking sight before me. Knowing I caused it.

My brother grabs Cade, pulling him backward. "Cut the shit, Huff," he yells into his ear. "We're just fucking worried!"

"Let me go!" Cade screams as he fights Hunter off.

Eventually, Hunter releases him.

Cade's eyes sweep from Hunter to Watson to me. "You're worried? You don't know the fucking first thing about me to be worried about." He shakes his head. "I'm fucking done with hockey. And I'm done with all of you."

As he grabs his keys from his desk and starts toward the door, I rush toward him. "Cade!" I scream, pure desperation in my voice. "Please, stop!"

He doesn't even stop to look at me as he walks out of his room and runs down the stairs. Seconds later, we hear the door slam as he leaves.

I crumple to the floor, wailing uncontrollably as my entire body shakes.

I can't help Cade. All I do is make things worse.

I'm in love with that broken, lost boy. And right now, he hates me. He really, really hates me.

CADE

I grip the steering wheel, unsure of what the fuck I'm even doing or where I'm going. I'm running, just like always. But running gets really fucking exhausting. And I'm tired of it.

And the worst part is, I'm running from the only thing that's ever brought me peace. Haley could have been my saving grace. And instead, I pushed her away. I cut her off like an extra fucking limb. She's attached herself so deeply inside of me; I know I am forever a changed man. My heart doesn't beat the same now. It probably never will again. And that's all because Haley Thompson woke me up and made me realize how much I had to lose. Yet, me being me, I fucked it all up.

When they all rushed in together—Haley, Watson, and Hunter—I could tell she had told them what was going on with me. And that was the worst kind of betrayal I'd ever felt in my life. I'd thought I could trust her. I guess I was wrong.

My entire life is a mess. Even if I wanted to play hockey, there's no way I'll be able to after Coach gets word of this. How I made it this far into the season without a drug test should make me feel fortunate enough, but it doesn't. Because like always, I'm never satisfied. I always need more.

I know I need help, but help is not easy to accept. My parents will ship me away to rehab. And just like last time, it won't work. My brain's too fucked up. Nothing can magically cure me and make me who I was before I started using. This is who I am now.

An addict. That's all I'll ever be. An addict who chooses drugs over the girl I love and over teammates who are like brothers to me and over a dream I've had for most of my life.

I continue to drive around. I left my phone at home, and for that, I'm glad. There's nothing I can say or do in a text or through a phone call to make it all better. I've left everything in shambles. This is my own doing.

I knew Haley wouldn't look at me the same way when she learned the truth. Turns out, I was right.

You can't change the past—that's a fact. But if you can't change the past ... how the hell can you rewrite the future?

Exactly. You can't.

15

CADE

I stuff my hands in my pockets nervously as I walk toward the arena. When Coach texted me that he needed to speak with me ASAP, I seriously considered not even coming here. I hadn't gone to practice yesterday. Instead, I drove around all day, ignoring everyone. And when I got home late last night and finally checked my phone, seeing Coach's message, along with countless others, I had been close to saying fuck everyone. But the thing is, Coach has done a lot for me. And I owe him an apology.

I walk inside and toward his office, finding the door half-open. Taking my hand out of my pocket, I hit my fist against the wood a few times.

"Come in," he calls out, and I force my feet to take the few steps inside.

Pointing to the door behind me, he says, "Close the door, Huff. Come, sit."

Doing as he said, I close the door and then take the seat across from him. He looks over his desk at me. His eyes look more sad than angry, which isn't something I expected from Coach LaConte.

"I'm guessing Thompson and Gentry talked to you?" I mutter, resting my fingertips on the side of my head.

"Sterns too."

Great. They even told Cap. Awesome.

"How long?" he asks softly.

I look down, scraping my finger over my jeans nervously. "Started this summer. During training." I swallow. "My knee was fucked. I didn't want to mess up the season."

"That's no excuse," he utters. "And the second your knee was hurt, you should have come to me, Cade. Playing with an injury only makes it worse. You know this."

"I know. I just thought … I thought I could handle it on my own," I murmur, ashamed. "I figured … if I could just make it through our season and not fuck it up for the team, my knee would heal, and I'd be fine."

"Well?" his deep voice grumbles. "Are you fine?"

I'm still for a second, feeling the tears gather in my eyes, blurring my vision as my finger continues to scrape that same spot on my jeans. "No."

"I'm disappointed that you thought you could handle your injury and your addiction on your own. I'm disappointed that you fell back into your old ways." His voice grows thick. "But you know what I'm most disappointed about?"

"What?" I barely hear myself answer.

"That you were struggling all this time and I didn't notice," he says. "And that you were injured, and I missed it."

When I glance up at him, I see the sadness on his face, tears filling his eyes.

"I'm supposed to be your coach. Since you've been on the team, I've spent as much time with you as anyone. And, for months—" He stops, his nostrils flaring. "For fucking months, it slipped by me when you needed me most." He shakes his head. "Cade, I failed you. And for that, I'm so sorry."

"Coach, no—"

"Yes, I did. Damn it, Huff, when I first offered you a spot on my team, I was aware of your past struggles. I knew you had been to rehab after the great loss of your best friend. I knew all of this," he growls, pounding his fist on the desk. "I got so into winning and performance that I never checked in with *you* to see how you were doing. I didn't hold you accountable with drug tests." Reaching across the table, he pats my hand with his. "I'm angry that you let yourself get this deep. But I'm mostly sorry that I wasn't there to help you. I love you, kid. You're one of my favorite knuckleheads I've coached. But you need help." He stops, his eyes looking directly into mine before he says the worst words I've heard in days. "Do you want to call your parents, or should I?"

Fucking hell. It's time to break my mom's heart again.

And I have to wonder, *Why do I keep hurting the women in my life I love most?*

LOST BOY

I stuff some shit in a duffel bag, moving around the room like a zombie with no actual soul.

I called my parents—in front of Coach because he made me do it that way, afraid I might not actually call them. My mom cried. My dad was angry. Once again, I ruined their fucking lives.

I wonder if they wish they had more kids. They just had me, and I turned out to be a fucking loser. If I were them, I'd wish I had other kids. Hell, I'd probably just give up on me altogether. Sometimes, I wish they would.

They promised me that I could come home and try to get clean there before going to rehab. Last time, rehab had been hell on earth, and I really didn't want to go back. I just wanted to go home.

My door creaks open, and Haley stands in the doorway.

"Cade," she whispers, her voice broken and defeated.

I don't look at her. I don't want to see the pain on her face and the sag in her shoulders. All caused by me. I had known it was inevitable.

I need to cut her off altogether. She needs to move on with her life and forget about me.

"I'm sorry," her voice barely squeaks. "I got scared. I just … didn't want to lose you."

"I wasn't yours to lose, Haley," is all I offer her. It's not true, but I want to push her away further. That's just what I do. It isn't personal; it's just what needs to happen.

I was hers. I'm still hers. Hell, I've never belonged to anyone more than I have to Haley Thompson in my entire life. But it's time to set her free. To rid her of me.

She reads romance stories. And maybe that's what she's looking for in me. But demons and angels don't make love stories. They just don't.

She runs to me, throwing her arms around my body as she pushes her face into my shirt. "I love you, Cade. Please. Talk to me," she sobs, her shoulders shaking, and I really want to console her, but I don't. "I need to know we're okay. You and me."

She doesn't need false hope. I *need* her to forget about me. Right now, what's happening … this is exactly what I didn't want.

"Haley, there is no you and me. There never was." I force the words out and hear a whimper rush from her throat. "Just … leave me alone."

Gently pushing her off of me, I reach for my duffel bag. But before I walk away, I decide that I deserve to be tortured. I deserve to feel pain. So, I look at her.

Her eyes are broken, and her body screams of defeat.

I robbed my angel of her wings. And now, she's just like everyone else in this fucked up world. Damaged.

Putting my head down, I walk past her and walk down the stairs and outside to my parents' car. Never sparing the guys a second look.

135

Because they shouldn't have to go through this shit just because I'm a fuckup. And maybe it'll make this sting less for them if I'm a dick. It'd give them a reason to give the hell up on me—and they should.

Putting my duffel bag in the trunk, I climb in the car and slam the door.

I had everything anyone could dream of. And I threw it away for pills that made my life worse.

HALEY

I want to puke. Or scream. Or maybe even break something.

But above all, I just want to go in my room, curl up in a ball, and never come out again. I feel so alone in this moment. Everything seems doomed, and I'm convinced I might actually die.

Not long ago, everything seemed fine. Now, I don't know what's going to happen.

I look out the window, watching Cade's parents' SUV pull out of the driveway and onto the road. I feel like I could pass out, and the walls seem to be closing in around me. Putting my hand on my stomach, I try to focus on what should be the simplest task. Breathing.

I hear Watson talking next to me, but I can't make out what he's saying. My mind is going a thousand miles an hour, but everything around me seems to be standing still.

I turn toward my brother, my heart breaking in my chest. Something inside me drives me to what I'm about to do next. Maybe it's just to feel less lonely. Maybe it's because I need someone to tell me it's all going to be all right. Or perhaps it's just because I can't continue to keep this secret any longer. It's eating me alive.

"Hunter, I'm pregnant," I croak.

His eyes widen, but he just stares at me. I look from Hunter to Watson and hold my hands protectively over my stomach. Almost like ... all this stress is hurting the baby and I need to save him or her.

"I'm pregnant ... and it's Cade's baby."

Watson and Hunter share a look with each other, both unable to form actual words. And before they can try, I run upstairs to my room and shut the door.

Collapsing on my bed, I pull my blankets over my head and cry so hard that my throat turns raw and my eyes swell shut. A thousand memories of

Cade rush through my mind—him kissing me, taking me to the bookstore, smiling at me, and everything in between.

It's like mourning a person who is still alive.

And maybe that's because it's *us*—him and me together—that's dead.

Somewhere in the midst of blurting out to my brother and Watson that I'm pregnant and right now ... I cried myself to sleep. My eyes feel swollen, and my face feels dry and crispy and, quite honestly, gross.

When I hear a knock at the door, I don't say anything. It's probably my brother. Or maybe even Sutton. If I'm lucky, they'll think I'm asleep and just go away. That's what I want. To be left alone.

"Hales, it's me," Watson says from the other side of the door. "Can I come in just for a minute?"

I sigh. I don't want to see anyone. I don't want to talk about it. And, yes, I know now that I should have just kept my damn mouth shut. But in the moment, it just sort of came out.

"Fine," I grunt, pulling the comforter over my head.

Watson doesn't need to see me looking like a zombie from *The Walking Dead*.

Slowly, the door opens, making a creaking sound. I hear his footsteps before the side of the bed shifts from his weight. Placing his hand on my ankle, he gives it a small squeeze to let me know he's here. And just that little action ... makes me cry again.

"How are you?" he whispers.

"I'm fine," I croak out, feeling my throat closing.

"Does he know?" He pauses. "Cade?"

I shake my head even though he can't see me while I'm under the blanket.

"Nope," I mutter. "He doesn't need to. Not until he gets better." My lip begins to quiver. "If he gets better."

"He'll be all right, Hales. Promise." He gives my leg another squeeze. "If you need something to take your mind off of it, I have an idea."

Peeking over the covers, I glare. "Seriously? He's been gone for, what, a few hours? And you're already trying to hook up?" I scrunch my nose up. "Ew. No. You're like family."

He frowns. "What? No! No. Fuck no." He shakes his head. "Wow, Hales. What the hell?"

"My mind isn't right today. What can I say?" I huff out. "So, if it doesn't involve me and you hooking up, then, yes, I could definitely use a distraction."

He looks down, blowing out a breath. Whatever he's about to tell me, I can tell he's scared to say it.

"Look, I'm going to tell you something I haven't told anyone else, okay?" He gives me a look, telling me this needs to be our secret. "Your life right now might feel complicated, and I guess I just don't want you to feel alone." He sighs. "I, uh … got married. To Ryann."

Shooting straight up, I suck in a breath so fast that I begin coughing. When I finally stop, I gawk at him as I say, "As in your dance partner? That Ryann? The one who I thought hated you?"

His lips turn up the slightest bit. "That's the one."

"Holy shit," I murmur, flopping back onto the bed and dragging my hand over my forehead. "I'm pregnant. You're married. What next?"

"Who fucking knows?" he whispers as he gives me one more pat on the leg and stands. "We're going to be okay, Hales. And Cade? He's going to be okay too."

God, I hope he's right.

As he leaves my room, I can't help but think of how insane the past few days have been. And then, without any warning at all, the tears start to spill from my eyes once again. So, I close my eyes and force myself to go back to sleep.

16

CADE

When we took a different route home, I should have known something was up. But I was too preoccupied with the monster in my brain to even put too much thought into it. But now that we're pulling through a gate, I'm starting to realize something.

I'm not going home. I'm at a fucking rehab. *Again.*

"What the fuck is this?" I growl, panic rising inside of me, spreading through my body like wildfire. Breathing becomes harder, and I don't know if that's because I'm feeling betrayed or because I know what's to come if I get dropped off here.

My mother's crying, and my dad's face pales as he continues to drive down the long, paved road before stopping in front of a large, dark gray building.

"Buddy," he says, turning and giving me a look of pity, "just get the help you need, okay?" His lip trembles as he looks at me. "Just get better, and then you can come home."

"No. No. No." I shake my head quickly. "Take me home. Take me home right now." I drag my hand over my head. "I'll be better, I promise." I begin crying like the pathetic bitch that I am. "Piss-test me every day, Mom." I stretch my arm for my mom, touching her shoulder. "Don't do this, Mom.

Don't leave me here. I promise, I'll be better this time." I look at the building. "Don't do this to me. If you love me, you won't do this. Please."

She cries harder. "I'm sorry, Cade. I'm so sorry." She forces the words out, wiping her eyes.

Dad tries to reach for me, but I pull away.

"Cade, we're only doing this to help you. We're doing this because we love you." Tears run down my old man's face. A dude who runs his own garage. He wouldn't go to the doctor if he cut his finger off—he's that tough. "Coach LaConte said that if you put in the work here, you might be able to come back and keep your spot. This place has changed so many people's lives for the better. It's one of the best programs in the South."

"No, fuck this," I say. "Take me home. I don't care what LaConte says. I don't give a fuck about being a Wolf," I lie to stop myself from facing what is coming. Withdrawal. Counseling. Meetings. Shit I'm not ready to do.

"You're not coming home, Cade," Mom whispers before she turns and looks at me. "Please. Please do this for me." Reaching back, she takes my hand. "I love you so much. But I can't live in fear anymore." She shakes as she cries, tears dripping in big drops down her face. "Every day, I'm scared I'll get the call that you're dead. You're killing me, Cade. Slowly, you are killing me and your father. Please, please … just give this place a try," she sobs. "My heart can't take much more."

I look away from my mother because I don't like the guilt I feel while watching her break down, knowing I'm to blame.

I don't understand why, but in that moment … Haley's face comes into my mind. She's sad. That beautiful smile is gone, and there's a lost look on her pretty face. Her bright light … burned out.

Before I can stop myself, my mouth opens.

"All right," I whisper, sucking in shaky breaths. "I'll go."

17

Haley

"So, you, my dear, are most definitely pregnant," Diane, the midwife, says, looking at my chart. Her short, curly hair is the most beautiful mix of salt and pepper, and her olive-green scrubs make her blue eyes almost glow. "Congratulations."

"Thanks," I mutter. "Can I go now?"

She frowns, opening her mouth to talk before my brother interrupts her.

"Hales, you must have some questions?" Hunter says from the corner chair.

I tried to leave him at home, but the asshole wouldn't take no for an answer. Remi was supposed to be here, but then she had to go get the stupid flu.

"Well, actually, no, you can't leave yet. We confirmed pregnancy with a urine specimen, but now, I'd like you to have an ultrasound." She glances at my brother. "Are you—"

"Her brother," he blurts out before the midwife can say partner or something really gross. "I'm her brother."

Diane smiles. "Wow, you're her brother, and you came to her first appointment. That's so sweet. I've been doing this for a long time, and I don't think I've ever had a brother come in."

"Yeah, well, the baby daddy is in re—"

"At home, sick," I blurt out, cutting Hunter off and shooting him a death glare. "He's sick, so I'm stuck with my brother, who talks too much and overshares."

"Uh, yes. Lots of crud going around, making everyone sick, unfortunately." The midwife frowns. "So, first off, if you haven't started taking prenatal vitamins, start today. And you'll need to stop at the desk and set up the rest of your appointments. After that, you'll go down to imaging, and they'll get your ultrasound all done."

"If that's done through my woman parts, sorry, bro, but you're going to be hanging outside," I mutter. "I love you and all, but ... no. Just no."

He scrunches his nose up and scowls. "Yeah, fuck that."

Diane watches our exchange before chuckling. "Lucky for you, you're far enough along that an abdominal ultrasound will be just fine." She gives me a reassuring smile. "Though maybe I should have lied. You know, just in case you wanted to keep your brother in the waiting room." She turns toward the standing computer, hitting a few buttons before looking at us over her glasses. "Do you have any more questions or concerns?"

"Nope, all set," I say quickly before hopping down from the exam table.

I don't say good-bye before I pull the door open and walk to the desk. My brother is hot on my heels, and I'm surprised he doesn't scold me for being a bitch to poor Diane. It's not Diane's fault that I haven't heard from Cade since he left a week ago. And even though that's not by his choice—because his parents told Hunter that Cade won't be allowed to contact the outside world for weeks—I still know in the back of my mind that even if he could call me, he wouldn't.

And that ... well, it puts me in a really bad mood. Because that man's penis impregnated me. He's away at rehab. He hates my guts. And now, here I am, with my freaking brother taking me to my first prenatal appointment.

It's fine. I'm fine. Everything. Is. Fine.

"Holy shit. That's your baby, Hales," Hunter whispers next to me. "Like, a real-life human-slash-alien is growing inside of you."

I look at the screen that shines bright in the dark room. It doesn't look like a baby, more of a blob. But we're told the flicker on the screen is a heartbeat. Which means ... I have two hearts beating inside of me right now. Which is ironic because it doesn't even feel like my own is working at the moment.

LOST BOY

As I continue to watch the little flutter on the screen, a rush of emotions hits me. This baby is part of me, but it's also part of Cade. We made this. Before everything seemed so ... hopeless.

But as I take in the image of the life inside of me, I blink back tears. This isn't how I ever imagined my first pregnancy would go. But somehow, the universe knew this is what I was meant for.

So, because of that, I vow, right now, to love and protect this baby at all costs. I also vow the same for this baby's father. Because without him, there wouldn't be that heart beating on the screen, reminding me I'm alive. And that my life is happening, ready or not.

"It's all going to be okay, Haley," Hunter tells me, giving my hand a squeeze. "I promise." He stops, swallowing thickly. "And Cade ... well, he is going to be all right. I know it," he says, knowing what matters most to me right now.

I give him a tiny nod, trying my best not to burst into a fit of tears. My chest burns, begging me to let every emotion inside of me out, but I keep it together. I have to keep it together. It isn't just about me anymore; I can't be weak and fall apart. Even if it's the only thing I want to do.

Hunter leans back and sighs. In an attempt to lighten the mood, he says, "Well, shit, you're growing a human, and Watson is a fucking husband. Everything is changing."

A few days after telling me, Watson told Hunter that he was married, and Hunter was absolutely dumbfounded. I couldn't blame him; it's a lot to take in.

Slowly, I smile, nodding my head. "I guess it is."

CADE

Two weeks. That's how long I've been in this place. It's far from hell, but I wish I could be anywhere else. This isn't like the last rehab I went to, which felt more like an old folks' home, only with piss tests and lots of *let's talk about your feelings* people in it.

This place is called Jace's Tomorrow, and it was started by a couple who had lost their son to drugs. Instead of being inside all day, we actually have to work around the property. Mowing the lawns—and not with riding mowers either. No, we've got ones that are like the first push mower ever invented. Lugging huge rocks to line the driveway. Cutting and dragging trees and brush, among other things. It makes for long days. I don't mind though. It's when I'm in idle mode that the demons living in my brain catch up with me.

The last program I did was only a month. This one … is three. Well, for me, it is anyway. Some people come for less time, some more.

Three months in here with a bunch of people I don't have a whole lot in common with sounds terrible. But this place also has horses. And surprisingly enough, taking care of them has been one of my favorite things to do, ever since I felt good enough to do anything after the first week.

I can't imagine the kind of money my parents had to come up with to get me in a place like this. And they did it, and I know they didn't think twice.

My nights often consist of a certain angel haunting my dreams with her sad eyes. In the dream, Haley is trying to reach for me, like she needs me. But just when I pull her toward me, I wake up. I wonder how she's doing and if she's thought of me since I've been gone. Fuck, her life is probably easier without my constant hot and cold attitude when it comes to her.

After showering quickly, I throw on my clothes and head toward Buck's office. I don't actually know what Buck's real name is. All I know is, he was hooked on drugs, living on the streets, and stealing from his parents, and he somehow got clean and wound up being a counselor here. I like him because unlike the counselors at the last place I was in, he actually knows what it's like to feel like you have no control over your life. To feel trapped in this tiny little hell, wanting to get out, but not knowing if you have what it takes to be able to.

I knock, and he tells me to come in.

With a big beard and a handful of tattoos, he doesn't look like your typical man for the job. But he's been sober for twenty-one years, so I'm not sure who else would be better at it.

"What's up, Cade man?" He grins, and I close the door behind me. "How did cleaning up the horse shit go?"

"Fucking smelly." I laugh, sitting down on the plush, large chair. "I swear that Beauty is more pregnant than y'all think. Her stomach is growin', dude."

"Could be," he says thoughtfully. "I'll have the vet come check her out." Sitting back in his chair, he puts his hands on the back of his head. "So, two weeks in. How do you feel?"

"Not puking anymore, so that's good," I say, trying to keep it light because that's just what I do. "And the night sweats haven't been so bad the past few nights. I was getting tired of waking up, thinking I'd pissed myself. That's hard on the ol' self-esteem. So, I call that a plus."

"Good, good." He nods. "So, you get to make a phone call today. If you want to, that is."

I think for a moment. An image of my mother gripping the phone tightly, waiting for it to ring, flashes in my brain. She knows I'm safe, but she'll still worry until she hears my voice. That much I know.

And then I think about how sad her voice will make me. She'll try to sound happy, but deep down, she'll be broken up inside when her grown-ass son calls and tells her about his pathetic day. The selfish part of me doesn't want to call. That's the same part that has shut out each and every feeling as much as possible since I came out of withdrawal. Because let's face it ... when you're going through that motherfucker, you can't help but feel *everything*.

I vaguely remember all the thoughts running through my head. I begged for Eli to come down from heaven and somehow make it better. And then I cried for the one person I wanted to hold because I knew having her body near me would dull the pain even if only a little bit.

Haley. God, I miss seeing that girl's face to start my morning. I miss her mismatched socks, baggy sweats, and sweet smile. And those eyes that looked at me with such wonder while I spoke. Like what came out of my mouth actually fucking mattered even if I knew deep down that it didn't. She looked at me in a way no one else ever had. Like I was the sky and she was stargazing.

"Cade?" Buck's voice interrupts my thoughts. "You good, man?"

Pulling myself from the land of Haley, I nod. "Yeah, I'm good. I'll call my parents." I sigh. "I'm sure they've been waiting to hear from me."

"What about you?" he asks, eyeing me over, but not in a way that makes me feel like I'm being observed. More like he genuinely wants to know. "Have you been waiting to call them?"

"Yeah," I say, but it sounds more like an echo. "Of course."

"You don't have to bullshit me, you know." He shrugs. "Remember what I told you. There's no point in trying to blow smoke up my ass. Just be straight with me, and I'll never judge you. Never."

I put my hand up to my mouth and chew the sides of my nails nervously. "Mom's going to tell me she's proud of me," I mutter.

"Well, that's because she is," he says matter-of-factly.

"Buck, I'm in fucking rehab. They probably used their life savings to get me here." I throw my hands up. "Why the fuck would she be proud?"

"Because you're still here." He smiles. "You're an adult. You know you could have left, and you didn't. You've stayed here. Do you have any idea how big of a deal that alone is?"

Guilt consumes me, just like it always does. If I had to choose one word to describe myself that would be etched into my forehead, guilt would be it. And the worst part is that the guilt I feel is what always makes me want to use again. I can blame my addiction on the knee injury, but the real reason I'm here is because I can't stand to be in my own fucking skin day in and day out. And the only thing that made it bearable was getting high.

"I don't know," I mutter. "I'm here because I chose to do drugs, Buck. So, at the end of the day, who cares if I'm still here? I got me here." I pound my palm to my chest. "Me. No one else."

He tilts his head to the side, narrowing his eyes a smidgen, and I know that look. He's figuring out my shit. Or trying to.

"And you feel bad about that?"

"No, I feel fan-fucking-tastic," I deadpan. "*Yes*, Buck. Of course I feel fucking bad."

"Well, until you understand that you can't change the past, that you can only create whatever future you long for and be the man you actually want to be and not the person you think you are just because of past shit, until then … you will not beat this," he says so straightforwardly. "I promise you that. If you keep thinking you're a pillhead, fuckup, loser, lowlife … that's all you're ever going to be." His lips turn up. "But the fact that you are sitting here, feeling bad and putting in the work, well, that means you're none of those things, brother. Are you an addict? Yes. Are you always going to be an addict, even when you're sober? Yes. Are you going to have to change the way you live and work hard every day to stay clean? Hell yes, you are. But you love your parents. You love your coach, your friends, and your teammates. And guess what. They love you too. They don't think of you as Cade, the drug addict. I know that."

"How do you know that?" I ask, narrowing my eyes. "How would you actually know what they think of me?"

He leans forward, his eyes smiling right along with his mouth. "Because, Cade, since you've been here, I can't tell you how many phone calls we've had from your friends and teammates, checking on you. We didn't tell you because for the first few weeks or until we see fit, we don't allow contact with the outside world." He taps his fingertips on his desk mindlessly. "The phone calls we've been getting, they aren't from people who think you're a loser or a pillhead. They are people who love you, man. You are blessed. And you have the support system to beat this thing—I promise you that." He reaches across, pointing toward my chest. "Now, you just need to believe that."

A lump forms in my throat, and my lips tremble. I know he didn't ask to hear about what first started my addiction, but suddenly, I feel the urge to do something I never have before.

Talk about Eli.

"When I was seventeen, the hockey team I was on beat our biggest rival. Not in just any game, but in the championship." My voice is barely a whisper as I look down at his desk instead of at his eyes. If I look at his face, I'm afraid I'll stop talking. And somehow, I know I need to get this out. "My best friend, Eli, and I were pumped. Together, we were unstoppable. I'd never had chemistry on the ice with anyone else as much as I did with Eli. It was like he knew my next move before I did. And vice versa."

The same picture flashes in my brain. Eli in my arms, bleeding out while I screamed for help.

"Later that night, we went to a convenience store just outside of town and closer to our rival school. He wanted to try to buy beer with a fake ID someone had made for him. His entire body was buzzing from our win. We were on a high that had absolutely nothing to do with drugs or liquor."

I pause, feeling my chest tighten. That entire night has replayed in my mind so many times. I know every single detail of that store. The clothes Eli wore. The sound the door made when the group of guys walked in, all wearing the colors of the team we'd just beaten.

"Some people—fans from the other team—strutted in and started talking shit." My voice grows hoarse, and I barely recognize it. "Just telling us we were nothing. That we sucked. Things like that."

In my brain, I see the asshole's face. "One of them walked up to Eli and shoved him backward into the aisle and against the bagged chips. Eli wasn't really a fighter. Sure, on the ice, he was aggressive and all, but off of it, he was a happy-go-lucky dude." I inhale a shaky breath. "I wasn't like that. I've always had a temper. Always quick to throw a punch or make a threat when someone wrongs me or someone I love."

I don't even realize that I'm crying like a bitch, my entire face soaked, until he hands me a tissue. I take it and wipe under my eyes and nose.

"I had that one guy by the throat. Reaching back, I landed a solid punch right in his nose. But then the clerk yelled that he was calling the police." I shrug. "We didn't want to get in trouble, Eli and I. So, we started to run."

My throat closes in, and I grab my chest as I sob. "The guy that I punched ... he yelled something at us, and we turned around real quick and saw he was holding a gun, pointing it at me. When Eli saw he was going to shoot me, he jumped toward me and pushed me out of the way."

I shake uncontrollably, and before I realize it, Buck is in front of me, wrapping his arms around my shoulders.

"He shot him in the chest," I whisper, feeling like I'm going to throw up. "And he died in my arms."

Buck pulls me against him, and I bury my face in his shoulder without knowing what I'm even doing.

"I should have been the one who died that day, not him." I sob uncontrollably. "It should have been me."

I lie on my back, looking up at the fan slowly turning above me. My face feels swollen from crying so much. And my abdomen is actually sore from shaking. I planned to get a second workout in today, but after meeting with Buck earlier, I'm too exhausted to even move.

I don't know if my teammates know about my past, but I know Coach LaConte does because when he first started watching me play, it was right before Eli was murdered. He told my coach he was interested in recruiting me, just like other colleges did. And then after Eli died, I went off the deep end. I walked away from hockey. I drank too much. I started experimenting with drugs. And finally ... I ended up in rehab. Word got out, and a lot of college scouts stopped asking about me. Not LaConte though.

I think back to the first time I officially met him. I was fresh out of rehab and looking at my final season of high school hockey, feeling like a fish out of water.

He showed up at my third game, walked up to me after we won, and bluntly said, "When you ended up in rehab, you fucked up your future with a lot of colleges, Huff. But … not with Brooks. Not everyone there will be on board with offering a scholarship to a kid who just got out of rehab. Lucky for you, I don't really give a shit what other people think."

And after we talked for a few minutes, he shook my hand, gripping it harder as he leaned in and said, "Don't make me regret it, Cade. I'll be watching you like a damn hawk watches a little mouse in a field."

And he held true to his word—for my freshman year at least.

Clearly, he thought I deserved more freedom than I did because after my first year with him, he stopped the random drug tests and wasn't checking in with me as much. He thought he could trust me, and I let him down.

I can call my parents today, but I'm going to wait a few more hours. If I called right now, I'd just start bawling like a little bitch, and then my mom would cry even harder than I know she's already going to. I don't want to make her even sadder. She needs to think I'm all right. Even if I know I'm far from it.

Haley

Cade has officially been gone for five weeks. Time is passing at a turtle's pace, but this pregnancy actually seems to be flying. Which makes zero sense, but whatever. After tomorrow, I'll be in the second trimester of my pregnancy, which scares the crap out of me. It's like I'm watching the grains fall in a sand timer, piling on the bottom. Making me realize there might be months to go, but it's passing quickly. And I'm afraid that I still won't be ready when July comes and it's time for me to give birth.

The holidays are usually my favorite time of the year. But even with lots of upcoming family time during Christmas next week and a baby *literally* growing inside of me ... I've never felt more alone. And knowing deep down that there's only one person who could make it better, and he can't be here right now. Well, it's like living in hell.

When it comes to Cade and his recovery, I don't know what to do. I've written him a dozen letters. Yet I haven't sent a single one. I'm afraid that I'll mess up his sobriety. I have no clue what the right thing to do is. But I also know it isn't right to keep this baby a secret either.

Besides, he was using drugs the entire time we were sneaking around. Now that he's sober and his mind is clear ... what if he no longer looks at me the way he did when he was high?

Remi looks over at me from across the table as we sit in the library, both silently working on our computers to send in any last-minute assignments. Slowly, she shuts her screen and sighs.

"You've been so quiet lately, Hales. Are you okay?" She widens her brown eyes, sending me a warning. "And don't even think about lying."

Closing my own laptop, I rest my face in my palms as I lean forward. "I don't know. I mean, personally? Yeah, I'm fine. I'm due in July, which means I can finish the school year and take the summer to settle into motherhood." I fill my cheeks with air before slowly letting it trickle out. "But by the time Cade comes back home, I'll be noticeably pregnant. I'm so afraid that this baby's existence will send Cade into a spiral. But I also hate—*hate*—keeping it a secret from him because I feel guilty."

"Have you considered going to see his parents?" She shrugs. "They might have some words of wisdom. They know their son better than anyone, right?"

I think for a moment. The last thing I want to do is for more people to know about the baby before Cade himself. But I also need to do the best thing for his recovery.

Slowly, I nod. "I haven't. Not really anyway. But I'm going to do that. I mean, today was the last day of classes anyway, and now, we're on break." I sit up in my seat, tipping my chin up to try to appear braver than I actually am. "It's about a four-hour drive. I'll leave tonight, get a motel close by, and go see them tomorrow."

"I'm coming with you," she says quickly. "I'll stay back at the motel while you go see them. But I don't want you driving there alone. Besides, that's sort of on the way back home to Tennessee. We can just make it one big trip since we planned to go home for Christmas anyway."

"You are the best friend I could ask for," I say softly. "For real."

"I'll be the best aunt too." She winks. "She'll know she can come to Auntie Remi when she gets into trouble."

"She?" I laugh. "You know, she could be a he!"

"Could be, but my money is on a girl. Shall we name her Wally—after Walgreens, where I took you to get that test?"

"Um, no." I scowl. "Let's not and say we did."

Getting up, I gather up my stuff. "Let's go. Before I change my mind."

I just hope his parents don't hate me. Or worse, think I tried to trap him into this.

CADE

I walk through the main lobby, and I smile because despite having to spend the holidays in rehab, I know my mom is going to love all the Christmas decorations in this place. I've never been one to care about shit like that, but when you're confined to a place, you appreciate things you probably didn't even notice before. In my case, it's shiny, bright, festive decorations and whatever smelly shit they've put out to make it smell like pine in here.

My parents will be here for Christmas Eve and will stay in a motel nearby and return Christmas Day. It's not ideal to spend Christmas in rehab. But if doing it this one time means I never have to do it again, so be it.

I've talked to my parents almost daily since I got my phone privileges. And Coach a few times, as well as some of the guys on the team, including Link, Hunter, and Watson. I've considered calling Haley I don't know how many times, but I keep thinking maybe she's moved on. Maybe she's dating someone new and hasn't thought of me. I mean, girls like her could do a lot better than a dude in rehab—that's for sure. Why would she wait around for my ass to get straight and come home?

I almost asked Hunter how she was doing, but I didn't want to make him feel uncomfortable. As far as I know, he has no idea she and I were as close as we were. And even though I don't care anymore if he knows the truth, she might not feel that same way.

I consider writing her a letter. If I send it out today, it will reach her just in time for Christmas. But what would I say? Tell her I love her even though I have nothing to offer right now? No, I can't do that. Not only because I am a mess, but also because Buck told me I can't be in a relationship until I've been sober for one year.

And by then, she'll definitely have moved on.

Tortured is a man who can't be with the only woman he's ever loved.

Well, besides my mom, of course.

"Heads up, Huff," Houston, another dude here for treatment, says, coming next to me. "My mom is coming to visit for Christmas, and you'd better believe she knit you a sweater." He cringes. "She's given me one every year since I was born. And before you say it's no big deal, thinking you won't wear it, she doesn't take no for an answer. So, you will be wearing it, my friend. Here's your warning."

"Uhh … Houston, we have a problem." I raise an eyebrow. "I'm not really the holiday-sweater-wearing type of dude."

He waves toward himself in his gray T-shirt and faded blue jeans. "And you think I am?" He shakes his head. "Nah, man. But there's no saying no to my mama." As he walks backward, he shrugs. "Hope you like green, my man!"

153

And then he turns, heading toward his room.

Houston is one of the people I've become close with in here. He's only a year older than me. He played football in high school, but after an injury, he got hooked on prescription pills and became addicted. He got here a week before I did and works out with me once or twice a day, every day. He isn't big on horses, so when we get paired up to clean out the stalls, he's about the worst partner to have.

Thinking about the horses makes me remember that I need to go check on Beauty, the horse that is indeed very pregnant. She's due anytime now, and as fucked up as it might sound, I kind of want to be there when she has her foal.

I look outside and see the sun shining bright, and I wonder … *Is Haley looking up at the sun too?* Even the thought that she might be somehow makes me feel closer to her.

Haley

I sit in my car and stare at the house that my GPS led me to. My brother gave me Cade's address and even offered to take Remi's place and come here with me. I told him no. I was thankful to have Remi for the company, but I needed to do this part alone, and Hunter wouldn't have allowed me to.

If I walk in there, I'm going to change their entire lives. I'm going to tell them that their son, who is not exactly stable, is going to be a father. They are just trying to help Cade, who is the most important person in their lives, get his life back. And here I am, about to drop a bomb and then walk off. I want them to know I love their son and that I want only the best for him. Even if I'm not it.

I let my gaze sweep the proximity of the house. The dark blue house with a pale yellow door and a farmer's porch is oddly welcoming. It isn't immense, like the one I grew up in, but it's beautiful, warm, and inviting. I notice the swing that hangs from the large tree, and I wonder if Cade ever swung on it when he was a kid or if it's new. I look at the second story, gazing at the windows, and wonder which one was his room. The plants in the front yard, matched with the perfectly manicured walkway, paint the idea in my brain that his mother is a gardener and that she probably likes DIY projects, maybe looking at Pinterest and finding the perfect yard she wants. Perhaps the Huffs are like my parents and hire people to take care of that stuff for them. But for some reason, I doubt it. No, this place looks like each stone, every plant, and each flower was put there with love.

Eventually, I push my door open and walk toward the house. My feet somehow carry me along despite my brain and heart telling them to stop. Though it's chilly outside, my armpits and palms sweat. And I'm thankful for Remi remembering to bring deodorant when I forgot mine.

Holding my fist up to the door, I knock. And when I stand there for a moment and no one comes to the door, I ring the doorbell. About thirty seconds later, Caden, Cade's father, answers the door.

He looks surprised to see me, and his eyes squint a tiny bit. He saw me at the house the day they came and took Cade to rehab, but I have no idea if he even remembers me.

"Haley ... is it?" he asks, and when I nod, he smiles. "I thought so."

"Hi, Mr. Huff." I give him an uneasy smile. "I'm sorry to drop in on you like this."

"Please, call me Caden." He looks a little worried, his brows pulling together. "Is my son okay? We spoke with him a little while ago. He seemed all right—"

Hearing the panic in his voice, I stop him. "Cade is fine. Well, I mean, I think he is. I haven't talked to him or anything. But, I mean, that's nothing new." I stop myself, knowing I'm a blabbering mess. "I'm ... I'm not really here about Cade." I pause. "Okay, that's not true. I am here for Cade. But not in that type of way. Sorry, I'm really nervous."

"Don't be nervous. Come on in, Haley. Kat is just inside." He waves his hand. "She'd love the visit, I'm sure."

I didn't really get a chance to talk to Cade's mom, Kat, when they were at the house. It was a whirlwind. And Cade was acting like he hated me the entire time they were there. But from what I saw, she was so warm and sweet.

Slowly, I trudge inside. And when I see how immaculate their house is, I quickly slip my shoes off before following Caden farther into the house.

"Kat," he calls, and I hear her clanging some pans around in the kitchen. "We have company."

The sound quickly stops, and she runs around the corner. There's a look of hope on her face that quickly falls when she spots me. I'm sure she was thinking, even for a second, her husband was surprising her with their son, and that makes me feel like an asshole for giving her false hope.

"It's Haley, right?" She wipes her hands on her black apron that says *#1 Mom* on it in white letters. "Hunter's sister?"

I give her a nod and take her hand as she holds it out for me. "Hi, Mrs. Huff. I'm sorry to drop in on y'all like this. If it's a bad time, I can come back."

"It's a fine time, Haley. But calling me Mrs. Huff makes me sound like an angry teacher or something." She chuckles. "Please, call me Kat."

"Kat," I say softly. "Well, I'm sorry to show up unexpected. I, uh, just wanted to talk with both of you."

"Don't be sorry at all," she answers sweetly.

I can see her son gets his eyes from her, and I wonder if our baby will have those same kind eyes.

"What can we do for you, Haley?" She waves toward the living room. "And please, sit down."

Yeah ... you're going to want to sit down too, I think, biting my lower lip as a way to cope with the nerves. It doesn't work.

Once we've all had a seat—me on the small love seat and the two of them on the couch—I sigh. "So, not many people know this, but before Cade went away ..." I stop, seeing the sadness that covers Kat's face from my words. "Well, Cade and I were sort of seeing each other."

I blush, hoping they don't notice. *Who am I kidding?* We weren't exactly seeing each other. We were hooking up. But I can't tell his parents that.

"Oh, really?" She doesn't hide the shock in her voice. "Yes, I'm sorry to say I had no idea."

"No one really did." I tuck my hair behind my ears anxiously. "Just my best friend, Remi. And I think Watson had his suspicions too."

"I see. Did you know he was ... using?" Caden asks, glancing at his wife.

"Not until just before he went away." I tell them the truth, still feeling the same guilt for not knowing sooner. "I should have told someone as soon as I saw. As soon as I suspected it, I should have gone to Hunter. Or you guys. But I told my brother and Watson when I knew he really needed help." Tears fill my eyes. "Before he left, I had been spending quite a bit of time with him, and I had no idea. I'm so sorry that I didn't figure it out sooner." I wipe my eyes. "Looking back, I see the signs I missed. I'm so mad at myself for not seeing it earlier."

"Don't be sorry," Kat quickly says. Her voice thick with sadness. "He's very, *very* good at hiding when he needs help."

"I keep wondering, you know, did I not pay enough attention to him?" I shake my head. "I don't know. I hate that he didn't—" I stop as a lump of emotion grows in my throat.

"You hate that he didn't think he could tell you?" Kat whispers, her eyebrows lifting.

I nod slowly. "Yeah. Like he thought ... he thought I'd walk away or something if I knew." I sniffle. "I would never."

"We've beaten ourselves up for years, trying to figure out how we missed it. Or what we did wrong to lead him to drugs in the first place," Caden says, staring off in the distance. "I still don't know the answer. But I'll tell you this much: this isn't your fault, Haley."

"He's right." Kat smiles. "So, if you're feeling guilty, don't." Her eyes gloss over with tears, and she covers her mouth. "I'm his mother, and for so long, I didn't know." She puts her hand to her chest. "It's my job to know when something is off with my child, and I had no idea."

Caden moves closer to her, pulling her to his side.

I curse myself for coming here. For causing them more pain. They are trying to heal, and I'm sure, every damn day, they are scared for Cade and afraid to lose him. And now, here I am, making it worse.

"I'm sorry," my voice squeaks. "I shouldn't have come. The last thing y'all need is me causing you more pain."

"We are glad you did," Kat is quick to answer. "But … I'm sensing there is more?"

My face falls as I look down at the ground and nod. "Yes." I wipe my eyes. "There's really no easy way to say this, but … a few days before you came and got him, I found out I was pregnant." I get the courage to look up at them. "With Cade's baby."

The gasp from Kat could be heard across the street, I swear. And Caden quickly stands, pacing the living room.

"Shit," he mutters. "Shit. Shit. Shit."

I sob, knowing I'm only making everything worse. "I'm so sorry. I swear, I didn't get pregnant on purpose," I whisper, barely hearing my own words. "I've been keeping it a secret because …" I pause. "Because I'm so scared that all this work he's putting in to get …" My voice cracks. "To get clean will be erased because this news will scare him. And that when he's scared, he'll spiral."

"Do you love him?" Kat says the question so softly that I almost think I heard her wrong. That is, until she repeats it. "Do you love him? Even now that you know the truth? *His* truth?"

"Yes," I say instantly. "I have loved your son since way before I found out I was pregnant. And maybe that's why I overlooked it all. The moodiness and his constant push and pull when it came to me. I just wanted him so bad." My lip trembles. "I just wanted to be with him. To love him and be loved by him. And I think I convinced myself it was all going to work out." I sniffle. "Even if there were so many signs that it wasn't going to."

Caden sits forward a little bit, digesting everything I told him. "Have you talked to him since he's been in rehab?"

"No," I say, shaking my head. "He knows I'm the one who told Hunter and Watson that he was using. And on the day he left, he would barely look at me, and he told me we were nothing." I force myself to carry on. "I don't think his love ever caught up to mine. And now … I don't think it ever will. He's too angry. He thinks I betrayed him when I told the truth." I wrap my arms around myself in an attempt to calm myself down. "And now … I'm betraying him again by keeping this secret."

LOST BOY

"Haley, you've kept this baby a secret to ensure he sticks to his recovery?" Caden asks, but it sounds like more of a thought. "You must really love him to do something like that."

"I do," I say, inhaling through my nose, trying anything to slow my heart rate down. "But I don't know what to do. No matter what, I feel like I'm doing the wrong thing."

"How so?" Kat says, scooching closer to her husband, almost like having him that much closer will help her calm down.

"If I don't tell him, I'm being dishonest. But if I tell him, I could compromise his recovery by putting too much pressure on him all at once." I lean back a little in my seat. "Either way ... I'm not doing the right thing. It's a catch-22." I look each of them in the eye, shifting from one to another. "I know you don't know me. I'd understand if you were wary of me, showing up here, telling you I'm pregnant with your son's baby. But I need you to know that I want what is truly best for Cade. Even if that isn't me. And whatever I can do to help him or you guys through his recovery, I'll do it."

"I believe you." Kat stands, walking over to me and holding her hands out.

Standing, I embrace her. And I cry. She cries. It's a sob-fest. I love my mom, but she's nothing like Kat Huff. Cade's mother is kind, soft while being strong, and clearly loves unconditionally.

I don't know what will come of Cade and me. But I know one thing: I'm thankful that this baby will have Kat as their family.

And when Caden hugs me next, promising me it is going to be all right and that Cade and this baby are going to be fine, I'm thankful for him too.

And for the first time in weeks, I feel something.

Hope.

Because with a family like his, I truly believe Cade can be stronger than his addiction. And somehow, someway, I want to be a part of his recovery.

A little while later, we sit at the table, finishing the sandwiches Kat made us. I didn't plan on staying this long, but when she insisted, I sort of didn't want to leave. Remi is waiting for me back at our room, but when I asked her if she was okay with me being gone longer, she assured me she was fine and that she had found a "bomb-ass mall" just down the road.

"From what I've read, Cade is going to be advised against being in a romantic relationship," Kat says, taking a sip of her tea and giving me a sympathetic smile. "However, maybe when you're pregnant and it isn't a brand-new relationship, perhaps that changes things?"

"No, no." I shake my head quickly, feeling the need to explain. "I don't expect him to break the rules for me. And if that's what is suggested when he leaves, I one thousand percent would like to stick to that plan." I sigh, putting my napkin on my now-empty plate. Eating hasn't been easy lately, but today, it didn't feel like a chore to do it. "I do really wish I could see him

159

though. To apologize, you know?" I sink into myself. "But I know that's selfish."

"It's far from selfish, girl." Caden grins. "I'd say that little shit is lucky to have you."

"I'd have to agree." Kat laughs the slightest bit, and I wonder how hard it's been for her to do that since dropping Cade off. "What about a letter?" She shrugs. "Nothing romantic, but something to let him know you're here for him. We could deliver it when we go out there for Christmas."

My heart breaks at the thought of Cade sitting in a rehab facility, celebrating the holidays. And then it travels to next year. And I can't help but wonder if we will be raising this child together or apart. Will he even want to be involved in his or her life? And worse … will he even be sober still? God, I hope so.

Reaching in my back pocket, I pull out a letter. I wrote a bunch, but I didn't tell him about the baby in any of them. This one is easy and friendly. I think it is appropriate too.

Sliding it across the table, I smile. "If he seems okay, if he's … strong enough, I'd love for him to have this." When I see Caden's eyes fill with anxiousness, I quickly add, "It doesn't say anything about the baby, I promise. I figured … we'll find a way to say that later."

He relaxes and gives me a small nod. "Yes, of course. Sorry."

After visiting a while longer, we exchange phone numbers, and I'm headed out the door.

And I'd give anything to be in the car with them when they go and see their son.

CADE

It's Christmas morning, and my parents are here. They stopped in last night and did some of the planned festivities, and even though I feel like I'm twelve years old when I say this, I really loved having them here. Almost felt like I was a kid again. Maybe my mind wants to take me back to that time—before everything got so complicated. We ended the night with a family therapy session, which I know, deep down, my dad fucking hates, like me. But he went. And he even shared his feelings, all that mushy shit.

Now, here we are, trudging down the hill because Buck just told me that Beauty is in labor and he knew how much I wanted to see her have her baby. I don't understand myself why I want to. I just know that I want to be there when that scrawny thing enters the world.

"I'm not going to lie; I didn't even want to be there when you were born. I ended up fainting and smashing my head on the floor. So, I really don't know about a slimy baby horse." My dad scowls. "Can't I just see it after the mom shits it out and cleans it off?"

"If you pass out, just make sure you don't land in some horse shit." I laugh, shaking my head.

I know he isn't joking. But my dad really hates anything that involves blood. And he really did faint while my mom was in labor.

The second Buck told me Beauty was in labor, my mom was up and out of her chair before she even had a chance to finish her coffee. She's always been an animal lover, and I can tell that she's happy with how much time I've spent caring for the horses lately. It's something unexpected—my interest in horses.

Jackie—who works at the rehab as well as helps with the horses—is crouched down. And when she sees me, she smiles. "Think we're going to have ourselves a Christmas baby, Cade. And guess what. You're just in time because that baby is coming out *now*."

I can't believe I'm standing here, wanting to watch this damn horse push a fucking baby out of its body. But since I started spending time with this horse, it almost seems like Beauty understands me or some shit. Her eyes look into my soul, and as dumb as it might sound ... she's sort of helped heal me. She calms me—although I don't have a fucking clue why.

My dad is somewhere in between watching and avoiding the entire thing as he continues to move around, looking at anything else before stealing a quick glance. But my mom stands next to me—we're a far enough distance to not make Beauty uncomfortable yet close enough to take in the whole thing. And minutes later ... out comes a foal.

Beauty wastes no time going to work, cleaning off her baby's black fur, followed by nuzzling her head.

I stare in complete awe because I just watched a creature come into the world. And that creature makes this place a little less dark.

My mom clutches my arm as tears fill her eyes while her gaze moves from the horses to me. "What a Christmas miracle that was." She throws her arms around me. "Thank you, Cade. Thank you for allowing me to watch that."

I smile, holding on to her. "Thank you for being here. Even if I don't deserve it."

Looking up at me, she reaches way up to do what she always does to me and Dad. Brush our hair to the side gently. "You deserve it, Cade. And I'll *always* be here." Stepping back, she opens her purse and pulls out an envelope. "We had a visitor a few days ago. Someone who wanted to check in on how you were doing." She smiles. "She wanted you to have this."

At the word *she*, my heart does some weird fluttery shit inside my chest. But I remind myself not to get too excited. It might not be from my angel.

I stare down at the letter that my parents left with me. They are returning in the morning before they drive back home, but since it's Christmas, I guess they wanted me to have this now. My fingers run over the edges of the folded

LOST BOY

paper. They already told me it was from Haley, and I hold my breath before I eventually unfold it.

Dear Cade,

It's been five weeks since you left. I hope you're doing well, and I think I can speak for the entire household when I say ... we miss you! We miss your goofy smile and your sometimes—okay, usually—inappropriate jokes.

I know you're mad at me. And I guess I really can't blame you. I'm sorry I betrayed your trust. And I'm even sorrier that you never felt like you could tell me the truth. Just please know that when I told Hunter and Watson, it was only with the best intentions for you. Because, Cade, you deserve to live a peaceful life. And I really hope, one day, you'll believe that.

I often sit in my room and stare at my bookcase. I picture you finding the perfect color blue—my blue—for it. And I imagine you putting it together. It is truly a work of art and my most precious, favorite gift anyone has ever given me.

I'm so proud of you for staying in there and putting the work in. There isn't a second that passes when you aren't on my mind. And I believe in you, Cade. After all, you're so much stronger than you know.

Thank you for making my time at the house ... interesting? To say the least. I had so much fun getting to know you. Even if you are a little shit sometimes.

No pressure, but I'm here if you ever need to talk. I miss you so much more than I could ever express in words.

Love,

Haley

P.S. Remember ... I'm just Haley. Not Haley baby. LOL.

Despite my heart being clear up to my fucking throat, I smile. Even though she always sassed me when I called her that, I know, deep down, she liked it. I never had to wonder if that girl cared about me; it was obvious in the way she looked up at me.

I wonder what she's doing today on Christmas. I'm sure she traveled home to be with her parents even though they aren't all that close. Just from

163

what I've observed, their parents are pretty tough on them. Basically the opposite of mine.

Sitting down at the tiny desk in the corner of my room, I pull open the drawer and take out a pen and pad of paper. And I do something I've never done.

I write a girl a letter. One I'm actually going to send to her and not just stuff into the back of my desk.

Haley. The only girl I would ever put words on paper for.

Haley

I rush into the post office, unlocking my box and pulling everything out. Since I received Cade's first letter weeks ago, it's become an obsession of mine to check the mail for his letters—often multiple times a day.

Our letters to each other are never romantic. Though, sometimes, he might flirt a tad, but that's just his personality. I was honestly shocked when I received the first letter from him. After I'd sent one to him with his parents, I hadn't expected him to actually respond. But he did. And now, we've been writing to each other for weeks.

When I walk outside, the chilly air hits my face. We're officially in the coldest month in Georgia, and I. Am. Freezing. Still, I don't even make it to my car before tearing open the envelope with my name and address in his chicken-scratch handwriting. And I wonder where he was sitting when he wrote it.

Being cold melts away in my brain as I lean against my car. Snuggling my nose further into my jacket in the nearly empty parking lot, I look down at the writing. His words have become such a comfort to me. My hand instinctively slides to my stomach as I begin to read. I smile because he starts the letter just like he did the first one and all the others that followed.

Dear Haley baby,

Damn, it's been cold out. I thought we lived in the South for the warmth, but lately, it feels like the damn North Pole. We even had snow flurries here early this morning when I was down with the horses. I guess it was better than sweating my ass off though, right?

Thanks for the package with all my favorite snacks. My buddies here were pretty dang jealous. I told them it sucked to be them. I'm kidding. I shared. A little. Just not the Kit Kat Bars. Those are mine.

You should see Beauty and Gaston. That horse is so cute—and, yes, I'm a grown-ass man, calling a baby horse cute. I wish you could see them when they run and play together. You'd love it. And, no, I'm still not sorry for naming Beauty's baby Gaston. I told you, maybe Gaston is just misunderstood. His whole life, everyone kissed his ass. Perhaps deep down, he's not actually a dick.

I did realize something when Hunter and the guys came to see me last week. Your brother is really scared of horses. And Watson, well, he loves farm animals. I caught him talking to the goats. Link stepped in horse shit with his new sneakers. That was the highlight of my week— no, month. You should have seen his face.

Having them here was kind of like when you're a kid and your school has an open house for your family to see the classroom. Except with my best friends. It should have made me feel like a loser, but honestly, I kind of liked showing them around this place.

You asked if I'm excited to get out of here in three weeks. If you had asked me that back when I was only a few weeks into being here, I would have said hell fucking yes. But now ... well, to be honest, I'm scared to leave. Everything here is scheduled. And I guess I've sort of grown comfortable with that. It leaves no room for me to fuck anything up. They hold me accountable here. What will happen when I leave? I want to believe I'm strong enough to not slip back into my old ways, but of course it's in the back of my mind that temptations will be everywhere and that real life will hit me like a ton of bricks. Oh well. Hopefully, I'll be fine.

I never really said it in the other letters, but I hope you know that you saved my life, Haley. I was so far into my addiction that I stopped caring about hockey, friends, or even myself. Thank you for pulling me from the darkness and waking my ass up.

LOST BOY

Now, since I know you're likely still in the parking lot, go back into the post office and ask for the package that couldn't fit in your box. And if you did leave the post office ... well, guess you'll have to wait and drive back over another day.

But something tells me you won't want to wait for this one.

—Cade

P.S. Apparently, your favorite author is a big fan of college hockey and will hook a dude up. Even a dude who contacted her from a rehab facility.

My eyes widen, and I rush back inside, asking the lady behind the desk if there is a package in my name. She gives me an annoyed look but walks to the back to get it. Moments later, she returns, sliding it across the counter.

"Thanks so much. Have a wonderful day!" I smile, unable to hide my excitement.

She says nothing. Just goes back to what she was doing, being the grump ass that she is.

Walking outside, I get in my car this time. Mostly because I'm freezing and I need heat.

I rip the box open, and my eyes fill with tears as I look at the stunning special edition covers of my favorite series that aren't even due to release until next week. Yet somehow, Cade had them sent to me.

Running my hand over each hardback cover, I literally can't get over how gorgeous they are. And when I open them, I can't believe my eyes.

"They are signed?" I squeal to the empty car before checking each of them.

All three are signed by my all-time favorite author.

I sniffle. Cade Huff is so thoughtful at times. Setting the box in my passenger seat, I rest my hand on my growing belly, knowing that before long ... I'll need to tell him about the baby. I mean ... if he plans to come back to Brooks, he's going to know the truth when he sees me. At week fourteen, I popped. And maybe to some people, I could put it off as one too many tacos, but to him? No way.

His mother was going to try to talk to Buck—his sponsor who also happens to be the head honcho at his rehab facility—about the best way to go about telling Cade about the baby. It's a delicate situation, and I just want to handle it with as much grace as I can.

I buckle my seat belt and look over at my box. Already planning my next letter to Cade.

CADE

A group of us lazes around one of the sitting rooms, sprawled out across the chairs and couches to get comfortable. No matter how many of these group meetings I've been to, I'm still not relaxed when it comes time to spill my heart out to everyone else in the room.

There are a few of the counselors here I really like. Others ... not so much. And those are the ones who seem to stare into my soul while I speak. It's probably just something they do without realizing it, but it makes my fucking skin crawl. Buck and another guy we all call Kobra—though I have no idea why—never do that. They listen without making it awkward as fuck. And then they move on to the next person. It's still uncomfortable, but at least it isn't awkward with a side of fucking cringe sprinkled on top. I also don't like the ones who wait too long to respond after I'm done talking. Like they want me to add more or something. I hate looking around uneasily while they digest the shit I said.

Today is Kobra's turn to lead our discussion. Where we have to share something that weighs heavily on our mind. For some, it's usually things we did to loved ones in order to feed our addiction. Stealing, lying, things like that. For others, it's the people we lost due to drugs. And when it comes time for me, I clear my throat, strumming my hands softly on my pant legs and looking toward the floor.

"A while back, I, uh ... I was at my dealer's house." I stop. "He's dead now," I say, not knowing why I felt the need to add that last part. "But there was a couple there. A girl and a guy. They were shooting up." My throat feels swollen, but I force myself to carry on. "She was so young. And pretty. *Really* pretty. And she looked like she was still fresh on her journey with drugs. Her eyes weren't dead inside yet. It was like ... like she was still in there. The drugs hadn't completely overtaken her."

I look up at Kobra, and he gives me a reassuring nod.

"I think about that girl all the time. I remember the red Converse on her feet and the zip-up hoodie she was wearing. I wonder where she is now. Is she alive? Did her parents get a phone call, letting them know that she had died?" My jaw tenses, and my heart squeezes inside my chest. "I think about how ... if I ever have a daughter, what if she goes down the same path that the girl did? That *I* did."

LOST BOY

I sit back, feeling my face heat from all the attention on me. I've always been one who likes to be the center of attention, but when it comes time for that here, it's not the same.

"I've seen countless addicts since I started using. But that girl ... she's stuck with me." I shrug. "I don't know why."

Kobra leans forward, patting my hand with his. "Sounds to me like, one day, you might make a good counselor yourself, Cade, because you clearly care about others, and you can help them, because you've been in their shoes."

I give him the look. It's the look I use when I'm done sharing and I want everyone's gaze off of me. He understands it, giving me a small smile before nodding his head. And then he moves on to the next person. I don't hear the person speaking because my mind is a thousand miles away.

All I can think about is that girl. And I wonder if it is too late for her. If that light in her eyes has gone out or if it still flickers.

Haley

After getting a call from Kat, I move nervously around the house and prepare to meet them at Cade's rehab a few hours away.

She spoke with his counselor regarding the baby, and he worried that if we waited to drop the bomb, Cade would feel betrayed since we kept it from him. He also worried that the news would be too much for Cade right when he should be getting back into the real world. That it would almost set him up for a chance to fail. Which is the last thing I want.

He has two weeks left now, so if we tell him today, Buck figures that will give him two weeks in the comfort of the rehab to get acclimated to the idea of becoming a dad. Rather than shocking his system the day he gets home.

I'm scared, and Hunter must sense it because when I slide my shoes on, he walks down the stairs and does the same.

"I'll drive you, okay?" He pulls me into his side for a half-hug—and my brother and I aren't the *hugging siblings* type.

"You don't have to do that, Hunter," I say, assuring him. "I'm sure you're tired."

He had an away game last night and didn't get home till quite late. I know he has to be exhausted.

"I'm fine. We'll take my truck." He grins. "You think I'd let you drive two hours each way to break the pregnancy news to your... baby daddy?" He shakes his head. "No chance in hell, Hales."

"You're too thoughtful, big bro. Are we sure you came from our parents?" I give him a funny look, scratching my chin. "Nah, definitely a stork."

Our parents are good parents and all, but they aren't the type that would interrupt their own schedules to run their kids around like Hunter is doing right now. No, they'd probably just pay someone to do it instead.

I follow him outside, and we walk toward his truck, where he instantly opens my door. Because that's my brother for you. The politest dude on the planet.

When he gets in, he glances at me. "Have you talked to them much? Since you told them the news?"

When I went home for Christmas, I told my parents I was pregnant. My mom cried. My dad paled before he scrubbed his hand across his face. I know I broke their hearts that day. What a Christmas present that was. But I guess I couldn't blame them.

"They've texted a little and a few phone calls," I mutter. "It'll take some time for them to wrap their head around it all."

"Yeah," he mumbles.

"Yeah," I echo back.

And then we're quiet. And I'm thankful for the silence as I prepare what the hell I'm going to say when I see Cade.

Or worse, when he sees me.

CADE

I let the words sink in, but I don't really retain them. Buck and my parents just explained that Haley is here. As in outside. Right now.

"Wait. She's here? Like, here at this rehab? And not to check herself in as a patient, but to actually see me?" I frown, looking at my parents before shifting my gaze to Buck. "Why is she here now?"

It's not that I don't want to see her. Of course I want to see her. But seeing her will make me want to pull her against me and bury my face in her neck. And after that, I'll want to kiss her, which goes against the *no romance* shit I'm striving to do. And after I kiss her ... forget it. Everyone might as well leave the room right then.

When it comes to Haley, I have little to no restraint.

I am so confused. Why would they choose to have Haley visit now—two weeks before I'm leaving this place? It makes no sense at all.

"She is," Buck says softly. "And, Cade, it's okay to walk away for a few minutes if you need to. It's all right to need time to cool off. But what isn't all right is shutting everyone out. Okay?"

I am so confused as I stare at him. *What the fuck would I need to cool off about?*

"Buck, I forgave her for telling her brother and Watson weeks ago. I'm not going to get mad." I lean back, resting my hands on my backward hat. "This is fucking weird. You're acting fucking weird." I look at my parents. "All of y'all are."

After a few moments, Haley walks in. Even though it hasn't even been three months since the last time I saw her, she looks different. More beautiful even. Her face glows, but her eyes are heavy with emotion. An emotion I can't really place, but I know it isn't good. Her baggy sweatshirt hangs from her tiny body, and I love that she didn't dress up but instead just went with something comfortable.

Haley might come from money and a family who cares about their image, but she's nothing like that. Hell, I swear her wardrobe is basically made up of crewneck sweatshirts, leggings, and hoodies.

"Hi," she squeaks, holding her hand up in a wave. Her eyes fill with tears when she takes me in.

I can't stand it. I need to go to her. Breathe in her sweet smell and hold her close to me.

"Hey," I say.

Standing, I walk over to her. Unable to stop myself, I put my arms around her and pull her against me. It's like feeling at home after weeks and weeks of feeling lost. But I notice right away that she feels different. And when I pull her closer and her stomach grazes mine, my eyes fly to hers. I stumble back and look at her abdomen.

"Cade," she whimpers, protectively moving her hands on her belly. "Please, don't freak out."

She's pregnant?

"You're pregnant?" I blurt out, putting my hands on top of my head. "When did you get pregnant?"

I whip my head toward Buck. "You thought … what? It would be a good idea to have the girl you know I'm fucking stupidly in love with visit me in rehab, just to tell me she's going to have another motherfucker's kid?" I can't breathe, my lungs sting, and jealous rage fills every blood cell pumping through my body. "What the hell, Buck?" I grunt, looking away. "Why torture me like this? What the fuck is the point?! I thought you wanted me to stay sober. Not drive me to the point of wanting to use!"

A million thoughts run through my head. But mostly, one sticks. *She's been pregnant with someone else's baby the entire time we've been writing to each other.*

She's moved on. I know it's what I wanted. I know it's why I pushed her away. I thought no way should an angel like her be with a lost motherfucker like me. But, fuck, deep down, I thought she'd be mine one day. Really, truly, wholeheartedly mine. It's part of the reason I've stuck it out in rehab. To be better for her.

She steps closer to me, putting her hands on my sides. "Cade, just listen to me! God, would you just listen?!" she pleads. "I'm not having another man's baby."

"I don't ... I don't understand," I say, sucking in a breath. Damn near on the edge of a full-blown panic attack. "What are you telling me, Haley?"

"Do you remember that night, um," she says before stopping and glancing nervously at Buck and my parents, "after that party, the one when Watson and I picked you up while you were walking home?"

When I finally grasp what she's telling me, my mouth hangs open, and my eyes must be the size of dinner plates. "Are you—" I stop, losing my breath. "Are you telling me it's *my* baby?"

Her eyebrows furrow as she looks up at me. "Yes! Who else's would it be?"

"I just thought ..." My voice is strained, and a lump forms in my throat as I look down at my biggest reason for getting me through rehab. Thoughts of her. Imagining being better *for* her. That's what has kept me here. It's why I've tried to trust this process and do what I need to. "I didn't know if you had moved on. And I don't have any idea how far along someone would need to be to be showing like ... that." I wave toward her stomach.

"Cade," she whispers, and I know she's trying her best to talk candidly, like there aren't three other people watching us, "even if I wasn't carrying your baby, I wouldn't have moved on." Tears pool in her eyes before running down her cheeks. "I told you that I love you. And I meant it. I *still* mean it." More tears come now even though I know she's trying her best to be strong. "I'm s-sorry that I didn't tell you sooner. I was just ..." She pauses, glancing at Buck before her eyes move to mine. Her lashes are soaked with tears. "I was so scared it would put too much stress on you. And that—"

"I'd relapse?" I whisper, barely audible.

She gives me a tiny nod. "It's not that I don't believe in you. Because I do. I believe in you with my whole heart, Cade. But a baby ... I know it's a lot." She sniffles. "And I didn't—I don't ever want you to feel trapped with me. Please, please know that. I really just want you to be happy. And healthy. Even if that doesn't include me and you. All I want is the best for you. I'm so sorry for not telling you," she sobs. "I just didn't know what to do."

"Shh, it's okay. I promise," I say, taking her hands in mine. "I'm okay."

Buck stands, speaking to us both. "I've grown really close to Cade. So, I felt a deep responsibility to be here for him when he got this news. To make sure he was all right." He looks between me and Haley. "But I think, now, you two can have some time to discuss things alone. If you'd like that, Cade."

I give him a nod, letting him know I would. And seconds later, he's ushering my parents outside the room.

"Do you hate me?" Her lip trembles.

"What? No!" I say quickly. "To be completely honest … I was way more upset when I thought you were pregnant with another man's baby." I stop, letting the words really soak in. "Is that crazy?"

"No," she whispers. "I just … I want you to be okay."

I stare down at her. And then I take my hands from hers and place them on her stomach. "I will be. I know that now more than ever." I say the words with certainty. I mean them more than I've ever meant anything else in my life. "I promise you, Haley, I'll be the person you and this baby need."

She breaks down, her entire face falling. "So … you're saying that you want this baby? You want to be involved?"

"Hell yeah, I want *our* baby," I tell her. "You won't have to worry about me. I might not know what the fuck I'm doing. I've never changed a diaper or any of that shit, but whatever you guys need … I'm going to be there. Promise."

"Cade," she whispers, biting her bottom lip nervously, "when it comes to him or her … you can't be in and out of their life. Or hot and cold. You can't be with them how you are with me. Okay? That would be too confusing for them."

I look down at her. I don't blame her for having that concern in her mind. Of course she does. I've always been so fucking flaky when it comes to her. She's scared I'll do the same with our kid, but I won't.

"Haley, I know I've fucked up … *a lot* when it comes to you. I know I would take and then give and then run away and shut you out." I reach out, brushing a tear from her cheek. "In my head, I did that because I thought it was best for you. I just thought … I thought your life would be better if I wasn't in it. But then I'd see you, and I couldn't stop myself. I'm sorry. But I swear to you, I will never do that to this baby. You have my word."

Through tear-soaked eyes, she peeks up at me before giving me a subtle nod. "Okay," she whispers. "I believe you."

It's shocking really. That I'm not freaking the fuck out over this news.

But I guess feeling that pain when I thought she was carrying another man's child inside of her body made me realize something. In that moment when I learned the truth, I realized that … my and Haley Thompson's story isn't finished yet. Far from it actually.

The way I see it, it hasn't even begun.

Haley

Hunter says his good-byes to Cade before waiting in the truck, just like he did for most of the visit. My brother is the best person in my entire family. There's nothing he wouldn't do for the people he loves.

Cade's parents hug him good-bye before getting into their car and driving away. I think they wanted to give us a minute to say our own good-bye.

He looks so good. He was never scrawny, but when he left for this place, he had lost a little weight and become run-down-looking. Gazing up at him right now, I have to remind myself not to ogle his broad shoulders, or his thick chest, or his eyes—which look clear for the first time since I've gotten to know him. His hat's backward on his head, but it doesn't make him look like a tool, like some guys do. He instead looks delicious, if I'm being honest.

"I just realized I never asked if you know what you're having yet. Well, what we're having," he says, stuffing his hands in his pockets and nodding toward my belly. "A girl or a boy?"

"I find out in a few weeks," I say, smiling at the thought of finally knowing. I open my mouth to say Ryann and Remi both think it's a girl, but I stop myself before the words get out. The last thing I want is for him to feel like everyone knew before him.

"If I'm home by then ... I'd like to go." He seems nervous, shifting his weight around on his feet. "If that's okay with you, that is."

"Of course it is. I actually made the appointment for the day after you come home just in case you wanted to be there." I smile. "Cade, you can be as involved as you want. I hope you know that was never the reason behind me not telling you. I would have loved for you to be there at all the appointments. I just don't want to overwhelm you."

The wind whips, a cold, assaulting breeze hitting my cheeks. I know we're both freezing, but I think neither of us wants to leave. It's like when you have your first crush and you talk on the phone way too late. Much later than your parents would ever allow if they knew. But neither of you wants to hang up. That's the way I feel when I'm around Cade.

"It's weird, but somehow, this news has made me more relaxed about getting out of here." His words are soft and meaningful. "I finally have something that I need to be accountable for." He bobs his head lightly. "You and this baby. I'm going to hold myself responsible for you both."

I give him a small smile, though deep down, I'm worried for him. Worried for the baby too.

LOST BOY

"I'd better not keep Hunter waiting," I squeak even though I'm sure my brother doesn't mind. But I know he has practice tomorrow morning. "It was really good to see you, Cade. I, uh … I've really missed you." I flick a tear away before it has the chance to roll down my cheek. "We all have."

"All I've done is miss you, Haley," he mutters before his eyes float to my lips. "I wish I could kiss you. I want to so bad." He blinks a few times, pulling himself from the thought.

"But you can't." I do my best to give him a smile even though it's weak. I know how he feels. I'd give anything to be close to him right now.

"But I can't," he mumbles back. "Because if I kissed you, I wouldn't be able to stop."

He pulls me in for a hug. His arms feel so good, wrapped around me, and he smells even better than I remember. I close my eyes and inhale, fully taking the moment in.

I understand the unconditional love his parents have for him because I'm realizing I have it too.

When he releases me, I reach up and touch his cheek. "I'm so proud of you, Cade." Tears fill my eyes, clouding my vision, and I blink them away. "So proud."

"I'm proud of you, Haley." His eyes are the ones glazed over now. "For months, you've been carrying our baby around in your body, probably going to appointments alone, and likely wondering if you were going to have to be both the mom and the dad." He places his hand on my stomach. "You're the strongest person I know."

"I don't know about all of that," my voice croaks.

"It takes a lot of strength to stand up to a drug addict and offer them help." His eyes shift between mine as his eyebrows pull together. "You could have just walked away from me or turned a blind eye. It would have been easier." His voice breaks as he gets choked up. "You saved me. And now … you're giving me a whole new reason to live."

I put my hand on top of his on my growing belly. "You gave me a reason too," I whisper.

After a few minutes, when he steps back, my body grows cold. And I miss him already even though he's just a few measly feet away from me. I'd give anything to be wrapped up in his arms again.

After an emotional good-bye, I'm in the passenger side of Hunter's truck as he drives down the long driveway, away from the rehab. But when I look out my window to see Cade running next to the car.

"What the hell?" Hunter mumbles when he sees him before coming to a stop.

I roll my window down. "What are you doing? What's wrong?"

He gives my brother a little smirk. "Don't worry, Thompson; I'm not trying to fly the coop or anything." He looks at me. "Can you just get out for one second?"

His chest heaves as he catches his breath, and puffs of smoke come from our lips from the chilly air.

Without question, I climb out of the car and look up at him. "Yeah?"

"In our letters, I wrote about how it's frowned upon to date right out of rehab. And that Buck and Kobra both suggested waiting a year." He kicks at the dirt driveway. "Just to, you know … work on myself and all that."

"I know," my voice barely chirps. I'm embarrassed at the possibility that he thinks I'm here to go against those rules. "I wasn't—"

"Shh, I know. I know you weren't," he says, swallowing. "A part of me wants to say fuck the rules that say I can't be with you now. Because deep down, I know that if anything, you'd keep me in line."

I hold on to his every word, having no idea what else is coming.

"I'd love to say I'll beat the odds of relapsing and we can ride off into the sunset together, living a fairy tale like the ones you read about in those porno books." He gives me a small smile before he cups my cheek, tears gathering in his eyes. "But the truth is, I don't trust myself. Not yet anyway. And I want to do it right this time, Haley. I want to do *us* right." He inhales, kissing my forehead. "For you. And for our baby. You both deserve someone you can count on."

"I understand," I rasp. "I want you to heal. More than anything, I want that for you, Cade."

"I know you do. And I'm not asking you to wait for me. I know I've put you through enough already, and I can't demand something like that." Dipping his head down, he presses his forehead to mine as his hand slides up the back of my head. "But just know that the day I'm one year sober, I'm coming for you. And I almost feel bad for any sad son of a bitch you might be dating by then because I'm not giving you a chance to say no. I'll be better, Haley. I'll be stronger." He swallows, his voice growing hoarse. "I'll be the man you both need."

I throw my arms around him, burying my face in his sweatshirt and squeezing my eyes shut, wishing I could freeze time. "I believe you," I whisper, my heart pounding in my ears.

We stand there, my body leaning against his, as we both openly cry.

"And I will wait. I'll wait as long as you need me to."

And I mean it. Because I believe in him. But more than that … I believe in us.

Cade

I finish reading Haley's letter and fold it up neatly. Pulling the top drawer of my desk open, I tuck it inside with the others. Treasures—that's what they are. Items I will forever keep safe because they truly are sacred to me.

Every word she jotted down is something she wrote just for me. She's taken time from her days to write to me while I've been here. I can't imagine why she would, but she has.

I take out a sheet of blank paper, already anticipating what I'm going to write to her before I even have a pen in my hand. I've never even been the type of guy to take a chick on a proper date. Yet here I am, writing fucking letters like that handsome fucker in *Dear John*. Which I only know about because my mother loves her some sappy shit like that. And I'll admit, I've been known to like a good tearjerker from time to time.

One week. That's how long until I join the real world. A place that has repeatedly proven to be too much for me to travel through sober. In here, it's easy. Everything I do is regulated. There isn't any downtime for my demons to catch me, and the things that keep me up at night, well, they somehow seem farther away.

I'm nervous to leave, but not nearly as anxious as I was before I found out I was going to be a father. And not just any father ... one to Haley Thompson's child.

How the fuck did I get so damn lucky?

Haley consumes my every thought. And ... yeah, I've fucked my hand to memories of her more times than I can count. The picture of her sprawled across the kitchen counter while I ate her like a starving man is perfectly etched in my brain. I mean, shit, I'm surprised the skin of my palm isn't raw yet. I'd give anything to make those fantasies a reality when I get out of here. But I'm not going to do that. Even if it wasn't for Buck's suggestion of waiting a full year of sobriety, I'm just not ready yet. She deserves all of me. And the truth is, there isn't all of me to give. Not yet anyway. With time, they say, I'll find my way back to feeling normal. Whatever the fuck that means. I can't remember the last time I felt that way. All I know is, when I make her mine, I'm going to be a better, stronger version of who I am right now. Because that's what that girl deserves.

I used to worry she'd be the one who got away. But now that the universe has permanently tied us together ... maybe she won't have to be.

I glance at the clock, knowing that in a few hours ... I have to come head-to-head with one of my biggest fears. I have to face my guilt head-on and not blink. My stomach turns, and I feel cold yet sweaty, just thinking about it.

Finding a pen, I pull it between my fingers and set the tip on the paper, and like always ... my angel named Haley saves me in a time of despair.

I want to look Eli's parents in the eyes so badly. I want to because that's what they deserve. But when I try, my body wants to go into a full-blown panic attack, and I look at the ground again. I've avoided them since the day he died. They've been nothing but kind to me, but I don't deserve it. And I know deep down, they know that too. They know I had a hand in their son dying.

Over the past few weeks, Buck has continuously praised me for how far I've come. And I believe him. I *feel* a lot better. But he's not stupid. He knows that I'm still holding on to so much guilt from the past. So, a few days ago, he came to me and said that before I graduated the program, he wanted to bring Ellen and Thomas, Eli's parents, in for a session. If they were open to it, of course. I told him absolutely not. The last thing I wanted to do was cause them more pain. I mean, for fuck's sake, they lost their son already. Why the hell should they have to travel hours away to visit an ex–drug addict and rid him of his guilt?

Yeah. Sounds pretty fucking stupid to me too.

But then I made the mistake of mentioning it to my mother—who loves to fix things for people because she can't stand anyone to be hurting. And since she still talks to Ellen a lot, she told her. And of course, Ellen, being the goddamn saint that she is, called Buck right away and scheduled a visit out here.

"Cade hasn't wanted to talk about this in too much depth, but it's been very obvious that he carries a great deal of guilt inside of him for what happened to your son, Eli." Buck says softly, leading the discussion. "Cade has shared some of his fondest memories of his time with your Eli. He sure thinks the world of him. He sounds like he was a great guy."

I'm thankful that he's taking charge because I don't know the first thing I should or shouldn't say right now. All I know is, I'm scared to make them sad. So, every time I open my mouth to talk, my brain convinces me that whatever I'm about to say is stupid and I should probably keep it inside.

"He was," Ellen answers, dabbing her eyes with a tissue. "And he thought the world of Cade too. Just like we do."

My throat burns, and my chest aches as I force myself to keep my emotions in check. If I fall apart on them … that'll make them feel bad for me. I don't want that. I don't deserve it.

"Cade is a pretty good dude—that's for sure. A pain in my ass at times. But he's a good one," Buck jokes, and out of the corner of my eye, I see him nod toward me. "And right now, he's doing great. He's been a model patient in this program. He's respectful. He works hard. And a big part of me thinks he is, in fact, ready to leave here. But what I worry about is that when he leaves this program and he feels that same guilt that he always has—which he will—I'm scared he'll try to numb it with drugs and alcohol." Buck sighs. "Cade is always going to carry that same heaviness around with him when it comes to Eli and that tragic, awful day. But if he continues to let it consume him, he will never stay sober. And if he doesn't stay sober, he could wind up dead."

"I'm sorry," I mutter, cupping my hand above my eyes. "You shouldn't have to be here."

"We want to be here." Thomas speaks this time. "Growing up, you were at our house as much as you were at your own. Same with Eli at your house. You two boys did everything together."

Ellen reaches her hand across the small gap between our chairs and places it on top of mine. "I knew my son enough to know that the last thing he would want is for you to hurt, Cade. You were the brother he never had. He loved you so much, and he would rest easier, knowing that you weren't carrying such a heavy burden on your shoulders." She gives my hand a squeeze, and finally, I dare to look at her. "That day was not your fault. Eli is not dead because of you. It's time to heal. For Eli, I need you to do that."

When she stands, pulling me up for a hug, I fucking lose it. Everything I've avoided for so long comes to a head, and I'm forced to feel everything. There are no drugs, alcohol, or even hockey to numb it. And as much as it hurts, it's also needed.

We hold each other, and I vaguely feel her hand patting the back of my head before Thomas joins us, hugging me too.

"We love you, kid," Thomas says against my ear. "He loves you too."

It hurts everywhere. But I guess pain isn't always a bad thing. Sometimes, it's just there to remind us we're still alive.

And that's something I'm not taking for granted anymore. The fact that I'm lucky enough to be alive.

CADE

I breathe the air into my lungs and let it out. It isn't like I have been cooped up inside the whole time in rehab or anything. Actually, I spent more time outside during my program than I probably ever had. But somehow, the air feels different today. Fresher. Better. And it feels like I'm on my way to a new start.

With my duffel bag in one hand, I hold my cell phone in the other. First time I've held the thing in twelve weeks, and surprisingly, I didn't miss it all that much. I found a calmness in being alone. Without the distractions of social media, texting, and calling. Before rehab, I couldn't stand to be alone, just me, but I grew sort of comfortable with it.

My dad throws his arm around me. "Proud of you, Cade." The emotion is thick in his tone. And he gives my shoulder a squeeze. "Not only for finishing this program, but also for handling the news about the baby so well. You're going to do just fine, son. No, you'll be great."

"Thanks, Dad," I say, turning back toward the door where Buck and Kobra are walking toward me.

"We'll be in the car," Dad tells me before he and my mom get into her SUV.

"I'm gonna miss you, you pain in the ass," Kobra drawls with a smirk. "Sometimes, when people leave, I get a feeling they aren't ready, and to be honest, it keeps me up at night." He pauses, swallowing. "I don't get that feeling with you though. You're ready, Cade."

"Hell yeah, you are," Buck adds. "And if you ever need us, we're here. All right?" Buck takes my hand, giving it a firm shake as he pulls me closer. "Keep working the program, okay? Go to your meetings. Call your sponsor, even when you think everything is fine. Don't ever get too comfortable, all right? There will still be hard days. Or things that set you off. But now, you've got all the tools to create the type of reality you want. For you and for that girl you're in love with and y'all's baby."

"Who said I'm—" I start to say, but then I remember when I thought Haley was pregnant with someone else's child and I blurted out that I loved Haley in front of Buck and my parents.

He raises his brows, and I shake my head and laugh.

"I know it'll be hard to not jump right in with her, but I promise, if you can keep working on yourself and get really comfortable with your sobriety, it'll be that much sweeter if and when you get together once you've got a year of sobriety under your belt. And even then, you might not be ready. But you'll know." Kobra's voice is soft yet strong as his gray eyes look at me, absolutely no judgment in them. "Trust the process. And don't ever try to deal with your shit alone. You've got us. Okay, my man?"

I nod. "I know. I will, I promise."

I hug each of them good-bye and thank them. Because, well, without them, I don't know if I would have stayed and seen this program through. But I'm glad I did.

When I climb in my mom's SUV, she turns backward to look at me. "Ready?"

I smile. "Ready."

And then I watch the rehab building, where I just spent the past twelve weeks rebuilding myself from nothing, as it gets further away. And I make a vow not just to myself, but also to Haley and our unborn baby that I'll never need to come back to a place like this again.

We're almost by the horse pasture when I point. "Can you pull over here, just for a minute?" I blurt out to my dad, and he stops the car.

"I'll just be a few," I say, pushing the door open and heading down the hill toward where Beauty and Gaston are standing, waiting for me.

"Hey, girl." I grin at Beauty, my hand rubbing between her eyes and down to her nose. I nod at Gaston. "Hey, buddy."

I bring my face closer to Beauty's. "Thank you," I whisper, aware that I'm talking to a horse, but honestly not giving a shit. "For giving me something to look forward to while I was here."

Her sweet, dark eyes look at me, and she nudges her head toward mine.

"You're going to help so many other pathetic bastards, just like you did with me." I laugh sadly. "I know it." Reaching down, I run my hand along Gaston's neck. "Bye, little guy. Take care of your mama."

Sober Cade is apparently a dude who cries. Talks to horses. And is excited that he impregnated his best friend's little sister. I suppose that's still better than the Cade who partied too much and crushed pills to snort up his nose though. Right?

HALEY

Setting a picture down near the fireplace, I look around my new place. It's a small house, just across the street from Cade, my brother, and Watson.

Last week, my parents came to Brooks, and we had a *come to Jesus* moment regarding the baby. They apologized that they had ghosted me but explained they were in shock. I told them the situation between Cade and me, and much to my surprise, they didn't freak out. They did, however, help me rent this house, getting it ready for me in record time.

I have the perfect spot for my bookcase in the guest room, where I'd love to make it my very own reading nook. But I felt weird, taking the beautiful piece of furniture with me without asking. Cade had built it, even attaching it to the wall so that it was extra safe and sturdy, and I didn't feel right about just packing it up without at least checking with him.

My brother pushes the door open—of course without knocking first. I'd expect nothing less though.

"Hey, Hales. Cade's about ten minutes out." He looks around. "Watson and I were talking; we think the three of us should be there when he gets home. You, me, and him. I know you already told Huff about this place, but ... he loves you, Hales. I know you guys are in a sensitive place right now, but this is a big deal for him. He's coming home. And it's the first time he's going to be at his house, sober, in God only knows how long. I think he needs us. You know, a united front or whatever they call it."

Reaching for my brother, I smack him with the back of my hand. "That's nice and all, *asshole*, but did you really think I wasn't going to do that already?" I shake my head. "You do realize I have his baby in my body, right? Of course I am going to welcome him home. Geesh. You really are a knucklehead sometimes."

He goes from looking proud of himself for his idea to annoyed as he rolls his eyes. "Whatever. Choppity-chop. Let's go. Get waddlin' across the road."

"I don't waddle!"

"Not yet," he taunts me. "Give it a few more weeks, and people will think you're a duck." As we head outside, he grins at me. "Speaking of the baby, Hunter has a nice ring to it, doesn't it? Plus, it could be a girl or a boy. I feel like Hunter could go either way."

"Go impregnate Sutton and have a baby with her," I deadpan. "And then you can name your own baby Hunter." I elbow his side. "And if you guys do have a girl, it can even be Hunter Haley. Or Haley Hunter." I wiggle my eyebrows. "Now, *that's* got a nice ring to it, doesn't it?"

"No," he mutters. "It definitely does not. I'm going to be a great uncle and all, and I'll love the piss right out of that kid. But a baby of my own? Nah. Not there yet, sis."

"Me neither," I mutter. "I've never even changed a diaper."

He pats my shoulder, giving me his best *supportive brother* voice. "You'll be great. But, uh … don't be asking me to change diapers. Because it's not happening."

"Well, thanks for the support." I snort, and we head toward his house.

CADE

When I step into my house, my parents right behind me, I smell one of Watson's damn candles and can't help but smile. *I'm home.* But then I remember it's just us three living here now, no Haley. And it doesn't feel quite as homey anymore.

Watson and Hunter waste no time coming toward me, pulling me into a big, cheesy group hug.

"Smells like a motherfucking bakery in here, Gentry." I laugh. "Your mom is really upping her candle game, huh?"

He smiles proudly. Watson Gentry isn't the type of dude who gives a shit if people make fun of him. He is who he is, he likes what he likes, and that's one thing I've always loved and respected about him.

"You love it, and you know it." He releases me the same time as Hunter, and we each take a step back, pretending we weren't just hugging like little bitches seconds ago.

LOST BOY

My gaze sweeps to see Haley as she waits in the doorframe of the living room, one hand resting on the wall as she offers me a small smile. Right away, I sense she's nervous, and I can't really blame her. She doesn't know her part in all of this. And I can't allow her to play the part I so badly want her to be because it goes against my damn rules.

My mother beelines toward Haley, throwing her arms around her. "Your belly has gotten even more adorable since I saw you last!" she squeals, rocking back and forth as she hugs her. "My Lord, you must be the cutest pregnant person I ever did see."

Haley's cheeks turn crimson red, and she giggles awkwardly. "Oh, I don't know about all that." Her lips pull to the side a little. "I officially can't wear any of my own clothes besides my sweats and leggings. And even those pinch my stomach."

"Well then, I guess it's time to go get maternity clothes!" my mom cheers. "I'm sure they've come a long way since I had Cade. They were so ugly back then. Now, pregnant women are so stylish and chic." She stops, her eyes growing wide. "Wait a second. Don't y'all find out tomorrow what this little bean in here is?"

"I'm no expert, but that ain't no bean anymore," Hunter says sarcastically, nodding toward his sister's stomach, which looks like half of a watermelon.

Haley throws a death glare his way, putting her hand on her hip when my mother steps back. And when my parents aren't looking, she gives him the middle finger.

In her letters, she wrote about how she felt like a "blob of jelly" because she was in that awkward stage where she wasn't hugely pregnant, but looked "chubby," but truth be told, I don't think she's ever looked more beautiful. And that's saying something because Haley *always* takes my breath away.

"Haley baby, as always, you look stunning," I say, smiling at her. "And, yeah, Mom, we're finding out tomorrow. So, I wanna know, what are y'all's predictions?" I look around the room. "Everyone who thinks it's a boy, raise your hand."

My dad and Watson both raise their hands.

I look at Hunter. "You want a niece, Thompson?"

"Nah, but I read somewhere that you puke your guts out with a girl. And Haley threw up every single day up until a few weeks ago." He grimaces. "Dude, she threw up *during* a hockey game. On someone's fucking shoes."

"Shut your mouth," she hisses. "We are so not talking about that."

I try to smile, but the truth is, it sucks to hear that she was sick and I wasn't here for her. And it blows even more that while I was away, life went on. It didn't stop just because I was gone. And I guess that's a tough pill to swallow.

Wow. Bad reference for a dude fresh out of rehab.

187

"Well, Ma, you told me once that you threw up every single day for, like, your entire pregnancy, and last I checked, I don't have a vagina," I deadpan, looking at Haley and winking. "Otherwise, how would I have put that baby in there?"

My mother puts her hand over her face, and my dad chuckles. Haley ... well, her cheeks just catch on fire a little bit more.

"Yep, there he is. He's back," Watson mutters before punching my arm. "Missed you, big guy."

I know exactly what he means by that. I've always been the funny one. The one who jokes around and makes people laugh. Floats through life, taking nothing seriously. Drugs will pull out every single piece of you that is lovable and leave you an empty shell. It feels good to be me again. Well, partially me. The rest will come with time, I'm sure.

"Yeah, well, someone's gotta loosen up you two sticks in the mud," I say lightly. "Might as well be me, I s'pose."

I'd be lying if I said being home isn't making me extremely anxious. And I guess the biggest reason why is because I feel bad for how much I hurt everyone I love the last time I was here. I'm not afraid of relapsing because I know deep down, I won't. I have a baby on the way. And I have a girl to win over.

It'll take some time, but when I'm one year sober, I'm getting my girl back. And when she's finally mine, I'll never do anything to mess that up again.

HALEY

After hugging me good-bye, Cade's parents head outside with him trailing behind. Through the window, I see his mom hug him tightly, the look of nervousness evident on her face. I know she's scared to leave him, and I don't blame her.

But when she hugged me good-bye, she whispered, "Look after him."

And that's something I plan to do. As best as I can—without overstepping, of course.

In so many of my books, I've read about gritty relationships and loving someone through the times when you want to give up. But none of the books had anything on what Cade and I are going through as a couple.

Yet I find myself thinking ... *What would those characters do in our situation?*

But the truth is, it doesn't matter. My and Cade's story isn't a novel. We're just us. And to a lot of people, I bet they'd look at our relationship and think we'd never make it back to each other. Not completely anyway. But I know they are wrong.

I love that man with my whole heart. And I'd wait for him forever if I had to.

A few minutes later, Cade walks back inside the house. He wipes his eyes with his sleeve and catches me watching him.

"Allergies," he says with a shrug. "You know … damn trees and shit."

My brother and Watson sit in the living room, laughing about something. They look relaxed, like a weight has been lifted, and they joke around like they're kids. All because their best friend is home and healthy.

I touch Cade's arm, and the shock that shoots up my hand, traveling through my body, has me pulling away from him, not wanting to overstep. "Are you all right?"

He lifts himself up onto the countertop, his legs dangling down, and he nods slowly. "I guess. I don't know. I just feel out of sorts. In rehab, as much of a pain as it was … everything was scheduled, down to the minute. Now, well, I just feel kind of—"

"Out of control?" I whisper.

"Yeah, kind of."

As his eyes stare into mine, I see that same look of sadness that's always been there, and I wonder if he'll always carry that with him.

"I gotta go talk to LaConte at some point this week. Figure all that shit out."

"Maybe you need to create a schedule of your own?" I shrug. "You know, block off certain times to do things, like work out, homework, things like that?"

He looks down, growing visibly embarrassed. "Remember how I told you that, at rehab, I spent a lot of time taking care of animals? Specifically the horses?" He exhales. "I actually liked that."

I open my mouth to answer, but there's a knock on the door, and when I peer around, glancing out the window, I smile at Cade. "It's Link. I'm sure he's here to see you."

He hops down, shocking me when he bends down and kisses my forehead. "Thank you, Haley."

"For what?" I whisper, weak in the knees from a damn forehead kiss.

"For saving my life," he says softly, his eyes lingering on mine for a moment longer before he walks around me and opens the door for Link to step inside.

Wanting to give them some time to talk, I head toward the stairs. "Going to go do one last sweep of my room," I say to my brother as I pass by. "In case I left anything behind."

Hunter gives me a look. "Hales, *of course* you left something. It's you we're talking about." He laughs, looking at Watson. "Now that she's moved out, we won't find random change, papers, and hair elastics everywhere." His eyes widen. "Or the five thousand water bottles."

"Eff off. I'm pregnant. I need the water," I grumble, climbing up the stairs.

Hunter has always been particular, neat, and put together. Me ... not so much.

A quick sweep ends up taking me over twenty-five minutes. I gather up a few odds and ends and a hoodie I found in one of the dressers. But for the most part, I have everything moved into my new place.

"As always, Hunter was right."

"Talking to yourself, Haley baby?" Cade drawls.

I yelp and damn near jump out of my skin, startled from him sneaking up on me.

I turn to see him leaning against my doorframe, and he looks so handsome. His hair is cut on the sides but a little longer on top. There's something about him that feels like home. And I so wish I could hug him, burying my face into it and breathing in his scent.

His eyes dart around the room before stopping on the bookcase. "You didn't want to take it?" He walks toward it, running his hand along the wood. "I can make it better. Or paint it a different color if you've changed your mind on the powder-puff blue."

"I *do* want it," I say softly. "It's my favorite thing ever. And you know that's my favorite color." My voice cracks the slightest bit, but I try to keep it together. I need to be strong. For him. "It's beautiful and absolutely perfect and everything I always pictured it to be in my mind, growing up. But it means so much to me mostly because you built it for me." I pause, my hands fidgeting together nervously. "But because you made it for me to have here, I didn't want to take it with me when I moved out." I shrug. "Besides ... Hunter and Watson probably would have put a dent in it or something when they moved it."

"Where are your books?" he asks, not looking at me.

"They are back in their respective boxes." I try to say it lightly, but it's actually painful to say the words.

I put so much work into unboxing them and setting them up just right. But I needed to move out of this house. He needs time and space to heal.

He walks toward me, stopping so close that it actually hurts to not be able to reach out and touch him. My entire body buzzes, coming to life because he's near me.

"This bookcase is and will always be yours. I don't care where you—or *we*—live. It's yours, Haley."

I've felt homesick since the day he left. And even now, having him here, but not actually with me … it's agony. If someone hated me and created a hell just for me, this would be it.

"It's so hard not to kiss you, Haley." His voice is tortured. "So. Fucking. Hard."

"I know," I whisper.

I open my mouth to say something else, but I feel a flutter. A feeling I was hoping and waiting for. A few times, I thought I might have felt it, but there's no denying it this time. Our baby just kicked me. Hard.

"Ouch," I breathe out, smiling a little.

Cade's hand flies to my arm, panic written all over his face. "Are you okay? What's wrong? Is something—"

Without explanation, I take his hand and place it on my stomach. And then I wait. And when his eyes widen and he looks down at me, an array of emotions flooding his face, the tears well in my eyes. Because that look of sadness in his eyes? It disappears for a second. And my heart swells just to see him in peace.

"Is that our baby?" he whispers just as he or she kicks again. "That *is* our baby. Holy shit, Hales. Holy shit." He looks at me, inhaling sharply. "Our baby can fucking kick. I'm going to be a dad. I'm going to be *someone's* dad."

I grin up at him through my tear-blurred vision and nod. "The *best* dad."

He kisses the top of my head.

And I silently thank the tiny human growing in my body. Because I know just how much their daddy needed this moment.

CADE

I climb out of the driver's side of my truck and rush around to help Haley down before she has a chance to get down by herself.

She looks down at me and laughs. "You know I'm not ninety, right? Just pregnant."

"You've got my baby in there, woman." I hold my hand out for her to take, and reluctantly, she does. "Besides, you had to do way too much by yourself while I was gone. I'm going to be on you like the Nerds on those gummy clusters you enjoy so much."

She steps down, giving me a pointed look. "I'm only five months along, Cade. I still have a ways to go before I need help getting out of a vehicle." When she sees me widening my eyes, she shrugs. "Fine. If you want to wait on me hand and foot … I like snacks. Books. And bubble baths."

"And oversize sweatshirts, crunchy Cheetos, and sweatpants." I wink. "Nothing but the best for my baby mama."

I want to hold her hand while we walk into the hospital, but I don't. We might be having a baby together, but we aren't romantically involved right now. So, instead, I hold the door open and rest my hand on her lower back when she walks into the office.

I've been gone for so long that I feel like a stranger in my own life now. For weeks, she's gone about life and done what she needs to do when it comes to appointments and such. And I've been away. I'm not missing anything else. Even if I drive her crazy, I want her to know that I'm not going anywhere. And that she can depend on me.

She checks in with the lady behind the desk, and we have a seat. I look around the room at the posters of birth and breastfeeding. There's a small fish tank in the corner and a kids section for the moms who have to bring other children with them to their appointments.

A couple walks out through the door. The woman looks like she's about to pop and sighs like she's frustrated. As she waddles along, he takes her hand, giving her a reassuring smile before opening the outside door and leaving.

He gets to be there for her without rules or limits. I wish I had that. I wish I were wired normal so I could just give Haley what she needs right now.

Haley flips through a magazine, but isn't really looking at it, and after a few minutes, a lady dressed in scrubs comes out and calls her name.

Standing, I follow her toward the lady.

Haley glances back at me. "Don't you dare look at the scale when they weigh me. Or this will be the first and last appointment you get to join."

"Regretting those two doughnuts on the way here already?" I whisper, and she shoots me a harsh glare. "I'm kidding, Haley baby. Honestly, you've never looked more gorgeous."

She rolls her eyes like I'm lying. But the truth is … I mean every word.

HALEY

The ultrasound tech tells us we're having a baby boy, and Cade wipes his eyes before picking my hand up and pressing his lips to it.

"I'll admit, I've been terrified of having a boy. I wanted a girl, who would be just like you. Not a boy who might be a little shit like me." He sniffles. "But seeing him? Seeing he's real and he's ours?" His voice cracks, and he shakes his head. "We're having a son, Haley. I love him so much already."

Tears stream down my face as I look from Cade to the black-and-white screen in front of us, and I nod. "Me too."

After the time I went to see Cade at rehab and told him the news that he was going to be a father, I expected him to be freaked out. But when he promised me he'd be here for our baby, I started thinking about names for either a boy or a girl. I thought long and hard about something. Eli was Cade's very best friend. He loved Eli beyond measure. And what better way to honor Eli than to name our firstborn after him?

I might not have known Eli, but I know he means a lot to Cade, so he's special to me too.

"Cade?" I whisper, nervous to tell him what's on my mind.

"Yeah, baby—Haley?" he says, correcting himself. "What is it?"

"What about Eli? Eli Hunter?" I reach up, wiping under my eyes. "Because, well, Eli was—is so important to you. And Hunter ... he's just really stepped up when it comes to being there for me during this pregnancy. And when it comes to your recovery, he's been so supportive."

"Really?" His voice is shaky as his eyes gloss over. "You'd be okay with naming our baby after Eli?"

I nod. "Yes, of course. If you want to, that is."

"I'd love that." He kisses my hand again. "And even though Watson might be a little bent out of shape and cry himself to sleep when he finds out ... yeah, I can't think of a better middle name than the guy who is responsible for bringing you—the best thing that's ever happened to me—into my life."

Cade

I head into the arena, somehow not nearly as nervous as I should be, and I think it's probably because I'm still on such a high from yesterday when I got to see my baby boy on the screen. And what made it even better was spending the day with Haley. But the closer I get to Coach's office, the more the nerves flood my body, the calmness quickly wearing off.

"Knock, knock," I say as I stick my head in Coach's open doorway. "Your favorite pain in the ass is back to put some more gray hairs on that head of yours."

He tries to give me a stern look, but can't hide his smile. "Gray hairs? What gray hairs are you talking about, Huff?"

I raise my brows. "Hey, if my son-in-law were Cam Hardy, I'd have some gray hairs too, Coach."

Standing, he walks around his desk and pulls me in for a hug. "Never thought I'd be so damn happy to see your face, ya asshole." He shakes me lightly. "You look good, kid. Really good."

Patting his back before he releases me, I take a seat in the chair across from him once he's back behind his desk.

I shift in my seat, fidgeting nervously because, truth be told, I've never felt so ashamed in my life. "I'm, uh … really sorry, Coach. I hope you know that."

"Tell me what you're sorry for, Cade."

"For lying. For doing drugs. And for letting those drugs come between you and the season you deserve. For letting you and my teammates down. For being an absolute moron." I stop. "I can go on, if you want."

Talking to LaConte has always come so easy to me. Aside from when I was high, of course. Because I was so fucking scared he'd notice something was up with me, I'd avoid eye contact as much as I could. Which, yeah, that was hard. But he's the best coach anyone could ask for. I hate myself for letting him down after he gave me a chance.

"Our season wasn't going to be perfect anyway, Huff. It's not easy to find our footing right away after losing so many big players on our team. I knew we'd have our work cut out for us this season." His lips fall into a flat line. "Did I think my best defenseman was on drugs and was going to be shipped off to rehab? Well … truthfully, no. I'm pretty good at seeing shit coming, but that one, yeah, I missed it. And, sure, it didn't help our season any, not having you. That's for sure." He bobs his head like he's thinking. "That's the way it goes in hockey—any sport, I suppose. Sometimes, you're on top. Other times, you're scrounging around on the bottom." His lips turn up the slightest bit. "Or like my college coach used to say, 'Sometimes, you're the windshield, and sometimes, you're the bug." He sighs. "But we've been holding our own. We miss you—there's no doubt about that. But the boys have worked hard, and if you ask me, this season hasn't been all bad. All things considering."

He stops, pulling in a breath and leaning over his desk a little more. "You know what I never got the chance to tell you, kid? Before you left, Boston called me." He tips his face up to look at me. "The Bruins, kid. The fucking Bruins wanted you."

My breath hitches as I let his words fully wash over me. And realize that … I blew it.

"Well, on the bright side of me fucking that up … I hear it's really fucking cold there. So, that might be tough on my nuts, you know?" I joke to lighten Coach's mood, but it doesn't work. "I'm more of a sunshine boy, to be honest."

"You play hockey," he mutters. "On *ice*."

"Yeah, but when I'm done, I don't have to walk outside to a fucking blizzard." I shrug. "Now, that would suck."

"Huff, are you forgetting that Cam Hardy plays for the Bruins? You'd be skating alongside him."

"You mean, I would have," I say, giving him a pointed look. "Before I did a bunch of drugs and landed myself in rehab." When Coach gives me a harsh glare, I shrink in my seat. "Sorry. Too soon?"

"I'm not convinced that they won't be calling again. I think they will. Maybe not this year, but next." He reclines in his seat, strumming his fingers on his chin. "You're *that* good, Huff. At least, you are when you want to be. When you're clear-minded."

"You can just say when I'm not on drugs. I don't mind," I deadpan.

"Goddammit, Huff. Stop trying to joke everything off and just be serious with me for five minutes, would you? Letting yourself feel pain isn't going to be the demise of you. Not feeling it? Well, that could be." He pulls his hat off, holding it above his head. "I'm pretty sure ten more gray hairs just popped up in the time you've been sitting here." Pulling it back over his head, he clears his throat. "If what you want is to play professional hockey, I'll do everything in my power to get you there, Cade." He pauses for a beat. "But if that isn't what you want? If being on the ice at the NHL level isn't your dream? Well ... that's fine too. Hell, Huff, I don't give a fuck if you want to be an astronaut or a NASCAR driver. Whatever you want to do with your life, that's what I'm pushing for."

I look away, ashamed as I gather the courage to open up. *It's Coach. I can trust him.*

"Eli, he, uh ... he always wanted to be a Wolf here at Brooks. More than anything, he wanted us to come here and play together. And after that, he wanted to be on any NHL team that would take him." My voice grows thicker. Getting the words out gets harder. "Least I can do is carry out part of his dream. He might not be able to do it, but I can."

"I didn't know him personally, but from what I've gathered, Eli had a bright future, Cade. He was a good kid. But things happen. Awful, fucking terrible, unfair things." His eyes soften. "You can't turn back time. And you also can't carry the guilt of that night around anymore. From what I've been hearing lately, you have too much to be thankful for." He pauses, inhaling. "I'm going to ask you, and you're going to be honest. Eli aside, do you want to play professional hockey?"

My chest tightens. And breathing becomes a little harder as I drop my gaze down. "No." I barely croak out the single word.

"Is that why you were joking around about losing a chance with the Bruins because you went to rehab? Instead of trying to think of a way to make them want you again?"

"No. Well, yeah. Maybe." I shrug, feeling embarrassed. "I don't know. I'm sorry I wasted your time, Coach."

"What in the hell does that nonsense mean?" His eyebrows shoot together. "Wasted my time?"

"You let me into this program even though you knew I was a fuckup. And you shared your knowledge and resources to make me good enough to be noticed by the pros, but I fucked that up without knowing it." I pull my lips to the side as my knee bounces. "Now, there's a possibility I could get another shot. And here I am, telling you I don't want it. No matter what I do, I fuck up."

"I don't give a shit if you want to work at McDonald's, Huff. I just want you to be happy and healthy." His head dips to the side. "But answer me this: have you always known you don't want that life? Or did you decide recently?"

I know right then that I'm done lying. To myself. To Coach. To everyone.

"I'm an addict, Coach." I say the words for the first time, almost not recognizing it's my own voice saying them. "Do you really think that type of lifestyle is what I need? Fame? Loads of money? Appearances and parties?" I shake my head. "It's not. All I wanna do is be the man Haley and the baby deserve. Not the strung-out one. Not the dude going to parties and getting fucked up off his ass. The one who doesn't know what he has." I swallow. "If you put me in the limelight, that's exactly who I'll be. I'm not strong enough to be anything else."

"So, you want to give up all aspects of hockey after your time at Brooks is over?" he asks, but there's no judgment in his voice.

"I love hockey. I love the way it feels when my skates touch the freshly groomed ice. I love the sound of the crowd and the buzz of their energy. I love how bright the lights are in the arena, and I love how unpredictable it all is." I smile sadly. "But I mostly love hockey because it's where I feel him most."

"Eli," Coach says, and I nod.

I drag a hand down my face, hating that I'm about to break Coach's heart. "My days of hockey are over. Not just my future in the pros, but my time as a Wolf. I'm sorry. I wanted to come back strong and help the team get to a Frozen Four. But I need to walk away." I exhale. "Even if that's terrifying. Because without it, I don't know who I am. But I also know I can't afford to get injured and need painkillers. So, the way I see it, it's a dead-end street. One that I don't want to continue on."

The room grows quiet, but the silence between us screams loudly in my ears.

Finally, Coach speaks. "I can't say I'm not sad because I am. I've coached a ton of players, and you're one of the most talented yet. But I respect the hell out of you for making this decision, Huff. It's not easy to set those tough boundaries you need in order to stay healthy. You're a good man. And I'm proud of you." He reaches over, patting the top of my hand quickly before pulling back. "You'll probably think I'm crazy. But I'll ask you anyway. Have you ever considered coaching?" He shrugs. "Might be something to look into."

"A coach should be someone the players look up to. An example of who they want to be." My head hangs. "Who the fuck would look at me and want to walk in my shoes?" I look up at the pictures scattered on his walls. Some of his daughter and granddaughter, others of his wife, but a lot of his team. "Your players trust you because they respect you. Why would anyone respect me?"

"Trust and respect are earned, Huff." His voice is suddenly somber. "Don't count yourself out yet. You've got work to do. That's obvious. But I believe in you. Besides, the best coaches have learned a lot of hard lessons. I dare to say you've certainly earned your stripes when it comes to that. So, what do you say? Maybe, down the road, you'll give it a try?"

"I don't know." I blow out a breath. "Everything is such a mess right now. Don't get me wrong; I know I'm to blame. I made it this way." I rub my eyes, wiping away the wetness. "I'm fresh out of rehab, trying to find my place on campus as a normal student instead of a Wolf. I can't be with Haley until I've been sober for a year. I'm going to have a kid, and I don't know the first thing about babies. I don't want to fuck up again. I'm fucking petrified, Coach. I'm scared that just me won't be enough for Haley and the baby. They deserve everything." I pause. "I mean, if I'm never an NHL star or inducted into the Hall of Fame, if I don't win some crazy award or have millions of dollars in my bank account ... what will that make me?"

He smiles a bit as he leans forward. "Well, that'll make you Cade Huff. Father to a beautiful baby. Hopefully future husband to Haley. A son to your parents. A friend to your teammates." He reaches over, patting my arm. "And I think that means you'll be plenty, my boy."

I look at Coach. His face shows he's not bullshitting. And LaConte isn't the type to fake something.

Eventually, I smile. "Yeah, I guess you're right."

"Boy, I'm always right," he says before the corner of his lips turns up a tiny bit. "I can't promise anything, but I'd like to make a few phone calls and figure out a way for you to still be involved with the team." He pauses. "If you want to be, that is. Because the way I see it, you're a huge asset to us. Even if you aren't on the ice."

"A huge asset or a huge pain in the ass?" I laugh. "And ... yeah, I'd love that—to be part of the team in some way." I nod, and then my face grows grim. "Plus, I need some sort of schedule. This being all over the place these first few days has been driving me mad."

"Like I said, I can't promise anything yet. But I'll find out this week and reach out to you." He chuckles. "Who am I kidding? As soon as you walk out of here, I'm going to start my phone calls on this."

Taking that as my cue to leave him be, I stand. I hold my hand out, and he takes it in his and shakes it.

"Thank you, Coach." My throat swells. "All of us are lucky to have you."

Coach has always been a hard-ass. Never one to show much emotion. So, when he nods his head and says, "Nah, I'm the lucky one," I've got to remind myself to keep it together.

He could have shitcanned me from the program altogether back when he found out I was using. Instead, he demanded I get help, and now, he tried to even get me my spot back. He's helping me by trying to keep me involved with the team. The man is a saint. No matter how much of an asshole he can be at times.

I let a lot of people down. But I'm going to make it up to them. I don't know how, but I will.

28

HALEY

After going home for the weekend to see my parents, I finally get back to Brooks and pull into the driveway. A yawn rips through me as I shift the car into park. Sleep has been hard to come by lately. I just can't seem to shut my mind off. As exciting as having a baby is, I'm scared. I don't know what to expect. And even though I love my parents dearly, and they weren't the worst parents in the world, they also aren't exactly people I'd turn to for parenting advice. They would be around for holidays and major things, but their minds would be thinking about work. I don't want to be like that with my son. I want to be present. Always.

Grabbing my bag from the backseat, I head inside. I can't wait to put on a baggy sweatshirt and sweatpants. These days, even leggings are too restricting.

As I head toward my bedroom, I walk past the room where I've started to put a few odds and ends of baby gear in and come to a dead stop. I turn my head, and my hand flies to my mouth as I step inside to what is now a beautiful nursery.

After the ultrasound a few weeks ago, I briefly mentioned to Cade that I wanted to do a woodsy theme in the baby's room. Looking around, I don't know why it surprises me that he listened to every single word. Of course he did. He's Cade. He missed nothing, even putting outlines of mountains with bears, foxes, and other creatures throughout the room.

Against the dark forest-green accent wall, above where the crib is, are wooden letters that make up the name Eli Hunter. Maybe it's the hormones or simply because Cade has the most beautiful heart, but I cry like a baby.

Walking to the corner of the room, I take a seat in the glider and look at the small bookcase next to it. It's filled with children's books, all handpicked by Cade.

I gaze around, unable to wipe the emotional smile off my face. This entire nursery was created with love, and it shows.

After God knows how long, I finally push myself up from the chair because like always, I need to pee. And after using the bathroom, I wash my hands and head toward my bedroom. Only to pass another surprise in the room across from the nursery.

My beautiful blue bookcase sits against the wall. But this time, my books are put away, all seemingly in the perfect place. And in the corner of the room is a cream-colored chaise lounge with a baby-blue throw blanket on it. I gaze around at the rest of the bookish decor that was never here before, and I stare in absolute amazement. Because Cade is so unbelievably thoughtful.

My very own reading area. No, my own reading room. As big as my heart swells, I also feel a pang of pain. Because as much as I know I need to walk across the street and thank Cade, what I really want to do is run to him as fast as my swollen feet will carry me. And to hug and kiss him. And never let him go. But the reality is, I can't do that. And that makes me feel painstakingly lonely.

I'm so incredibly in love with Cade Huff. And I'm counting down the days until I can show him.

CADE

An hour ago, I watched Haley's car pull into her driveway, but I still haven't seen her. I'm sure she'll come over eventually. And I know I'll have to settle for a hug, but that's better than nothing. Anytime I get to hold her close, even for just a moment, is worth it.

I sit in the recliner while Watson occupies the couch, and Hunter's sprawled out on the love seat. Sometimes, I get the impression that they feel like they can't leave me alone or something. I've been home for weeks now.

LOST BOY

I'm settling into a routine, and I'm fine. I don't want them—or anyone—to feel like they need to spend their days babysitting me, like I can't be trusted.

Out of the corner of my eye, I see Watson's phone buzz, and he checks it before tucking it back in his pocket.

"You know, guys, I appreciate the whole babysitting thing and all, but you can go hang out with your women now. Who says I want to look at y'all's ugly faces anyhow?"

They both shift uncomfortably in their seats, but Hunter tries to joke it off as he says, "What the hell are you talking about, fool?" He shrugs. "If I was babysitting you, I'd be charging your ass a fee."

Watson doesn't respond. Instead, he looks at his phone once more before he inhales sharply. Standing abruptly, he shoves his phone into his pocket and wrings his hands together.

"Gentry, do you have ants in your pants or what?" I ask before widening my eyes. "Or do you need a little trip to the free clinic to clean up your crabbies?"

"I don't have fucking crabs, Huff," he grunts, annoyed.

"Nice to hear since we share a toilet seat and all. And now that Haley's moved out, I'm not entirely sure who's cleaning that bad boy." I sprawl my arms out. "Well then, if you don't have crabs, what in the fuck is with the sudden fidgeting?"

"Go on, Watty boy. Tell him," Hunter tosses out lazily.

Watson stops fidgeting, and he takes a deep breath. "Huff, you know how, like, you're going to be a dad now?"

"What, Gentry, are you knocked up too?" I grin, not knowing where the hell he's going with this.

"Well, no. But I'm sort of a husband," he mutters, shifting around on his feet. "I, uh ... kind of married Ryann." He swallows hard, dragging a hand through his hair. "Hunter knows already. It happened while you were at rehab, and I just never knew when the right time to tell you was. I didn't want you to feel like you were in there, missing everything. But now, well ... I could be in a bit of a mess." He cracks his fingers nervously. "Say something, would you?"

"Well, if you have a belated bachelor party ... I'll probably have to sit that one out." I shrug. "Unless you're planning on having sparkling cider or soda pop. But a cheese platter? That I could get down with."

"I'm so fucking confused," Hunter says, dragging his hand down his face. "I knew about the marriage shit, but now, I don't get it. Why are you in a mess?"

Before he can respond, I can't help myself as I throw something out there to lighten the mood. "Damn, Gentry. That's a big commitment just to have sex."

"Well, that isn't why we did it, dickwad."

205

"I know. I'm just fucking with you," I say, standing to give him a quick side hug. "Congratulations, Gentry. Looks like we both skipped some steps with the women we love, huh?"

"I never told you I love Ryann," he says, his eyes narrowing at me. "Guess you love Haley though?"

"That woman is fixing to have my baby. Of course I love her." I look at Hunter, feeling the need to add something. "But whether I slipped one past the goalie or not … I love your sister, Thompson, just FYI. So, don't kill me."

"I might kill you for saying shit like *slipped one past the goalie.*" He grimaces before standing. "Okay, Gentry, stop dodging my question. Why are you in a mess?"

"It's a long story," Watson huffs out. "I'll tell you more when I can."

"But if you're married, why isn't she ever here?" I narrow my eyes. "Or why aren't you with her?"

"Dude, she's been busy since you've been home. Besides, we wanted this to be your chill zone. I didn't want to bring someone over you don't really know when you're fresh out of rehab." He smiles. "But trust me, I spend a lot of time at her place."

Before we can pester him for more information, there's a knock at the door.

"I'll get it," I say nonchalantly, hoping like hell it's my baby mama. Seeing her is always the best part of my day.

Strutting toward the door, I pull it open, and there stands Haley in an oversize crewneck sweatshirt with some bookish saying above a picture of a stack of books, paired with black sweatpants and those ugly but adorable-on-her UGG boots. Just the sight of her has my heart skipping a beat, and I suck in a breath.

"Hey, beautiful." I smile. "Why did you knock? We've all told you this is still your place. You can just come in."

She stares up at me, her eyes growing mistier by the second. "Cade … thank you." Stepping toward me, she throws her arms around me and buries her face in my shirt. "My reading room, our baby's nursery." She weeps, pushing her face against my chest. "It's all perfect," she whispers. "I love them both so much."

Stunned, I don't react for a moment, but finally, I wrap my arms around her. "You're welcome, Haley baby. I just wanted to make you smile." When she peers up at me, I swipe my thumbs across her cheeks to wipe away her tears. "Smile, not cry, beautiful."

"I'm just so happy," her voice squeaks, but she gives me a tiny smile. "No one has ever done anything like that for me."

"Well, no one has ever put a baby inside you either, have they?" I wink before kissing her forehead. "You deserve that and so much more. I promise, now that I'm back, I'm going to do my best to keep you smiling—even if I can't do it the way that I'd like to. I'll be the best baby daddy and friend you've ever seen."

"You're so much better of a man than you give yourself credit for," she whispers. "I wish you'd see yourself through my eyes."

My heart squeezes, and I hug her against me tighter. "By the way, I'm sorry if I screwed any of your book places up. I was going strictly by memory with that. And I was running out of time."

She breathes out a laugh against my shirt. "It was fine. No, it was perfect." She gazes up at me, looking at me with those eyes that tell me she's holding back because she has to. "Come over for dinner tonight? I can show you some of the adorable baby clothes I picked up this weekend." She rolls her eyes up toward the ceiling and nods. "I dare say we're going to have the best-dressed babe around."

"I'd love that," I say, raising my eyebrows. "But you have to let me take care of dinner."

"But you don't cook," she says, giving me an inquisitive look.

I shrug. "Yeah. But I'm the best ever at ordering takeout."

"Orange chicken and spring rolls?" she gasps, widening her eyes.

"Anything for you." I tip my chin up before she steps back. I ache to keep her body close to mine and kiss her lips. But at least having dinner with her means I get to be near her longer today. I'll take what I can get.

"I'll see you in a bit?" she asks softly, and I nod.

"Yep. I'll be over with Chinese food in hand for the prego lady." I wink. "See you soon."

"Bye, Hales!" Watson hollers from the living room before she leaves.

"Yeah, fuck you, sister. We just chopped liver?" Hunter yells. "Don't worry about coming to see us!"

She shakes her head but smiles. "Hi, boys. Bye, boys!" Holding her hand up, she waves before walking back across the road.

To a house I wish I lived in with her.

HALEY

The pride I feel in my chest as I watch the Wolves win the Frozen Four and become champions is huge. But it doesn't compare to how big my heart swells as I watch Cade down there with them, basking in the accomplishment. Only now, he's behind the glass as a student coach for the defensive players instead of out on the ice. And the best part about it is, because Coach LaConte is a literal saint, he fought for Cade to keep his scholarship, and won. His argument was that players who are injured are often given the chance to keep their scholarships. Cade's injuries might not be seen with a set of eyes, but they are still there. His addiction is something he'll always have to fight against. But LaConte truly believes that, even though Cade isn't laced up and on the ice anymore, he is still a huge part of the team. And could be a very valuable piece to the defense program at Brooks.

Though the game was intense, there's a look of peace on his face that I never saw when he was a player. A sense of contentment maybe. Whatever it is, I love it. And it makes me so happy for not only him, but our family too.

If I said everything has been easy since he got home nearly ten weeks ago, I'd be lying. Finding a way to cope as friends and not cross any imaginary boundaries, well, it's hard.

The way I love him makes this non-romantic relationship we have incredibly challenging at times. Especially when there's that magnetic pull between us, where our souls just want to collide with each other. I can't say it gets easier, but I guess we're learning what works for us. Which seems to be just being transparent. Talking to each other when one of us feels frustrated with how things are with this whole *non-romantic, but having a baby* thing. I try not to mention how badly I want to be with him because that somehow feels like I'd be pressuring him to go against the rules he's set in place. And I'd never do that.

I'll wait as long as I have to, but I'm already counting down the days for when I can hold him like he's mine. If that day ever comes, that is. I suppose a lot could happen in the next seven months while we trudge toward his one-year mark of sobriety.

The baby jabs his foot into the wall of my stomach, and I cringe. "Wowzer, you're active tonight."

"It could have been that humungous soda you downed," Sutton says, her lips in a line and her eyes wide. "Just sayin'."

"Or all that candy," Remi adds, looking at Sutton and shrugging. "If someone fed me that shit, I'd probably have my underwear on my head, dancing right now."

"Thank God no one did then," I mutter. "Also, it's not like I eat candy all day, every day, jerks. Just for special occasions." I wave my hand out to the ice. "This qualified as special."

"Oh, yeah? What was yesterday's occasion?" Remi snorts before I shoot her down with some daggers, and she shrugs. "Sorry."

I'm thirty weeks pregnant, and even though I still have ten weeks to go, give or take, I feel like a whale. And my ribs hurt. And I pee every half hour. And my ass has now doubled in size, and I'm pretty sure it's starting its own website because it's so large.

On top of all of that, women still throw themselves at Cade right under my nose. He, of course, turns them down. At least, from what I've seen, he does. But apparently, the fact that he's been to rehab only makes him hotter to the female population at Brooks.

But at the end of the day, it's me who he's delivering treats and things to weekly. Whether it's with a new sweatshirt, a baggy pair of sweatpants, or some sugar-and-butter-packed baked goods … he makes me feel special. So, I'm thankful for that.

Feeling his eyes on me, I find him down below and wave. He gives me a thumbs-up—something he's been doing at the games lately as a way to make sure I'm feeling okay. I smile and hold my thumb up for a second before dropping it down.

God, he looks so good.

He's more muscular than ever. And there's just a glow on his face and a light in his eyes that was never there before. I'm sure it was at one time, before I met him.

All I have to do is look at Cade, and I somehow feel safer. And I hope, one day, he feels the same way about me.

CADE

"Is this how you thought you'd end the season?" Coach asks, clapping his hand on my shoulder.

"About to have a kid. Off the team. Sober as a nun, sipping Coca-Cola instead of downing shots?" I tilt my head to the side. "Absolutely, Coach."

He chuckles, and his hand squeezes my shoulder before releasing it. "Proud of you, Huff. You make a damn good addition to the coaching staff."

"Thanks, Coach," I say and look toward the team celebrating. "They deserve this. Each and every one of them."

"They do. And you're still one of them, son. Once a Wolf, always a Wolf." He smacks my back lightly before walking away.

And I watch the best group of dudes I know completely freak out because they've worked their entire life to get to this point.

I don't feel jealous or envious. And I'm not beating myself up inside that I'm on this side of the Plexiglas and not out there. But what I do think about is how much Eli would have loved this. And how I wish he could have been here with me, celebrating this day that will never be forgotten by any of us here.

And I tell myself that he's with me. Right now and always.

30

Haley
Nine Weeks Later

I stand in the spray of the shower for God knows how long. I don't feel well today, but I'm not having contractions. At least, I don't think I am.

I feel crampy. Like I have my period, but times ten. The pain can't be timed, and it doesn't stop and start back up. It's continuous and annoying. I've chalked it up to likely just being some Braxton-Hicks, that my body is just preparing me for what's to come, but when I become lightheaded, I realize something isn't right.

I blink a few times, wondering why my head feels so fuzzy and thinking of how to make it go away, coming up with nothing. I turn the shower off and grab my towel. I only make it a few steps before I feel like I'm going to faint, and I quickly sink to the toilet seat.

The pain in my abdomen worsens, and I cry out in agony. I know I need to call Cade and have him take me to the hospital, but my phone's in my room. I'll be strong enough to move from this spot in a few minutes. I'll regain my strength and then call him, and he can take me to the doctor to be checked. It'll all be fine.

This is normal, I'm sure.

CADE

I knock on the door for the fifth time, and still, no answer. I don't like to just barge into Haley's house—it doesn't feel right—but right now, knowing she could go into labor at any time ... fuck it, I'm going in.

Pushing the door open, right away, I notice how quiet it is. Maybe she's sleeping though.

"Haley?" I call out, not loud enough to scare the absolute shit out of her if she's sleeping but enough to hopefully cause her to stir. "It's Cade. You all right?"

No answer. *Great.*

I check each room, my heart beating faster when I find another empty. Finally, the only room left is the bathroom. The last thing I want to do is invade her privacy, but it isn't like her to not answer the door. Maybe she's out on a walk, but I'm not taking any chances.

I knock on the door. There's no answer, but I push the door open anyway. And when I do, my heart leaps into my throat. I bolt toward Haley, who's lying on the floor. Her skin is so pale, and her body is only partially covered with her towel. But that's not what has my body turning to ice. What does is the blood on the floor, telling me something is clearly wrong.

Very wrong.

I shake her a few times before putting my ear to her chest. Tears of relief fall from my eyes when I hear her heart beating.

"Baby, wake up," I cry, lifting her into my arms, but she doesn't respond.

Taking my phone out, I dial 911 and yell frantically into the phone for them to send help.

I break down, holding her close to me, begging her to just open her eyes.

I look down at Eli before shifting my gaze to his mom. A few hours ago, they delivered him by emergency C-section, and now ... he's in my arms while Haley still hasn't woken up. The doctors said that what caused her distress was her placenta detaching, but they are confident she'll be fine. So, now, here I sit, holding our son and praying to a god that I don't even really know exists for her to just wake up from the anesthesia and meet our boy.

"You're so lucky," I whisper to him. "Your mama is an angel."

"Is that right?" Haley's voice croaks, making my eyes fly to her.

I'm on my feet and at her side in seconds, kissing her forehead.

"It is, but I'm still a little angry with you right now. So … for today, I might call you a major pain in my ass." My vision gets blurry from the tears that she always brings out in me, turning me into a giant pussy. "You scared the shit out of me, angel."

"Sorry," she whispers before holding her arms out for Eli. "He's the most perfect thing I've ever seen."

Gently, I position him on her, setting pillows at her sides so that she's more comfortable before sitting on the edge of the bed.

"More perfect than me?" I narrow my eyes at her. "He's been here for a few measly hours, and already, he's shit his pants, and yet he's more perfect than me? This is bullshit."

She starts to giggle but then stops. "I'm not going to lie; I'm worried about how awful this scar is going to feel when the epidural or whatever is blocking the pain wears off."

"Are you in any pain right now? Do you need me to get you something?" I start to get up, but her voice stops me.

"No, I'm fine. Just stay here." She looks down at Eli, brushing her finger against his cheek. "A few hours on Earth, and your mama missed it." She brings him closer, inhaling him. "From now on, I'll be right here."

I look down at the two of them, and I feel every bit as happy as I do sad. Because this is a moment we'll never get back. And if I hadn't made the choices I did in the past, I'd be able to kiss Haley right now. But I can't. Not right now.

I'm so in love with this woman, and I can't even tell her. Not yet anyway. So, instead, I press another kiss to the top of her head.

"I'm so proud of you, Haley. Thank you. For giving me the chance to be his dad." I close my eyes. "I promise, I won't mess this up."

I feel her head nod softly. "I know," she whispers. "I know you won't."

And I mean it. For once, I won't fuck something up.

31

HALEY

After bringing me a bottle and setting a can of Dr. Pepper and a muffin next to the remote on the coffee table, Cade heads toward the door before he stops—just like he always does.

I bring the bottle to Eli's mouth, and per usual, he quickly starts feeding. Nursing wasn't something my body wanted any part of. Neither was pumping or really anything that involved a milk supply. And as frustrating as that was, what mattered to me was that Eli was fed. So, with Cade's reassurance that it was fine, we made the call to switch to formula.

"You sure you're going to be okay?" Cade says—which, since I had the baby, is the same thing he asks before every time he leaves me. "Because I can totally tell LaConte that—"

"Cade, we're good," I assure him, knowing he can't just tell Coach LaConte he isn't coming in now that he's actually working as a coach. "Go to work before you're late."

He widens his eyes. "Yeah, and then they'll think I'm back to—"

"Don't you dare finish that sentence," I warn him. "We're good."

Walking over to us once again, he kisses Eli's head and then mine. "I'll be back in a few hours. Text me what you want for a coffee order today since you've been changing it so dang often that I can't even keep up, woman."

"You know, you don't always have to bring me coffee. I know you're busy with hockey training." I cringe. "And staying up with this little man so often."

As many times as I've told Cade to go to sleep and that I'll take the night shift with our two-week-old, who has no interest in sleeping during the night hours, Cade insists. Which often leads to us binge-watching shows all night. Okay, Cade binges. I usually pass out and wake up hours later, somehow tucked into my bed.

Cade has been staying over since we brought Eli home. He sleeps on the couch since my spare bedroom is a gorgeous reading nook. He is the epitome of the perfect partner. My hormones are a mess. I cry at the drop of a hat. But having him here has been a saving grace. I think spending time with the team as a student coach has given him a sense of pride. He's also started a job—which he is loving, teaching kids how to skate on weekends and some weeknights at the arena. He's never said it, but I know it's because he wants to provide for our son. And even though we aren't in a relationship right now, we're still a family. Cade is my family.

Both of our parents have come to visit multiple times since Eli was born. My mother's always had a hard exterior, but I swear I saw it soften when she saw her grandson for the very first time. And Kat and Caden ... they are obsessed. They FaceTime daily.

Hunter stops in far too often and has been deemed a baby hogger by Sutton. Watson won't say it out loud, but he's terrified of holding the baby. And Remi, well, I'm slightly worried she might actually try to steal him sometimes.

We have the greatest support system. And Eli is surrounded by the very best people.

Haley
Four Months Later

Something wakes me up, though I was in such a deep sleep that I'm barely conscious, so I can't figure out what the hell it was. I blame that on the fact that I didn't get Eli down until nearly eleven tonight after he fussed for basically the entire day. I'm wiped.

The sound starts again, and I shoot up in bed to find my phone vibrating on my nightstand. When I see it's a few minutes after midnight, I frown.

Why the hell is Cade calling me this late?

After the first month of Eli's life, I made Cade move back to his house across the road because my couch was far from comfortable and I felt terrible, watching his huge body trying to fit on it.

Dread fills my gut, and I feel guilty that I'm instantly scared that he's off doing something he's not supposed to be doing and has now gotten himself in a mess.

Sliding my finger across the screen, I bring the phone to my ear. "Cade? What's wrong?"

"What's wrong is … it's raining out. And since it's November, that means it's pretty fucking cold. But here I am, outside your door, getting my ass wetter than a sponge in a kitchen sink," he drawls. "And, yeah, I would have just snuck in, but I know you keep a baseball bat beside your door, and I didn't feel like getting my nuts cracked tonight."

"I don't—" I start to say, but he stops me.

"Are you going to let me in, angel? Or what?"

"Yeah ... yeah!" I say, standing up quickly. "But don't you dare wake your son up. That little guy was grumpy today."

"Must get it from his mama," he teases. "Kidding. Hurry up, babe."

I race down the short hallway, my feet padding along the carpet, and I yank the door open. And when his eyes fall to my body, I look down and blush when I remember I'm wearing one of his shirts that I stole when he was away.

"Nice shirt." He smirks. "Tell me, did you get yourself all hot, wearing that in bed while I was gone—"

"Cade," I hiss, "stop." I wave my hand toward him. "What are you doing here?"

A few pieces of wet hair peek out of his hood as he steps through the doorway. He's so damn handsome; it should be illegal or something. He grins at me, showing me that subtle dimple, but when he moves closer to me and closes the door behind him, I can tell he's about to be anything but goofy.

"A year ago on this date, I snuck my pills into the bathroom and got high one last time. Then, the next day, I got in the car with my parents, heading home—or so I thought. I remember every single thing about that day, Haley. Like you coming into my room and trying to talk to me."

"You were angry with me," I utter, biting down on my lip. "Because I'd betrayed you. Or ... you felt like I had."

"Was I mad that you had told everyone the truth about me? Yeah, I was. I was fucking pissed." He stops, his lips wet from being out in the rain. "But you know why I couldn't look at you? Do you know the real reason why I had to walk away that day?"

"Why?" I ask weakly. Not knowing if I even want to hear it. After all, I've always been so in love with him. I'm not sure he'll ever catch up to the way I feel. So, right now, I have no idea what is about to come out of his mouth.

"Because I was so fucking in love with you, Haley, that I knew that if I didn't walk away then, I never would. And you are the best human being I have ever met. You're the sunshine that comes after a heavy rainstorm. The kind that lights up everything it touches. And there I was, a drug addict." He shakes his head.

"The only way I can explain it is, being an addict feels like you're drowning, but you're so consumed with getting high just to feel normal that you stop caring that you're slowly dying and giving up on yourself." He gives me a sad smile, his lips turning up the smallest, tiniest bit. "When I was sitting in rehab, I realized something. The only times I didn't feel like I was drowning in the months before that point were when I was with you. But you needed more than what I was back then. I knew that.

He cups my cheeks. "A year is a long-ass time to wait when it comes to kissing you, Haley Thompson. Or holding you the way I need to. I'll never fuck up from here on out because I never want to go through that again.

"That day you came to see me at rehab, I told you that the day I was one year sober, I was coming for you. Well, here I am. Ready to tell you all the reasons why you should give me a chance even though I know you could do better than me. I'm far from perfect. But I've looked at enough of the descriptions on the backs of those books you love to read, and I know that your idea of a fairy tale often comes from the most flawed beginnings."

He's so close now, sliding one of his hands so that it pushes some of my hair away from my face. "I love the way your face lights up when you talk about Eli. And I adore watching you read one of your porno books, especially when you get to a dirty scene and you blush, glancing around to make sure no one is watching. I love that your hair is frizzy when it rains and that you prefer sweatpants and an oversized sweatshirt to any other article of clothing. And I really, *really* fucking love that you always wear mismatched socks. And it's not on purpose either. You just literally can't find the match for any of them. Your cell phone is never over ten percent charged because you never plug it in at night. Or that someone could give you a million dollars and you'd potentially lose it because you're so dang unorganized that it's painful. And don't even get me started on the places you leave your laptop, car keys, and hair ties." He chuckles. "But as frustrating as it might be to others, I think it's the cutest thing I've ever seen. And I want a lifetime of it." His thumb slides over my bottom lip. "I want a lifetime with you, Haley."

A lump lodges itself in my throat as tears well in my eyes. "If this is only because you feel a responsibility to be with me for Eli … please, don't do this."

"Why would you think that?" He cradles my face in both hands, forcing me to look up at him.

I try to look down, but I can't. So, instead, I squeeze my eyes shut. "Because I've always loved you more, Cade. I've always chased you … and waited for you to stop running so I could catch you." I sniffle. "And for you to actually see me."

"See you, angel?" His voice is raspy now. "All I see *is* you." Bending his neck down, he gazes into my eyes. "Before I even knew there was a baby in our story, I knew we weren't finished. I wanted to let you go because, deep down, I knew you deserved the world, and I was scared I couldn't give it to you. But, Haley, I promise you … those weeks of me fighting my demons, playing in games when I was high off my ass, going through withdrawal, and feeling more alone in rehab than I had my entire life? It was you who got me through it. It was knowing that if I was ever going to get my shot to make you happy, to be the one putting a smile on your face again … I had to get my life together. I'm here today because of you, Haley. Because your love saved my life and I'm ready to be everything you deserve. You and Eli both." He pauses. "My life might not sound like much to a lot of people. No future in professional hockey or being a famous athlete. But in my eyes, spending my life with you and Eli … if you ask me … I won the lottery."

"Do you mean that?" I whisper.

"Yes. It's been one year, Haley. One year without kissing those sweet lips and worshipping your beautiful body." His nose grazes mine. "The longest year of my life. And I can't wait another fucking second."

All at once, his lips are on mine. It's not a slow tease, leading up to something more intimate. It's zero to one hundred in seconds. And before I realize it, my back is pushed against the wall, and my legs are around his waist. His rain-drenched body soaks my shirt, but I'm too drunk off of his kiss to care about how cold it makes me.

I've missed every part of him. His minty kiss, the stubble on his face, the way his body is always warm and makes me want to snuggle into him, the woodsy scent of him when he is this close. Everything. This past year, I'd lie in bed and fantasize, but couldn't actually *feel* him. I felt so homesick because I had to stay far enough away from him to keep myself from leaping into his arms and making him break his rules. Finally, I'm home.

He pulls away. "Fuck, I've wanted to do that for so long," he growls against my lips, his growing erection pushing against my body and making me ache between my legs, to the point of pain. "I need to be inside of you, Haley. If not, I might actually die."

Even given how turned on I am, I giggle against his lips. "Die, huh?"

"Babe, I haven't had sex in a year. My balls might fall off, and then I could bleed to death."

"I don't think it works that way." I smile, peering through my lashes at him. "You haven't been with anyone since me?"

He pulls back, frowning. "Fuck no. I haven't wanted anyone else." He kisses me again. "Have you, uh … been with—"

"No!" I say quickly. "I haven't even looked at another man."

He wiggles his eyebrows. "So, you've just been reading your naughty books? And getting all horned up by yourself?"

My cheeks burn, and I gaze downward, not wanting to answer.

"You have, haven't you?" he grunts. "Fuck, that's hot." Gripping my chin, he smirks. "Did you touch yourself?"

"Sometimes," I barely whisper. "This is embarrassing!"

"What did you imagine when you slipped your fingers inside of yourself, angel?" His voice holds no humor in it now. It's husky, gritty, and filled with desperation.

"You. And me." I swallow. "You doing the things to me that I was reading about. Or ... vice versa."

"Did you get yourself off?" his voice croaks. "Did you come on your fingers, imagining it was my cock?"

"Yes," I breathe out.

"Fuck," he groans. His eyes glaze over as he walks us toward my bedroom.

I'm afraid that if I blink or if I breathe wrong ... I'll wake up and realize I'm dreaming. So, I'm just going to enjoy this. Enjoy it and pray it's real.

CADE

I lean down, setting Haley on the bed before standing over her. I spot the book on her nightstand, and I grab it. I've read the backs of a few of them, but I've never actually opened one of her books to see what's inside.

I open it, flipping through it until I find a page where the dude is going down on his girl, telling her how good she tastes.

Reaching up, she grabs the book and tosses it to the side. "I don't want what's in the book. I want you and me. I've waited a damn year. I want Cade Huff. That's it," she says, suddenly sounding brave.

That is, until I reach for the hem of her shirt.

"Can't I leave it on?" she whines, stopping my fingers from pulling the fabric up. "Please?"

"Angel, I've waited three hundred sixty-five days to fucking worship this perfect body. You think I'm going to let you keep my baggy shirt on when I fuck you for the first time in over a year? It's basically like I'm a virgin again. I need to see you."

Her cheeks turn the deepest red I've ever seen them, and that's saying a lot because everything makes the girl blush.

"Cade ... my body looks different. I have stretch marks and a scar from my C-section." She looks away from me. "What if you don't like what you see? What if it ... turns you off?"

Hovering over her, I lean down and kiss her before placing my hand on her stomach. "Haley, you grew a baby—my baby—in this body. I love every fucking inch of you. I don't give a fuck if you're covered in stretch marks. This is mine. Don't cover it up—ever."

Reaching down, I grip the center of the shirt. Without warning, I rip it right down the middle, leaving her breasts and stomach completely exposed.

Her hands fly to cover herself up, but I catch her wrists, pinning them at her sides against the bed.

"I said, don't cover yourself up. I want to see my beautiful girl." I let my eyes rake down the length of her body. "Fucking perfection. You're even more gorgeous than before."

"Cade," she whimpers, her lips trembling.

"I mean it." Taking her hand, I graze it over the hard bulge in my sweatpants. "Do you feel that, angel? That's what you're doing to me. You're making my dick so hard that I can't think straight. That's how badly I want you. How much I like what I see."

Bending down, I run my tongue between her beautiful tits, taking her nipples into my mouth one at a time before my mouth continues downward. Stopping at the scar from her C-section, I press my lips to it. "You're so stunning," I murmur against her skin. "So. Fucking. Beautiful."

I don't look at her and see stretch marks. I look at her and see a woman who grew a human inside of her. I see a person who went to appointments alone because she loved me so much that she didn't want to burden me with the truth. Even if it was the furthest thing from a burden. I see an angel— my angel. The most stunning woman in the entire world. Now more than ever, even if she doesn't feel like it.

I know she got an IUD after having Eli because I went to the appointment and sat in the waiting room with him while she was in there. And one thing I can't wait to do is fuck her raw. To have nothing between us as I bury my cock inside of her, fucking her into the morning hours to make up for all I've missed.

Time has robbed us of so much. *I* robbed us of so much. No more though. I'm giving back for all I've taken.

Reaching up, she tugs my sweatpants. "Please, Cade. I just need you right now."

I know the feeling. There're so many things I want to do with her, but at this second, I feel like if I don't bury my cock inside of her, I truly might die.

Pulling my sweatpants and boxers off, I climb on top of her, sinking into her heat slowly. She's so fucking tight, and she feels so fucking good. I'm worried I'll blow my load right now.

She lifts up, catching my mouth with hers, and I kiss her, never coming up for air.

"I love you so much," I grumble against her lips.

I plunge into her deeper, and her legs wrap around my waist. I take her hands, lacing my fingers with hers and pushing them against the mattress.

As I pump inside of her, our lips meet again as she stares up at me. Her honey-blonde hair is a beautiful mess.

"I love you so much," she breathes out before kissing me again.

Her head falls back as her hands grip mine harder, her eyebrows pulling together. "Cade. I ... I can't—"

Her chest heaves as she grinds herself harder against my cock, tilting her chin up as she sucks in a breath. "I'm—"

"Come all over my cock. Show me how much you missed me fucking you, angel," I growl in between pumps. "I'm going to come inside of you, filling you so full of my cum to remind you that you are all mine."

As she clenches around me, crying out a muffled scream, I fucking lose it. Of all the times I've imagined this over the past year, none of it came close to actually being balls deep inside of my girl, watching her eyes haze over while she comes undone on my dick.

While our hands squeeze each other tightly, I bury my face in her neck, spilling myself inside of her body, claiming her once and for all.

"I love you, angel," I grunt against her skin, kissing her neck. "So fucking much."

Everything feels so right. And perfect.

33

Haley

I'm snuggled, warm and cozy, in my bed, and it takes me a moment to realize that Eli never woke me up this morning for a feeding. And then last night's events hit me. Cade. Me. Lots of emotions, followed by a bunch of sex. I shoot straight up, and my heart sinks when I realize there's no Cade next to me. Climbing out of bed, I pull some sweatpants and a baggy T-shirt on and head toward the baby's room.

I push the door open, and I see Cade cradling Eli in his arms while he rocks in the rocking chair.

As I walk in, he looks up and smiles. "Morning, Mama."

A shirtless Cade rocking my baby boy is enough to make my heart swell inside my chest to the point that I have to suck in a breath.

"Good morning. How long have you been up?" I look up at the clock. "Holy cow. It's after eight? He usually wakes me up at—"

"Five?" he coos, cocking his head to the side playfully. "I figured you could use more rest. You know, after the night you had." He winks. "You can thank me later. It's fine."

I cross my arms over my chest. "You cannot just leave me in bed alone anymore. Do you understand that?" I tip my chin up. "I literally have PTSD from waking up alone after anytime you and I … connected."

His eyes dazzle with amusement. "Connected, huh? That's what we're calling it?" He glances down at Eli before looking at me again. "I'd call it a lot of things. But, sure … we can go with *connected*. Even though that sounds like I'm connecting a charger to its port." Suddenly, his smirk grows. "Actually, that doesn't sound half-bad. Considering my dick was pound—"

"The baby is literally right here!" I hiss. "None of your filthy words right now, jerk!"

"Babe, he shits himself every few hours, spits up all over me every time I'm holding him, and smiles when he farts. Do you really think he can understand my *filthy* words?"

"Maybe." I shrug. "Either way, cut it out. And for the last time. Do. Not. Leave. Me. In. Bed. Alone!"

"But you were sleeping so peacefully," he says, frowning. "And I haven't been able to help nearly as much as I should have since he was born. I just wanted you to get some sleep. You deserve that."

I lean against the wall, uncrossing my arms and letting them hang at my sides before sighing.

Cade Huff is impossible to stay angry with. I used to think that was a bad thing. Now, I'm realizing maybe that's just what makes unconditional love … well, unconditional. Because what I've learned is that maybe the deepest love doesn't have limitations. At least, the real kind doesn't. And truth be told, I'd follow Cade anywhere. I wouldn't even question where we were going. Just as long as we were going there together. I love him that much.

"Fine," I sigh. "Just promise me that you'll always come back. No more running."

"I promise you, Haley, I will always come back. Every single time." He grins, and I know he's about to soften the mood with something lighter. He always does. "I had to let you rest. How else would you have the energy for when I rail the fuck out of you during naptime today?"

I bite my lip and clench my legs together as I continue to ogle him while he's shirtless, holding our son protectively against his chest. He's a sight to behold. I'm a lucky girl.

"If you've got him, I think I'll go shower." I roll my eyes. "A certain someone got me all sweaty last night, and I smell."

He looks down at Eli as he snores softly. Lately, he's been waking up at the ass crack of dawn, and by eight or nine, he's ready to go back to sleep. People aren't joking when they say motherhood is the most beautiful yet tiring thing on earth. Some days, I feel like I'm running on empty.

"I've got him, babe," he assures me. "Go read one of your dirty books while you take a bath. I've got a few hours before I need to be at practice."

I try to hide my smile. Little does he know that I have an entire day planned for him later on today. Maintaining sobriety for a year is a huge accomplishment. And I know it's just the beginning of his journey.

To be honest, I assumed that after his surprise party to celebrate his year of sobriety, we would sit down and talk about our future. I wasn't sure if he would need more time or if he'd decide that he didn't want to pursue a relationship with me. Either way, what I wasn't expecting was for him to show up minutes after midnight, declaring his love for me. I have to admit, I like how it went a whole lot better than what I had imagined.

"I think I'll do that," I say, nodding once. "He'll be down for at least an hour."

I twirl a strand of my hair on my finger, trying to seem more confident than I am. Truthfully, Cade still makes me nervous. He's stupid hot and obnoxiously charismatic.

"So … if you find yourself bored … you know where I'll be."

His eyes darken. "Oh, angel … if you really thought for a second that I was going to let your sexy ass soak in that tub, naked, and not join you, you clearly don't know me that well. I was just trying to play it cool." He pulls his bottom lip between his teeth. "You've got about five minutes to get ready for me. Clock's a-ticking, baby."

Stepping backward, I head out of the room and bolt toward the bathroom. I begin filling the bathtub before I pull my sleep shirt and panties off, already anticipating being naked with Cade again.

After putting some bubble bath in the running water, I glance in the mirror, frowning at myself. *What a mess.* Pulling my hair into a messy bun, I quickly wash my face and brush my teeth. And then I climb in the tub, and butterflies flood my stomach while I wait for my man to come in.

CADE

I fondle Haley's perfect tits. Even though she isn't breastfeeding, they have swelled up since she became a mother. She thinks they are ugly, but I can't keep my hands, eyes, or even my mouth off of them.

With her ass sits just above my cock, I grow against her. And with every stroke of my fingers against her nipples, every ounce of blood rushes to my dick, making me ache to be inside of her.

Her back rests against my chest, her head just below my shoulder. She isn't reading like she planned though. Instead, we're just sitting in the bathtub in comfortable silence as I run my hands all over her body. But the longer we're in here, the more my cock needs her wrapped around it.

Subtly, she nudges herself against me. And when she does, the tip of my cock presses against her ass, begging to slip inside of her.

I felt like I waited an eternity to be with her again. And now that I've got her back ... I can't get enough of her.

When she wiggles against me again, I know she wants me just as badly as I want her. Placing my hands on her hips, I lift her up enough to position my aching cock at her entrance. I pull her body toward me, inching myself inside little by little. Once I'm all in, I move her in a rhythm. The water slapping in the tub as I fuck her.

Leaning my head forward, I kiss her shoulder blade before biting down. Her tits bounce as I move in and out of her, and I so badly wish I could have my mouth on them.

"Cade," she breathes out. Turning her head, she looks up at me, her eyes filled with desperation, as she moans again before pulling her lip between her teeth.

"God, I missed fucking you," I growl against her neck. "I had to fuck my hand in the shower while I pictured your lips wrapped around my cock."

Taking a bath is great, but the water is just another thing between us that I can't fucking stand. Getting up quickly, I pull her bare body up with me and step out of the bathtub. Spinning her around, I press her front against the glass of the shower next to where the tub sits and plunge inside of her. One hand tangles in her hair, giving it a little yank, and the other wraps around her neck.

Moving her hand upward, she cups it over where mine grips her neck, and she pushes down on my fingers. Her message isn't lost on me, but it sure makes my cock even harder.

"You want to be choked, angel baby?" I growl against her ear as I bend her over a little bit more, fucking her deeper. "You want to feel a little pain while you take my dick like a good girl?"

Craning her head, she peers up at me through her lashes and nods.

"Fuck, you're so hot," I groan.

I grip her neck tighter while also fastening my hold on her hair, and she cries out a muffled sound.

"Cade," she manages to croak. "Yes. Fuck ... yes."

My hips smash against hers, and my balls smack against her ass as I plunge in and out of her. She's so close. I feel her begin to tighten around me, which only makes my balls start to tingle. Releasing her neck and hair, I knit her fingers with mine and slam our palms against the glass of the shower door. My mouth stays against her ear as she cries out.

LOST BOY

"Come all over my cock, angel," I grunt into her ear. "You ready to feel my cum drip from your pussy and down your legs? Because I'm going to unload inside of you. Inside of what's mine."

My hips jerk as I come undone, spilling my cum inside of her.

"Mine," I rasp, pulling back and then laying my face between her shoulders.

Once she's milked me for all I'm worth and I know she's come hard, I pull out of her and turn her to face me. Sliding my hand up her cheek, I kiss her.

"I don't think I'll ever get enough of you, angel." My lips are on hers again. "I love you so fucking much."

"I love you," she whispers before the tears start flowing.

"What's wrong?" I dip my forehead toward hers. "Why are you crying?"

"I've waited for this for so long," her voice squeaks. "I'm so scared it'll get taken from me again. That you'll get taken from me again." She squeezes her eyes shut. "For so long, all I've wanted is you. I'm scared that if I go all in, I'll lose you."

"Open your eyes, angel," I demand softly, and reluctantly, she listens. "I'm not going anywhere. This thing right here? It's forever." I kiss her forehead. "You don't have to worry anymore."

I hug her naked body tighter. "The entire time in rehab, I told myself if I ever got another chance with you, I'd never mess it up. I hated being away, but I'm a better man for it. I appreciate what I have now. And for a guy who should have lost everything long ago, I have a lot." I smile. "Way I see it, I'm the luckiest bastard alive."

She sniffles before her arms hug me. "I love you so much."

And when I open my mouth to answer, I hear the most beautiful sound.

Our baby boy crying for us.

34

Haley

"I meant what I said, Haley," Kat says as she moves around the kitchen, setting up the rest of the food. "If you need a night of uninterrupted sleep, you let me know. I don't mind coming up to help."

"I might just take you up on that." I smile, looking between her and where her husband sits, cradling Eli as he stares down at him in pure adoration.

When Cade got home from rehab, they began making the drive to Brooks more frequently. But once I had Eli, I swear they've been coming once every few weeks. I know Kat wishes they could move closer, but since Caden owns a garage, it's not that simple. And maybe we would leave Brooks and move closer to them if Cade didn't love being a part of the coaching staff so much. But he does, so we are here to stay for now.

"Everyone should be here in the next half hour," I say, glancing at the clock. "Do you think Cade will be upset with this surprise? Should I tell him?" I fidget nervously. "I don't want to make him anxious."

Cade knows his parents are in town, but he has no idea that I've invited the rest of his friends and loved ones to celebrate his one year of sobriety. And now, I'm wondering if it's a good idea.

Coming next to me, Kat pats my shoulder. "Honey, he's going to love this surprise. Besides, it's not like there's going to be keg stands and piles of weed to be smoked. It's at three in the afternoon. There's soda and fruit punch and loads of food." She glances toward me, a knowing look on her face. "You know ... since it has been a year of sobriety for Cade, does that mean things are, well, different for y'all?"

My cheeks heat up like an oven as my mind travels back to last night and this morning. Him showing up here in the pouring rain and declaring his love. And then showing me that love. *Multiple times.*

"Well ... maybe," I answer softly. "I guess we will see." I straighten a few of the dishes out and wipe the counter.

"Baby girl, I saw the way he was looking at you earlier. And the way he was hugging you when you were washing dishes." She gently nudges her elbow into my side. "Y'all aren't fooling me. But you know what? The little man is now five months old. Caden and I are in town for the weekend. What do you say you pack an overnight bag and you and Cade go away for the night? After his party, of course."

"Well, the team plays tomorrow night," I say, thinking out loud, even though it does sound nice. Just Cade and me ... alone.

"So, be back a few hours before game time," she says softly. "Just think about it. Talk to Cade about it and let me know. Either way is fine. But just know that leaving Eli overnight, with his *grandmother*, does not make you a bad mom. Parents deserve some time for themselves, you know. And Lord knows, between classes and being a mom, you haven't had much time for that."

I offer her a smile. "Thank you, Kat. I'll talk to Cade and let you know."

As she busies herself getting everything ready again, I look over at Caden with Eli and realize how lucky my son is to have Cade's parents. My mom and dad still come to visit as well, but for them, work will always come first. But I know that Eli will never feel unloved because of all the amazing people he has in his life.

I think of how everything has finally begun to fall into place. I decided what I wanted to be in school for—which was, in fact, not a doctor. But instead, I hope to one day work at a publishing company. Or maybe even as an editor. Something to do with books for sure. And Cade is in a great place. He's enjoying coaching, and he's also become a sponsor to a few people who just began their path to sobriety, and I can tell he loves it.

When I look at Cade, I don't see an addict. I see the funniest person I've ever met. The best gift giver. A sturdy shoulder to cry on. A lopsided grin that lights up the entire room. A strong set of arms that gives the greatest hugs. And mostly ...

I see the world's greatest dad. And the man I love.

CADE

I ride home with the guys from practice. It's kind of weird now because I'm more of a helper than a player this season, but I'm actually enjoying it more than I ever did playing. I get to work with the defense, and when I stand back during the games and watch the things I've taught them play out before me, shit, it's rewarding.

"So, uh ... I couldn't help but notice you weren't home this morning," Hunter drawls with a smirk. "Where'd you run off to bright and early?"

"Early? I heard him leave in the middle of the night in the pouring rain," Watson tosses back. "But I didn't hear his truck start. Which means ... fucker didn't go too far." He pretends to cough. "Across the street."

"You chasing my sister, Huff?" Hunter says, tipping his chin up. "Thought I warned you about that."

"Oh, you did. But in Cade language, he apparently thought you meant *impregnant my sister*." Watson laughs. "Which, by the way, still pissed about the middle name."

"Uncle number one, right here." Hunter winks at Watson. "Don't be jelly."

"Yeah, but once Eli can walk and talk, he'll know who's the real number one uncle," Watson throws back. "Santa won't have nothing on me."

I just sit back and listen to them go back and forth like two old women, fighting over who is or who will be the better uncle.

Today marks one year of sobriety for me. And I dare to say ... it's been the best year of my entire life. I broke down, felt like the world was ending. Went to rehab, met some damn good people. Found out I was going to have a baby with the only woman I'd ever loved. Came home, had to learn to love her from a distance while also being there for her at the same time. Became a dad and watched Haley step seamlessly into the role of a mother, and then, as of this day ... we get to finally be a family.

I've done a lot of dumb shit in my life. But getting her pregnant wasn't one of them.

We pull in front of the house and all pile out.

"I'm going to see Haley and the baby. I'll see y'all later. Matter of fact, consider this my notice. I'm moving out. Daddy's going home." I hold my hand up to wave, but notice they are following me. "What are you doing?" I frown.

"We want to see our nephew, duh," Hunter says as the three of us cross the road and walk along the sidewalk to Haley's place.

I pull the door open, and my ears are instantly assaulted with the sound of people screaming, "Surprise!"

My eyes shift around the room, taking in the sight of my parents, Haley and the baby, the entire hockey team, Coach LaConte and his wife, Cam, Addison and Isla, Brody and Bria, Haley's parents, Buck and Kobra, a few of the other guys from rehab, and finally … my eyes land on Ellen and Thomas, Eli's parents.

Haley walks toward me, carrying Eli in her arms before she kisses me on the cheek. "Happy one year of sobriety, Daddy. We love you so much."

"Call me Daddy again," I say, wiggling my eyebrows. "It does all sorts of things to me."

She laughs and shakes her head. "You're too much."

I gaze around again, letting the emotions flood through me. "Thank you, angel. Without you, I wouldn't be here right now." I kiss Eli's head. "Without both of you. You gave me a life worth living."

She starts crying, wiping under her eyes before giving me one last squeeze. "Don't make me cry. I'm actually wearing mascara for once." She gives me a quick kiss, whispering in my ear, "Your mom and dad offered to watch the baby tonight. For the entire night."

When she steps back, I grin down at her. "Well, what are we waiting for? Kick these fuckers out right now so we can go."

She swats my chest but giggles and steps away, and I look around the room, blown away that all of these people are here for me.

I'm the luckiest son of a bitch alive.

And the day is only going to get better.

See, I have a surprise up my sleeve too. One that I hope she'll love as much as I love her.

My mom hugs me, kissing my cheek. "I'm so proud of you, my boy. I hope you know that."

I hug her back before looking down, amused. "Guess you've been keeping secrets for more than just me, huh, Mama?"

Her eyes widen as she releases me. "First you with your grand plan for tonight. And then Haley with this party." She runs her hand across her forehead. "I thought for sure I'd blow one of your covers."

A month ago, after talking to Buck and Kobra, I told them I would follow the *one year sober* rule, but that the second that time was up, I was getting my girl back and we were going to be a family. I told them that not only did I want to be with her, but I also wanted to marry her. To be a family with her and my son. They, of course, wanted to make sure I was ready and that I wasn't putting myself in a situation that would compromise my sobriety, but after an hour-long chat, I think they realized that Haley and Eli were probably the best thing for my sobriety. So, tonight, not only am I going to propose, but I hope we can get married too. Because I can't go another day without making her my wife.

I just pray she'll say yes.

35

Haley

"You know, for literally a few hours' notice ... you really pulled together the night." I smile at Cade as he opens the passenger door, letting me out. "It's almost like you ... planned it or something."

He gives me a mischievous grin, but says nothing. He doesn't have to; I know that he didn't just happen to have a dress in my pre-motherhood body in the back of his closet. Or a room booked at the nicest, swankiest place this side of Georgia.

"What are you up to, Mr. Huff?" I wrap my hand around his arm as we walk into the gorgeous lobby.

"The things I'll do to get eight hours of uninterrupted time with your body without Eli crying is kind of pathetic, huh?" He smirks. "But what can I say? I want to fuck you six ways to Sunday."

A shiver runs up my spine. He might have snuck in at midnight, and we might have had sex this morning, too, but I'm already ready for more. When you wait so long for someone, it's hard to not feel this way.

Cade stops, turning toward me. "How long do I have to wait?"

I frown. "For what?"

HANNAH GRAY

"To marry you. How long is the appropriate time to ask? Because, Haley … I'm so fucking ready."

I'm in shock by his words. Obviously, I'd love nothing more than to be married to Cade. And not just because he's the father of my child, but also because I've been so stupidly, crazily in love with him for so long.

"Cade, I'd marry you right now if I could." I smile, never expecting what happens next to happen.

"Will you then?" He slides to one knee, keeping my hands in his. "Will you marry me tonight?"

I stare down at him in complete and utter shock. And then I wonder if I'm dreaming and I'm about to wake up. That would suck. But even if this is a dream, I'm not ready for it to end.

"Just promise me something," I say, my emotions finally catching up to me. "That you aren't just doing this for Eli. Because, Cade … I want the best for you."

"Haley, before I even knew there was going to be an Eli, I was all in." He nods slowly. "I was going to let you go because, well, I thought that would be best for you. But there wasn't a single second when you weren't on my mind. You're it for me, Haley. I want to be your husband. And I hope I can somehow trick you into being my wife."

"Yes," I squeak. "One million times over, yes!"

He stands, cupping my cheeks and kissing me. "I love you so much. And thank you. Because if you'd said no … that would have been embarrassing."

As he tugs my hand, walking toward a large archway, my heart speeds up when I see his mom holding Eli, wearing a dress shirt and pants.

"Cade?" I croak, covering my mouth.

He stops. "I thought about how I'd do this. What you'd want when it came time to getting married. A big part of me wanted no one but us and our son there. But then I remembered all the people who had gotten us here. Who were there for you when I couldn't be. Who had believed in me when they could have given up." He lifts my hand, kissing it. "If this isn't what you want, we can do something different. I swear to you, I'll go tell everyone to leave right now. But the sooner I get to be your husband, the better. You're my family, Haley."

I peer around the corner. There aren't too many people in the room. Probably twenty or so. It's still small and intimate. But he's right. Without so many of these people here … I don't know if we would have made it.

"It's perfect," I say, smiling up at him through teary eyes. "You're perfect."

He leans down, putting his lips against my ear. "I'm not, but you might say that when you're straddling my face later, angel." He pulls back, his eyes darkening. "What do you say, Haley baby? Let's go get hitched?"

240

I burst into tears, nodding my head. "Yes. But, Cade, if this isn't real ... if it's a dream ... please don't wake me."

"I promise, this is the realest thing you'll ever know." He kisses me before leading me into the room.

Dreams really do come true.

CADE

I hold Haley's hands in mine, and my body trembles. I look at her, and I see nothing but an angel. Somehow, with an insane amount of luck, I'm about to become her husband.

"I know I sprang this on you about five minutes ago. Maybe you're in shock, maybe you feel bad for me ... either way, I'm going to hurry up and get this going before you change your mind." I smile at her, hearing a few laughs in the crowd.

My throat swells, a lump lodging itself there, as I blink back a few tears. *I'm already being a little bitch, and I haven't even started to tell her my vows.* This is going to be harder than I thought.

"Haley, you came into my life at a time when I needed you the most—even though I maybe didn't act like it. On the outside, I seemed fine. But on the inside, I was in a dark place. Just having you around brought some light in, keeping me going."

I wipe my eyes before returning my hand to hers. "I've heard a lot of people say things like, *They saved my life,* when talking about their significant other. But the truth is, you really did save my life. You saw a broken, lost man who needed help, and you got it for me. You led me to safety before I was gone for good. You did it because you loved me, even then. You loved me more than I deserved."

I swallow before dragging in a breath. "I know I'm no longer Cade Huff, future hockey star, like maybe I thought I would be one day. I'm not going to have fame or boatloads of money. But, Haley, when it comes to you, to us ... we have everything we need right here. You, me, and Eli. And when we're eighty years old, if my old ass is still driving you to the bookstore and following you around for hours while you look at your dirty books, I'll be a happy man." I smile at her through my tears. "I don't need a big, elaborate life, Haley. I just need you and me and Eli. And that's more than enough."

She looks up at me, tears spilling from her eyes before rolling down her cheeks. She's the most beautiful piece of art I've ever laid eyes on, and I really don't know how I could be this damn blessed.

"I love you with all that I am and will ever be. For the rest of our lives, I'll listen to you and cherish you. You'll never have to wonder where I stand when it comes to you. That I promise you, Haley." I give her hands a squeeze. "Every single day of my life, I'll choose you. Always."

When it's her turn to talk, her eyebrows pull together, and she sniffles. "Damn you, setting me up to fail," she croaks out, and everyone chuckles. "Unlike you, I'm not all that good at speaking in front of people. And Lord knows, I'll never captivate a crowd quite the way you do." She stops, swallowing. "All I can do is speak from my heart. Which isn't hard to do when my heart beats for you and our son." Her voice cracks, and she blinks away the tears from her vision.

"Watching you struggle was the hardest thing I've ever had to go through. But feeling that crippling pain when I knew you were hurting made me understand something." She drags in a breath, letting it out slowly. "True love is not conditional. It's constant. And always. It's through the really dark times, and it's in the best times. It's patient when it needs to be, and it's showing tough love when required." Her fingers squeeze mine. "Our love might not look like everyone else's. Or even sound like the fairy tales I read about. And that's because … it's not. It's ours. It's us." She gives me a smile. "And I love us. I love you. And I'm so proud to stand by your side—now as your wife—and watch you continue to help others with your story."

My eyes drink her in, and the corner of my mouth turns up. "Preacher … can you say whatever needs to be legally said so I can kiss my wife?"

"Soon, son. Soon, she'll be your wife," he utters, and I hear the humor in his voice.

He finishes up the ceremony before declaring us husband and wife. And when it's time for him to say I can kiss my bride, my lips are already on hers before he gets the words out.

I cup her face, and I kiss her so hard.

A year ago, I was getting checked into a rehab facility, and I wondered if I'd ever get the chance to do this again. Now, she's my wife.

Pulling back, I press my forehead to hers and grin. "So, fairy tales? That's what you're calling those porno books you read?"

She giggles against me, rolling her eyes. "What can I say? Your wife likes smutty books."

Looping my arms around her, I drag her closer, kissing her again. "Wife. I like the sound of that."

"Yeah," she says, grinning. "Me too."

Not all too long ago, I felt like I had fallen too far to ever be saved. I didn't think I'd ever find myself again or be capable of going through life and feeling things like joy. And then an angel came along, proving she was tough enough to walk through the depths of hell as long as it meant she could be by my side. She swooped me up and delivered me to grace.

So, here's to the lost boys like me. May they also find their one and only to love the darkness right out of them.

HALEY

"Cover Me Up" by Morgan Wallen plays as Cade holds me close, smiling down at me, and I can feel his heart beating quickly against mine.

"I'm so fucking lucky," he whispers, blinking back the tears in his eyes. "I can't believe you're mine."

"I've been yours long before today, Cade." I smile. "I think from the day I moved into the house, it was all over. There was no going back."

"I know I haven't made it easy. No matter how much time passes with my sobriety, I know you'll still worry about me, and I'm so sorry for that. And I'm sure our life is going to look a lot different from a lot of our friends. With no pro hockey, there's no fancy mansion or jet-setting around the country. But I meant what I said. I don't need all of that when I already have everything I need right here." He leans down, kissing the top of my head. "My angel."

"I have more than I could ever need." I nod. "Also, I have no idea how we fit your *one year sober* party, a wedding, and a reception into one day. But I'm impressed with your planning."

He smirks. "You forgot to mention all that good sex earlier." He leans down, putting his lips closer to my ear. "And I can assure you, there's lots more of that coming. Mom's watching Eli tonight. Which means … you and me. Alone in a swanky hotel room."

I feel my body heat as a shiver runs up my spine just before he kisses me.

When he pulls back, Kat cuts in, passing Eli to Cade, and we hold him between us. And how lucky are we? We get to finish our first dance as a married couple, holding our son.

A year ago, I felt like my entire world was ending. Now, I'm realizing that was just the path we needed to take to get to this moment right here. A moment that I wouldn't trade for anything.

I've read hundreds of romance books in my life. But our story, even after the pain, is my favorite.

THE END

acknowledgments

What a ride this book was. Sometimes, I was happy, and sometimes, I was sobbing while typing out the words. I'm not going to lie; this was hands down the hardest story I've written yet.

The layers of addiction are so much more complex than I think a lot of people realize. How much it can affect literally every aspect of yourself and everything you know. I didn't want to throw this book together and release it into the world. It needed to be done right. At least, I hope that it was.

There were a few times I wondered if it was too much. If anyone would want to even read something like this. My first four puck boys have been so incredibly loved, and I've feared so much that this one wouldn't be received well because, welp, Cade Huff was a whole other animal to channel. But when I typed *the end*, I realized something. I loved Cade and Haley's love story. It was, by far, my most flawed fairy tale yet. But it was theirs. And it was real. And raw. And I hope it shows that no matter what, love can heal. Whether it is love from a significant other or love from a child it has the ability to save lives. Love does it every single day.

So, thank you for reading this one. Thank you for trusting me, even after I warned you it was going to be gritty and cause some pain.

At the top of my list, as always, is my family. My daughters and my husband because this book took a lot out of me. When I finally finished it, I felt like I could sleep for a week straight. Thank you for being patient with me during that time. And for celebrating each victory and goal reached with me. I love you all so much. You make my world go round.

Next is my mom because, well, she really is my rock and my best friend. For my whole life, she's been my biggest cheerleader. That hasn't changed. I'm not the type of person to get into my feelings too often. I guess I never have been. But, Mom, thank you for raising me to see that love will always defeat hate. That forgiveness feels a lot better than staying angry. And that being the bigger person doesn't make someone weak, but instead, it makes them strong. I love you more than I could ever write down. The world needs more souls like you in it.

Thank you to my dad for giving me the greatest second job on Wednesdays, where our lunch breaks are filled with conversation and lots of laughs. In so many ways, I'm a lot like you. And I hope that you see it, too, and that you're proud. Love you lots.

My brother—I'm so proud of the husband and father you have become. I'm proud of the obstacles you've overcome and the man you are today. I love you so much.

My sister-in-law, who is also one of my very best friends—Thanks for being one of my biggest cheerleaders. (You and Mom are tied for that number one spot.) Life gets busy between work and kids, sports and school events. But I know we'll always have each other's back. And I love your messages when you read my latest book and send me your review. Love you.

Candice Butchino—There aren't enough words to describe how much I adore you. Thank you for listening to my long, cringeworthy voice messages. And for always dropping everything just to lend a hand. You're a rare gem, and I'm happy to have you as a beta reader, proofreader, sticker slinger, swag creator, badass bookstagrammer, but most importantly ... a close friend.

Tatum Hanscom, who has literally been rocking with me since book one— You are a damn good friend. You're honest when I need an opinion. You're a laugh whenever I need one. And you're the best proofreader a girl could ask for.

Autumn Gantz ... the boss lady—You're a woman who wears many hats. You wake up daily to a list most people would need a week to complete. You don't go to sleep until the job is done, and no matter what you have going on in your personal life, you make sure that your authors are taken care of. We've been together for three years now, and I can't wait to see where this road takes us. Thanks for taking a chance on me and letting me join the Wordsmith family. Love you big.

Jovana Shirley at Unforeseen Editing—I'm hoping I made you cry at least once in this story. Whenever I get notes back that a scene made you cry, I basically leap with joy. Chanting, *Victory is mine!* I love you so much. It's not common to work with the same person for three years and only have good stories to share. But that's exactly how it is with you. Thank you for being a huge piece in what has gotten me this far as an author.

Amy Queau, Q Designs—Thanks for another gorgeous cover! I love it so much, as usual!

Renie Saliba—Thank you for providing me with the beautiful cover picture. It's perfect!

Sarah Grimz Sentz with Enchanting Romance Designs—Thank you for another beautiful discreet cover! I can't get enough of them.

There're so many bookstagrammers I want to thank, but I'm afraid I'll forget someone, and that's the last thing I want to do. Because truthfully, each one of you is the reason why my books have been getting the love that they have. You all work so hard to not only share the stories you adore, but to promote the authors you love too. This community is growing because of you. You are changing authors' lives every single day. And you aren't asking for anything in return. So, thank you. My heart still flutters inside my chest every single time I watch one of your reels or see one of your edits. I love and appreciate you all so much.

about the author

Hannah Gray spends her days in vacationland, living in a small, quaint town on the coast of Maine. She is an avid reader of contemporary romance and is always in competition with herself to read more books every year.

During the day, she loves on her three perfect-to-her daughters and tries to be the best mom she can be. But once she tucks them in at night—okay, scratch that. Once they fall asleep next to her in her bed—because their bedrooms apparently have monsters in them—she dives into her own fantasy world, staying awake well into the late-night hours, typing away stories about her characters. As much as she loves being a wife and mom—and she certainly does love it—reading and writing are her outlet, giving her a place to travel far away while still physically being with her family.

She married her better half in 2013, and he's been putting up with her craziness every day since. As her anchor, he's her one constant in this insane, forever-changing world.

Made in the USA
Monee, IL
16 March 2024